I Hope You Find Joy

A Story of Love and Forgiveness (Book 1)

A Novel

By Eliza Mae Albano

ISBN Number: 978-1-7775120-0-2

Dedicated to my parents and sister who always support me in prayer. Thank you to God the Father, Son, and Holy Spirit.

CHAPTER 1

Passengers of AIR TRANSAT flight 325 to Toronto from Montreal, your flight has been delayed. Please stand by for your gate number.

Emma closed her eyes and counted to ten. Her heart was racing, and her hands were shaking. When someone or something hijacked her plans, her anxiety skyrocketed. Though her breathing helped to endure her flight being rerouted to Montreal, the sound of rolling wheels and the high-pitched voices of teenagers in the overcrowded Pierre Elliot Trudeau Terminal, breathing could not help her now.

As she inched closer, she watched Christopher Gomes Riley sip his coffee as he sat inside the Brûlerie St-Denis cafe. Squinting her eyes, she tried to convince herself that the brown-haired, handsome, and well-dressed man metres away wasn't the same hip-hop wearing boy who taught her how cruel human beings could be to each other. It was difficult to ignore how her shoulder muscles tightened, and her knees buckled underneath her as she watched him chew his danish. She never wanted to see him again, especially wearing oversized black yoga pants and a worn-out, V-neck t-shirt.

Leaning her head back in disbelief, she knew her appearance wouldn't matter to him. For a whole summer, she was always sweaty from entertaining campers under the oppressive sun and had matching unruly black hair that told of the humidity level outside. And despite how she didn't exhibit any runway model qualities, he would spend time with her watching the sunrise, discussing literature, and debating the merits of religion and science. Always ready with a compliment about her intelligence before her appearance.

Although it had been over fifteen years since she saw him, she never forgot how his dark hazel eyes had stared at her with wonder and awe when she explained what she read, experienced, or thought. She had engraved every line and curve of his chiseled face and sarcastic and booming voice to memory, memories of how he scratched his left brow with his index finger to admit he was wrong or smiled when he had impressed her. He bit his lower lip when she amused him and silently sat with her when she had a rough day. Those recollections brought her joy. But, as another group of annoying snickering teenage girls passed her, her happy memories faded. The truth of the matter was, he was the boy who broke her heart and the only person she had intentionally humiliated and destroyed for emotional retribution.

The first time she met him, his charisma intrigued her, but his arrogance repelled her. She hated how he flirted with every girl who crossed his path and told her how fun it was to work with Charice, who laughed at his jokes, or how much he liked Michelle's openness. Other times, he would barrel ahead with his ideas without considering another person's feelings or opinions. Yet, she would find herself talking to him until the wee hours of the morning, wondering if he acted this way because someone he loved had hurt him.

Her instincts weren't wrong. As they became friends, she learned how his parents' divorce affected him. Being treated like a toy prize to be won, he learned how two people could love each other and, in a blink of an eye, hate each other with equal intensity. As his parents showed him, he learned how material goods became substitutes for missed quality time between parent and child. It was evident to her that his reckless behaviour was caused by his parents' divorce. He was a boy who avoided being in love like the plague or accumulated things to feel valued.

Yet, his clairvoyance and charm made everyone love him. He was a natural leader who swayed others to follow him into reckless schemes. She never took part in these plans because she never craved to be his giddy groupie. At one point, she didn't even want to be his friend. It was an instinct she wished she had followed if it meant not feeling like an acrophobic ascending to the peak of a rollercoaster when she saw him again.

However, as she gawked at him now like an obsessed fan, she was relieved when he lowered his head. He didn't recognize her. She could walk away and leave the past behind her. Yet, her heart sunk like a child watching her most treasured toy given to a younger sibling. She inched closer to him, hoping that he would glance up from his phone to see how beautiful she had become despite having her black hair loosely tied back to hide her disheveled appearance after sitting on a plane for over ten hours.

As if God heard her pleas, Christopher raised his head again. He cracked a smile as if he was unsure if he should acknowledge her presence. Anger percolated in her veins for not following her instinct to leave, but his wave melted the bitterness from her heart. She wanted to turn away, but something in his eyes urged her to accept his invitation.

Banging her leg on the table, she spilled his coffee on him.

"I'm so sorry."

"Emma?"

"Christopher!"

She dropped her oversized, star-patterned shoulder bag on his feet as she tried to help clean the coffee off of him. He winced in pain and bit his lower lip. Smiling, she wiped the stains on his shirt and let her hand assess his toned body. As her trembling fingers lingered on his fit physique, she forgot how to breathe.

He yelled at her over the cacophony of the café. "I assumed it was you. Now I know it's you. Don't worry. What has it been? Fifteen years? What are you doing here?"

Rediscovering the ability to speak and pulling her hand off his chest, she replied, "I'm flying back from Vienna. Yourself?"

She wondered if he was as nervous to see her as she was to see him. Unlike Emma, he had no difficulty in holding her gaze nor remembering how to speak.

"My boss wants me in London. He's an eccentric man. He needs to hear my voice and see me. I'm the guy he trusts with his affairs, business acquisitions, stocks, futures, and all that stuff. Money begets money. I'm not sure if I want to move to another country."

Admiring his well-tailored suit and well-groomed, matured, and defined face, she had only heard pieces of what he said. From his appearance, she concluded that he had grown into a confident and successful businessman, but his eyes had lost that playfulness and fearlessness, which always enchanted her. The only response she could muster was a fake expression of interest.

"Are you okay?" Christopher pulled out a chair for her to sit with him.

"Sorry, you were saying?"

Leaning back on his chair, he quipped, "You're not listening."

"Sorry, it's been a long day."

"Travelling alone? Arguing with your husband and kids? Or your boyfriend?"

Emma noticed how his eyes scanned her bare left hand.

She lifted his left hand to examine it. "Seems you've followed your dreams. Living life large as a free and single man."

His charming grin faded as he drew back his hand. Scratching his brow with his left index finger, he looked down and sighed. She noticed that her comment offended him. But it didn't give her pleasure to do it.

He took a sip of his coffee and leaned forward. "Well, we still know how to push the wrong buttons."

"I suppose we've always been sensitive to the other's opinion and always ready with a disparaging critic of the other." She crossed her hands across the table, trying to sound witty and indifferent to their past.

"But in your case, your opinion of me has always been accurate."

She gawked, unable to respond to his matter-of-fact response. His statement wasn't true. When she believed he was a nice guy who only said and did reckless things to be popular, her intuition and faith in him blew up in her face. Leaning forward, she wondered whether she should believe him or her experience.

"Are you, Charlotte, and Sonja still friends?" He relaxed into his chair.

"Still friends. Sonja is getting married."

"And yourself? How are you?"

Drawing her shaky and cold hands from the table, she placed them on her lap. She didn't want to answer his question. It was complicated. But she wasn't going to tell him that. Instead, she replied, "I'm doing well. How are you?"

"I have to decide about my future. Remember?"

"I was listening. Your work sounds exciting, especially how you represent a multi-billionaire who accumulates wealth."

"Go on, say it. You've been dying to comment." He cracked a grin.

"One guy makes a profit while others become poor."

"Feel better?"

"Yes."

They both laughed and stared at each other. She turned away. This was too familiar and comfortable when she should be filled with righteous anger.

"Let's say I create opportunities," he clarified.

"Does that help you sleep at night? Do you enjoy treating people like a commodity and using them?"

"No, that's not what I do. I learned the consequences of treating people like that…Emma, I—"

Now boarding AIR TRANSAT flight 325 to Toronto at Gate 39. Please have your boarding pass ready.

Relieved, she stood up. "Finally, my flight is here."

"It was great seeing you again." He jumped up from his seat.

"I'm surprised you remembered me."

"How could I forget you?" he murmured as he handed her purse to her.

"I have to get to my gate." She jerked her hand away as his hand grazed her fingers. Swallowing her breath, she turned to leave.

"Wait!" He gently grabbed her elbow.

She yanked her arm from his grasp as if she placed her hand on a hot stove.

"Sorry. If we don't see each other again…I… hope you find… joy in your life." Christopher stepped back and raised his hands in surrender.

Emma could no longer hear the constant reminders overhead that informed passengers not to leave bags unattended and the white noise of travellers getting to their gates. The tables, chairs, and passengers around her resembled a Van Gogh painting. All she saw was Christopher's mouth moving, asking her if she had joy in her life.

"You okay?" He snapped his fingers in front of her.

Unbeknownst to Emma, she had been staring blankly at him. When she realized it, she swatted his hand away and replied, "Thank you."

"I wished we stayed in touch so I could make it up to you. But I get it. I hurt you. I've always wondered if you're happy. Found love. Married with kids. Writing—"

"I need to go. Have a safe trip. This was nice. I really didn't expect you to remember me."

"I remember everything," he divulged in an enticing, husky, and sincere voice.

"Then, I hope you make a wise choice about your future." She backed away and offered her hand.

"Same to you." He grinned and shook her hand, but he didn't let it go.

Staring into those hazel eyes, she forgot a million things she wanted to say to him. Her flight number blared through the intercom again. Finally releasing his hand, she said goodbye. As she headed towards her gate, she fanned herself, hating how distance and time hadn't healed the wounds or severed the connection between them.

CHAPTER 2

Exiting the baggage claim area at Pearson Airport, to the arrival foyer, she scanned the welcome home signs. But all she saw were tour company names welcoming tourists to Canada. She had hoped that Martin would be holding up a sign or flowers to welcome her home. Even though she had told him how sentimental gifts and gestures were unnecessary for their relationship, deep down, she wished he hadn't listened to her.

"Emma Alamayo?"

A young, blue-eyed, twenty-two-year-old man welcomed Emma at the exit gate. He was holding a sign with her name printed in bold capital letters.

She squinted her eyes, hoping that she didn't need glasses. "Yes."

"Please wait here. Can I take your bags for you?"

"No. Who are you?"

"I'm Ravi."

"Ravi?"

"Yes, ma'am! He didn't tell you who I am?"

Emma grimaced beside him as she felt ancient near his youthful energy. "No, I've had a long flight, and I don't want to play twenty questions. Please, tell me who you are before I yell for help."

"There's my girl. Welcome back!" Running towards her, Martin yelled over the heads of passengers, trying not to trip over their bags.

He picked Emma up and gave her a heartfelt kiss as Ravi took a picture of the reunion. Relief surged through her as being in the arms of her tall, darkish brown hair and GQhandsome boyfriend meant she was home.

"These two weeks have been brutal. You could use another holiday. Rough flight?"

"They rerouted my flight to Montreal."

As they stood in each other's arms, she buried her head on his shoulder. She was uncomfortable having Ravi watch them. He was holding a light above their head to take another picture as an elderly, white-haired, serious-looking man joined them.

"Sir, can you kiss her again?" Ravi suggested.

"Martin, who are these men? Why are they taking our picture?"

He kissed the top of her forehead. "I wanted to tell you, but it was impossible to reach you."

"I'm Leon. He's right. You were inaccessible."

"Nice to meet you, Leon. But, who are you?"

"I work for the Conservative Party. Ravi and I are vetting Mr. Torcoke."

"Martin?"

"Leon, we can talk later," Martin instructed Leon through pursed lips.

"She had two weeks," Leon grunted as Ravi showed him the pictures.

"I understand, Leon. Give my girl time, and she'll answer your questions. You don't want to see her pissed. It's not a pretty sight."

"Martin?" Emma squeezed his hand.

Tilting her head to check the angles of her face, Leon remarked, "Emma, with your beauty and success as an advertisement executive and his as a constitutional lawyer, the media is going to fall in love with you. I can't wait to see the polling numbers."

"You can sell her the idea later. I promise she'll be in a

better mood." He swatted Leon's hand away from Emma's face.

"Don't take too long. I have other candidates."

As Leon and Ravi's phones rang, the men left them alone.

"Before you say anything, I had to give them an answer. I didn't want to decide without you." Martin kissed her before she could respond.

"Can you please bring me home?"

"Let me take this for you."

She relinquished her bags. His quick peck on her head told her he was sympathetic to her whims and attuned to her fatigue. It soothed her nervous spirit.

As she sat in Martin's souped-up Mercedes SUV, her thoughts ran like a newsreel in her mind from Martin's announcement to Christopher's well wishes. Yet, her thoughts about Christopher seemed to have her full attention. It made her stomach turn. Running into him again opened memories she never wanted to revisit.

Damn it! Damn that five-hour delay! Breathe!

Shaking her head, she turned her attention to Martin's news. Before she left, he made it clear that he wanted a life with her. But the future he was offering had changed in two weeks. She wasn't prepared to have voters scrutinize her life nor dissecting the meaning in her words. She wanted to vomit.

I hope you find joy in your life.

"Aha! Get out of my head!"

"What did you say?"

Emma stopped tapping her finger on her lap. Taking a calculated breath, she returned to the present. They were on the stretch of the highway at the highest peak, where you were treated to a stunning view of the Toronto skyline. As the sun set, the rays of light cascading over the skyscrapers were calling her home. It was a breathtaking sight that made it easy to forget the last few hours.

"Nothing," she murmured as she pulled her hands together.

As he merged onto the Queen Elizabeth Highway, Emma focused on the skyline again. The Toronto horizon had changed with each new condo being erected. As a new building went up, there was less sky to see. In her youth, she always enjoyed seeing how light played on the waves of Lake Ontario. Yet as she aged, she only noticed how the towering condos distorted any natural light to shimmer on the water or on the city sidewalks below.

With her attention on the Toronto skyscrapers, her thoughts went back to her life. A writer would describe Emma's career as lucrative and her boyfriend as ideal. Her life was perfect on paper. Yet, in Emma's eyes, she judged it as an incomplete life. Every time she scrolled through family or friends' pictures on Facebook or Instagram, envy boiled in her heart. They appeared happy and fulfilled. She yearned for that happiness and was ready to have it with Martin. He offered her a life of 'happily ever after.' But, seeing Christopher again reignited the self-doubt and fear about Martin and the future she was planning with him before leaving for Vienna.

"You okay?" Martin asked as the traffic came to a standstill.

"I love coming home and seeing how beautiful Toronto is," she replied wistfully.

"Even as we sit in traffic." Martin chuckled and moved the car an inch forward. "Have you called your parents?"

"I can only handle one person's joy at a time."

"Do you want to listen to music?" Martin touched her hand gently.

"Hmm. Sure." She waited for him to choose something as she watched a family arguing with each other in the car beside her.

"Great. The silence is killing me."

She recognized the curt and frigid tone. As he was searching for a station, his fingers tapped the screen as if he wanted to punch someone.

"I'm sorry," she whispered. She placed her hand lightly on his forearm.

"I'm sorry too. They needed a decision and it —"

"Was an opportunity. It's not your news. I'm tired."

"Of course. How was your trip?" he inquired.

"It was great."

"I missed you. Two weeks without you is an eternity."

Emma tried to resist the urge to smirk as his attempt to be romantic lacked sincerity.

"She smiles. I wanted to plan ahead and hoped you would see it that way."

"A future together in politics?"

"Yes."

If there was a quality in Martin she always admired, it was his ability to make a definitive decision. His confidence in their future together endeared her towards him.

She met him when she was shopping at Ikea, trying to decorate her condo on a budget. They were in the Billy Bookcase section when he solicited her opinion. Emma was cautious. His tact and pick-up line lacked any finesse. He listened to her point of view and weighed the pros and cons of buying a Billy over an Expedit bookcase. Once she finished explaining the differences between bookcases and touring the section with him, he continued to shop. His response confused her. Her gut told her Martin was flirting. But, when he waved goodbye, extracting no personal information, she was disappointed until she rammed her cart into him.

"I'm so sorry," she uttered, embarrassed at her clumsiness.

He massaged his ankle, trying not to swear. "Not a problem. You didn't hurt me because I wanted your opinion and didn't thank you?"

"I was lost in my thoughts and didn't notice you stopped. Are you okay?" she asked him.

"I should let you pass me so I can still move tomorrow."

"Sounds wise. I've injured many people with a cart."

"Impossible; not with that angelic face."

She tilted her head, trying to read his body language for clues. Was he being polite, or was he flirting?

"I've lost my chance to get your number, haven't I?"

"Are you asking?"

"I wanted it when I saw you upstairs in the bookshelves section. I was waiting to run into you here since I didn't have the nerve to ask you up there."

"That sounds creepy."

"I swear I'm not crazy. If you want validation, you can call my therapist."

The same lightness and friendly manner had remained between them, but it never put her mind at ease. Although there was a comfort and an electrical, physical attraction between them, she wasn't sure if she could vow to love and honour him in sickness and in health for the rest of her life.

As they entered her condo, Martin was trying not to laugh. Her open concept condo had a stunning view of High Park and the city skyline in the distance. With her off-grey walls and modern stainless steel kitchen, light bounced off the walls and floors. But you wouldn't see that now, as her unpacked boxes were piled against the wall, and the opened ones were scattered on the floor like an obstacle course.

"Don't even say it!" She tried to cover his mouth.

"Are you moving?"

"Funny. I've—"

"Had no time to do it before you left," he nickered as he finished her sentence.

"I kept it this way so you could use it for your election headquarters," she commented, noticing his campaign posters scattered on the floor.

"They hope to run me in this neighbourhood. Leon wants me to set up residence here, eventually."

"Living with your girlfriend?"

"I know, not your ideal. But, I told Leon I'd live here for a better reason."

"You said that it had too many mom and pop shops, and you felt you were living in a small village."

"You showed me the error of my ways. I could learn to love your neighbourhood."

Martin stumbled to her room, dodging the boxes in his way. "It gets better in the bedroom," he yelled sarcastically.

With a high-hearted sigh, she peered at her unpacked brown boxes and reviewed Martin's political mock campaign boards and list of potential financial support.

Mrs. Martin Torcoke, can you tell us something you love about your husband that will be good for the city? Is this possible, Em, a life in politics?

Emma shook her head and cleared Martin's stuff from the floor. As she tidied up under the setting sun, she surveyed her space. Over the last year, she had tried to make it a home by purchasing a simple beige couch, two matching Poang chairs, as well as refurbishing stools for her breakfast bar. But with Martin's political banners and posters filling parts of her space, it resembled a campaign office.

"Do you want wine?" she asked.

"Sounds good," he yelled back.

As she was pouring the wine, she noticed how Amalie, her mentee, had been in her condo, trying to organize her books and photos. She recognized the framed lake photo and the pile of unmatched books and wondered if the memories and thoughts encased in them would still affect her. Groaning, she turned her head and pondered the way Amalie decorated her fridge with her to-do-list and recent photos. She mulled over the picture with her and Martin at the summer family picnic. It was a portrait of happiness, which made her wonder if he would be her husband at the next family one.

Downing her wine, she turned her attention from the pictures and returned her attention to the unfinished business around her. Amalie had managed to place some of her books away, but from Emma's experience, she knew the contents inside the box distracted her protege from finishing the task.

In a daze, she bumped into a stack of other boxes. With little reaction, she watched letters and pictures fall to the ground. She gathered the items and sorted them on the floor. Finding a stack of napkins, she stopped to read her poetry. Her fingers trembled over the words. Words that expressed her ideals and dreams for the future were now the musings of her naïve aspirations on disposable napkins.

As she sat on the floor organizing the other items, she found the ideal celebrity husband list. A scornful snicker left her mouth as she remembered how foolish and idealistic she used to be in her youth. She was a girl who believed her future husband would have George Clooney's dark and charming humour, Mark Wahlberg's body, and Denzel Washington's faith and wisdom. She downed another glass of wine before moving the contents back into the box. But a rock caught her eye. She held it in her hand and examined the grooves and the water lines on it, trying to recall its significance.

"Are you okay?" Martin placed his hand on her shoulder.

"I wish I'd eaten something before drinking. As you can see, I knocked over that box, and everything fell out."

"Are you trying to organize your stuff? Another glass of wine?"

"Why not? What is this?" She held the rock to his face.

"A rock."

"What else?" She rested her chin on her other hand.

"Is this a trick question?"

"Humour me?"

"Paperweight? No?"

"I worked with someone who studied this rock and declared he saw erosion, time, and sentiment. Rocks weren't his thing. Human anatomy fascinated him."

"What do *you* see?" He smiled down at her.

She responded like a preteen girl explaining her crush to her friends for the first time. "Life. Notice each watermark. This one is the person who held the rock and made a wish. It filled her heart with anticipation and hope for the future. The second line is when a young woman named Diane picked up the rock and threw it at the boy who broke her heart."

"And what did your coworker say after you displayed such a vivid imagination?"

"It's a rock."

She handed Martin the rock and watched how he examined its' grooves and colour again. Emma yearned for an answer that would tell her he was the man of her dreams. She wanted him to tell her that it was more than a rock.

"Seeing that you have all those pictures around you, and the way you're interrogating me, I would say this rock is important to you. A portal to your past?"

She pulled him to sit beside her. Kissing him lightly, she tasted the wine on his lips. It made her dizzy, and she forgot all her problems.

"I guessed right?"

"It's a keepsake from my summer job as a camp counsellor."

"I never thought you were nostalgic."

"It was a long time ago." With Martin's help, she got off the floor and placed the pictures and rock on an empty bookshelf. She meandered over to the kitchen to find something to absorb the wine burning through her blood rather than to dwell on the past or the future.

"You should call your parents." He leaned on the counter and turned his phone to her.

"Thanks, Mom!" She shoved the phone back to him.

"They worry."

"Didn't realize you were on my parents' team?"

"I'm always on your side, but I'm trying to get your parents to love me. If I can't convince them, then how can I even consider running for political office. Remember, I answered the door in a towel."

"Well, they assumed the worst. Trust me, the choices I make for myself is what they hate, not you."

"What are these?" He examined the remaining papers and books on the floor.

She glanced down and recognized the blue and detailed art on the back and front cover. She drank more wine before answering the question. "Those thoughts are of a teenage girls' naïveness."

"You write?"

"I used to."

"I've learned two new things today. Here you go." Topping off her glass, he handed Emma her journals.

"Not curious?" She peered over the rim of her glass.

"I am. But I'm more interested in the present." He kissed her forehead. "And the future. Should I leave?" he asked, grazing her lips and then tracing kisses down her neck.

"Why?" she murmured, feeling his need pressing against her stomach.

"You're not smiling. Do you need to tell me something?"

"I'm going back to work. Plus, my boyfriend told me he plans to move here because he's running for office. It isn't romantic." She straightened as her shoulders tensed up.

"So, you're angry at me?"

"It's not you. It's work. Things fall apart when I'm not there."

As he leaned in to kiss her, a twinkle of desire stirred in her heart. She knew what he wanted, and her need to forget the day outweighed her reservations about physical intimacy with him. As his lips moved to her neck again, reason went out the window as her feelings took over to physically respond to his kiss.

He whispered into her ear, "Perhaps we have a future ahead of us where you don't have to work anymore."

"Sounds tempting."

He took her wine glass and placed it on the kitchen counter. Resting his hands on her hips, he drew her close in a way that made her forget her present concerns and future worries.

"I don't have to leave. I can welcome you home properly." He paused and searched her eyes for her response.

She began to unbutton his shirt, forgetting her desire to discuss their future. Lifting her in his arms, he kissed her again and eased her back into a future with him.

CHAPTER 3

As the daily human cattle travelled briskly on the street, Emma stood outside the Gilles Marketing firm holding a Venti Pike Place and a briefcase of dread. She wished she was at home still in bed, but Martin, the early riser, made sure she was out the door before he left at sunrise. He had prepared a blueberry oatmeal muffin and vegetable smoothie to help her conquer the day. But, his breakfast didn't offer the caffeine jolt she needed to manage her absent-minded team. Behind those doors, the Ice Queen reigned, and pushing her subjects to work tirelessly was her path to success and happiness.

She was the best marketing strategist in her firm. She had a gift for creating campaigns that inspired consumers to believe happiness was in things. It wasn't her dream job, but she was an effective manager. She was a manager who learned that every time she left the office, her staff veered off her plans, causing unnecessary work and tension on her team.

The time she dedicated to managing their problems was an unnecessary nuisance. She tried to create a cohesive professional team, but her staff wanted it to function like a family. Hence, they treated her as the mother-hen. They trusted her fairness in distributing work and understanding when they missed deadlines. It explained why her staff wasn't at their desks as she meandered around the unit. Her team was hard-working and talented people, but she wished they were professional. Despite being disheartened, she opened her office door to an empty room.

"You're early!" Richard yelled as he ran towards her.

Richard was Emma's youthful and blond executive

assistant. An energetic bunny when it came to finishing his work, he was someone who always needed the carrot dangling in front of him to get him started. She loved his energy, but as she learned when working with him and her eagerness to please staff, mistakes and lapses in judgements were bound to happen without her watchful eye.

"Where are my things?" She interrogated Richard with laser eye focus.

"Not here. We've moved up in the world. Literally. We're on the seventieth floor."

"Richard?"

"Follow me. Charlie and Christine are upstairs."

She followed Richard to her new office. It was a spacious area for her to work on a long desk and a place for her team to meet and sit in cozy chairs and a comfy couch. But she didn't foresee any work getting done, especially on a clear and sunny day in the city, when you could see planes leaving the Billy Bishop airport, the magnificent height of the CN Tower, and the blue waters of Lake Ontario. At this height, one could get lost in their daydreams and accomplish nothing during the day.

Her team was in the process of hanging congratulations banners and balloons over her view. It was typical for them to leave everything to the last minute and cover up the best feature of her office.

"Surprise!" everyone yelled half-heartedly.

"You're back. Thank God! How do you like your new office?" Charlie screamed with relief as he guided her to her new executive chair and patted her down to sit.

"About what?" She sat, stunned, touching the surface of her shiny grey and white granite desk.

"Your promotion," Christine stated.

"I didn't say yes."

"You're a Vice President."

"No. I'm not," she declared as she checked the drawers of her desk that already contained her favourite pens and secret wrapped cappuccino chocolate truffles.

"Don't worry. Your new boss will love you. We were bought while you were on your trip. Charlie and I had to step aside, but they wanted to keep you and your staff," Christine explained.

Her mind reeled, and she couldn't breathe. Vomiting seemed like a good idea to relieve the butterflies in her stomach.

"Don't worry. Christine and I were planning to sell," Charlie added as he patted Emma's hand.

"Am I still a manager?"

"No! Listen. You're a Vice President," Christine repeated as she showed Emma her new desk nameplate.

"Of Marketing?"

"No!" Charlie shoved her new business card into her hand.

"What am I, then?"

"It's a long story. You'll be a fantastic Vice President of Philanthropy and Development."

She squinted her eyes. "What does that mean?"

"Where is Richard? He'll explain everything." Charlie scanned the room.

"Can someone explain what's happening?" She stood with her arms crossed in front of her chest like a conductor trying to figure out what to change in the score for the orchestra to sound harmonious. It didn't help her mood to see Charlie and Christine cracking jokes, indifferent to her feelings.

"The new owner doesn't need you to work on his Fortune 500 accounts. Your style doesn't work for those projects. He believes your talent will serve his charities and personal projects better," Christine explained with a reassuring tone.

"Where is Shane or Leslie? They have experience."

"Relax. It's a lot to take in. But when you strike gold, dig and leave," Charlie asserted as he placed his arm around Emma.

She jerked away from Charlie and wandered around her new office, trying to control the tremor in her hand. Touching the advertisement awards and memorabilia from her past marketing campaigns, which her staff had hung on her walls and placed on her shelves, didn't calm the chill in her spine.

God, why me?

Returning to her desk, she picked up one of her family pictures. Her staff had decorated her desk with photos of her nieces and nephews as well as her parents and siblings. It showed that they understood her very well to keep family portraits nearby. A picture of them all together at a family reunion managed to settle her nerves.

"He'll love you. You'll be fine." Christine handed her a file and encouraged her to open it.

In a blink of an eye, Christine and Charlie hugged everyone goodbye and left her with a new boss and job title.

"Richard, what is this?" Emma passed the file labelled *St. Michael's Family Service Centre* to him.

St. Michael's Family Service Centre was in the lively and multicultural area of Toronto known as Parkdale. Parkdale was a section of Toronto where you could taste the world, see colourful graffiti street art on the exterior walls, and discover vintage furniture and clothes to make your living space unique. It was an area where a centre like St. Michael's helped the impoverished inhabitants access mental health services and opportunities to find work, attend classes to enhance your working skills, or groups to support you as you rebuild your life.

"Our first project," Richard announced as he handed her back the file on the Centre.

"This is a prank, right?"

"Interesting word choice." He pointed at her as if he was a professor showing the class that Emma had given an original insight.

She glared at him with full knowledge that he was lying to her. "We need a plan."

"Usual caffeine shot?"

"Yes."

"Further details are on your desk. Welcome back."

Emma plopped down in her chair to stop her dizziness. She was sitting in her worst-case scenario; a Vice President of a made-up division that had to oversee a fundraising campaign for the St. Michael's Family Service Centre. Her stomach turned. This was the place where her sister Annabelle worked.

Tell me, God, this isn't happening.

She slumped over. Her world wasn't this complicated two weeks ago when her personal and professional life were separate. But, she was sitting in a strange blue-and-grey office, watching her two worlds collide. It was a situation she had no power to control when all she wanted to do was wake up from this nightmare.

She avoided working with her family. For her, working with family was the path to bruising someone's ego. Working on the St. Michael Centre campaign meant working with her sister, who was the senior social worker and liaison for the Centre's fundraising efforts.

Now, Emma loved her sister, but she wasn't so keen on

working with her. As the youngest of three, Emma was either being protected by the eldest Annabelle or teased by Lillian. When it came to Annabelle, she always made sure Emma felt safe and loved to the point that Emma hated it. Her sister took to protecting her like Canadian troops deployed by the UN to protect civilians in worn-torn countries. Sometimes it felt oppressing, but she felt safe in her care.

"You have a delivery!" Richard shouted, carrying yellow roses and white lilies for her.

"Martin is so sweet," she gushed over her favourite flowers.

"No, he didn't pick these flowers." He rolled his eyes at her.

"Who is it from?"

"No idea. Here's the card." Clearing his throat, he handed it to her.

Welcome to the team. I can't wait to see you soon.

"No name?"

"Not important. The flowers are stunning in your office. Oh, your mother, Annabelle, and Amalie called. They claimed it was urgent." He snatched the card from her, then jumped around her office, trying to find the best spot for her flowers.

"Let me guess; my mother called to lecture me. Annabelle wants to plan, and Amalie was having a faith crisis."

"Your trip has made you sharper."

"Richard, who sent the flowers?" She crossed her arms across her chest.

"It's a long story. Let's answer your messages instead."

He sat with his iPad in hand, ready to take notes. His attentiveness and eagerness to run down Emma's appointments made her more suspicious.

"Do you need to tell me something?" She watched Richard fidget with his tie.

"It could be the reason your sister called."

"She didn't call to congratulate me?"

"Sure." He lowered his head and tapped senselessly on his iPad.

"Richard! What are you hiding from me?" Sitting up straight in her chair, she waited for him to respond.

"This new title has taken to your personality." He avoided her steely glare.

She narrowed her eyes as she approached him like a seagull waiting for a three-year-old to drop his ice cream at a carnival. Circling him, she knew her position, and silence would force him to tell her the truth.

"It's the new owner. We started on the wrong foot. But, we're still working. What did you use to say? Let's consider the positive before delving into solutions."

"I've never said that."

"You sure?"

"Richard!"

"What were we talking about?"

"The flowers!"

Richard started making fish sounds with his mouth. She waited patiently, knowing that her assistant was about to tell her the truth.

"The new owner has concerns. There's a reason Charlie and Christine were quick to leave. You see, everyone appeases our new owner's requests because if he likes you and the work, he supports your projects. You have full access to his donor list and business ventures."

"Okay. Not the first time we've dealt with eccentric wealth and ego."

"Right."

"And?"

"In your absence, the millionaire requested we send him a work sample. We did, and we didn't." He nodded and avoided her lethal stare.

"That's confusing."

"We thought you, Charlie, and Christine were testing us and assumed you were playing a practical joke to make sure we were working. We sent you a parody of our work. Inventive, right?"

She was astonished at his stupidity.

"Explain." Her voice felt tighter than a wrestler, ready to attack her opponent.

"But then you weren't you, and well, we assumed we lost our jobs, then we're still here. Now, we have flowers."

"Richard, did you fix this?" Her tone was steady and lethal as she towered over him.

"We fixed it, and we didn't. That's why the card said see you soon. 'Tight Ass' is coming." Richard's tone was even as he scrolled through his notes.

"Come again?"

"Eccentric millionaire doesn't leave his house, so he sends a representative."

"Is 'Tight Ass' a nickname?"

"Rumour has it, he has a figurative and literal tight ass."

"Richard!" Her head was starting to throb as if rocks were rolling around in her head.

"Right. We're still working for the eccentric millionaire, provided 'Tight Ass' approves us."

"Does 'Tight Ass' have a name?" Grinding her teeth, she grilled Richard for information.

"My source couldn't get me that information."

"You don't have the new boss's name?"

"The new boss swore Charlie and Christine to secrecy. Part of the deal."

"Did your sources tell you how we wow the millionaire and the henchman?" She controlled her pitch and volume as she noted Richard's vibrant spirit deflated like a car tire running over a nail.

His face was turning green as he fidgeted with his perfectly aligned tie. "No."

"Is that why Annabelle left me a message?"

"Several messages."

"Are there more?"

"He'll be here on Wednesday for our presentation."

"That's in two days!" She clenched her fists as Richard kept adding on to the bad news. "And the flowers?"

"The flowers are from him." He pointed to the flowers dramatically.

"The eccentric millionaire?"

"No. 'Tight Ass.' I've heard when 'Tight Ass' sends a bouquet, it's a gift to remind you he can fire you."

"Let me get this straight, your source can tell you why 'Tight Ass' sends flowers, but you don't have 'Tight Ass' name or picture?" Throwing her hands up, she slumped down onto her desk chair.

"Both keep a low profile."

"You're joking, right?"

"No. I'm not CSIS. I'm not a spy."

"You're right! Spies wouldn't give the enemy intel on how to kill you. What did you send?" She closed her eyes and counted to ten as he retrieved the package. As he placed it on her desk, she had to count to one-hundred. Without even opening the contents, her blood boiled, seeing the unpolished presentation.

"We thought you needed to enjoy your holiday before getting back to, well, here." Richard pointed around the room as he stepped back to the other side of her desk.

"You wanted to wait till today?"

"Well, you didn't answer your phone. Martin told us that you were resting, rough flight, and, well, you didn't answer your emails. Figured we would solve the problem on Monday. We're still here. As you can see, our boss is merciful, right?" His pitchy and nonchalant voice broke Emma's resolve to remain patient and calm.

"Richard! This is serious. They could fire us. If you sent me this, I'd fire you."

"We appealed to the new owner's humanity and explained how you were returning from Austria. We sent a long list of successful projects. They must enjoy our work, because they kept your team intact and promoted you. Besides, we trust that you can fix our mistakes. Does the Ice Queen want to talk to her staff?"

She glared at him, trying to control the expletives exploding in her mind.

"I'll gather everyone," Richard mumbled as he dragged himself out of her office.

As her team filed into her office, she recited a Shakespeare sonnet in her head. It was an ideal way to deal with her frustration. Her room was full of stupidity, a room that might not even belong to her if she could not rectify their incompetence to save everyone's job.

"Welcome back! You seem well-rested." Lois tried to sound excited.

Emma growled, and with a twitch in her eyes, the members of her staff were standing straight around her desk.

"Too soon. I'll shut up now and let you continue."

"It's good to see that you have common sense. Cancel all your plans. We'll be working late till I can forgive you for embarrassing me."

She dropped the package on her desk and watched how everyone in the room quivered at the sound. It was time for them to understand why people called her the Ice Queen and not mother-hen.

CHAPTER 4

St. Michael's Family Service Centre offices were housed in a refurbished Victorian home. With its beautifully maintained craftsmanship of detailed woodwork on the ceiling and stairs, couches, and warm, muted colours, the Centre felt like a home. Even with the floors creaking throughout the house as clients and employees moved on each floor, it was a peaceful place for people to find refuge from the problems and stresses of their lives. It was a place where people could change their lives if they opened up their hearts to acknowledge the truth and work towards a better life.

She gripped the cell phone as she spoke to Martin. "I'll meet these people, but my sister needs to talk. I'll be there." Emma hated sounding like a whining child.

"You promise?"

"Yes. I'm at Annabelle's office," she whispered into her cell phone. Taking an exasperated breath, she found her composure as she listened to Martin.

"Emma! This is crucial to our future. Leon needs you here."

"Okay. I promise."

She plastered a face of confidence and calm for the people passing her in the hallway. She hated how their eyes judged her appearance and speculated why she was yelling in the hallway.

"Don't bail on me this time!" he ordered.

Emma noted how Martin was in his vigilant and uncompromising lawyer mode.

"I'm sorry. When I was away, everything changed."

"It's a sign. Quit. You didn't create this mess. Fire

your team. Your new boss will realize you can lead his Fortune 500 Marketing team rather than his philanthropy department."

"Martin! I can't. They're still my staff. They made a foolish mistake."

"They're adults."

"Martin! I have to impress my new boss."

"Don't you hate your job?"

"Hate is a strong word."

"Okay. I get it. Be here in an hour."

Before she could, Martin hung up the phone. The dial tone rang like French sirens in her ears, annoying and unbearable to hear. Clenching the phone in her hand and holding her head between her legs, she controlled her need to scream. After an exhausting team meeting, his disapproving tone deflated her last ounce of confidence and patience. But she didn't have the energy nor time to call him back and make peace with him.

Sitting outside Annabelle's office, she focused on her breathing to help her prepare for the current task. On the exhale, she allowed the tension in her shoulders to relax.

You have a plan. Convince your sister everything is okay. Trust in your team. O, God, make everything okay.

Shaking her hands out, her pep talk silenced the misgivings of her heart. For a moment, she embraced being alone with her thoughts. She let grace embrace her soul to study her surroundings and the people around her.

Observing people was a skill she had gained in a theater class. Theater class was where she studied the art of storytelling or, as her professors used to say, sharing stories in your life that you have embellished with your imagination. She laughed again. In her creative writing class, she learned the same lesson. The truth was present if she opened her eyes. Life had its own unending narrative.

She closed her eyes, remembering the hours she spent captivated by her characters' dreams and failures. It filled her spirit with a blissful peace. Working on her storytelling craft was the place where she learned to understand a person's soul and how fragile it was when they risked their heart for love. But after her experience with Christopher, her eyes were opened. Her imagination was dangerous. It was her imagination that kept her from seeing who she was and could never be. This epiphany influenced her to switch her major from Theatre to Business Administration. There she found a safe place to rebuild her confidence in black-and-white rules, where emotions were suppressed for economic success.

"I have good timing," Amalie squawked as she sat beside Emma, offering her a coffee and a chicken avocado wrap. "What are you contemplating about today? A regret story?"

Biting into her sandwich, Emma chewed her food slowly. She enjoyed Amalie's innocence and her ignorance but did not like how she could read her mind. After a few years, Amalie had become a close friend who saw beyond Emma's successful and confident executive woman facade. She recalled a time when Amalie was in her condo unpacking boxes with her. Amalie, being ever curious of her mentors past, rummaged through her university notebooks and always asked about the meaning of her random thoughts in the margin. In university when Emma got bored in class, she would write quirky limericks or outlines for stories instead of taking down notes in class. Emma thought she convinced Amalie that those were studying techniques to help her memorize literary form and criticisms from Chaucer to Beckett.

Emma swallowed her food. "Sorry. I used to journal. I was wondering why I stopped."

"You used to write?" Amalie giggled and popped a chip into her mouth.

"If you mean writing unsophisticated poetry verses and short stories, then yes," Emma replied, trying to sound indifferent.

"Anyone ever read it from cover to cover?"

"One person, but he read it because he wanted something from me."

"To know you better?"

Emma rolled her eyes. "Not in the way you think."

"I'm intrigued. Tell me more." Amalie rested her chin on top of her two clasped hands.

Amalie's child-like curiosity was something Emma wished still resided in her as opposed to adult suspicion. Actually, there were many things about Amalie that Emma admired. She marvelled at the different hairstyles and colours Amalie tried in a month. One day she was a blond punk girl, and the next day, she would be a brunette beatnik. Today she was a fiery redhead who didn't care what others thought, nor afraid to share her opinion with others even when they did not want to hear it. With that hair and look in her eyes, Emma knew Amalie was determined to unravel her life story

"Why are you here?" Emma observed Amalie's reaction over the brim of her coffee.

"I'm here for you. Your sister suggested it was a way to pay you back."

What bothered Emma about Amalie was her relentless mission to pay her back. After helping her find the courage and desire to live her life without alcohol or drugs, Amalie felt she was an indentured servant to Emma. In Amalie's mind, without Emma, she would still be in an abusive relationship, shooting up in a drug house. Or, as Amalie kept reminding Emma, she could be dead and not on the cusp of finding love again and on her way to a successful career in photography.

However, it never stopped Amalie from trying. As much as Emma tried to squash Amalie's quest to repay her, she had made it a point to always bring up the story ideas she had found in her university notebooks. Recently, Emma was dodging more questions about her occupation and explaining why she was using her writing skills to peddle products instead of publishing her anecdotes and stories. But, Amalie's admiration and persistence could not sway her in sharing her past nor the real reason why she stopped writing. Emma explained to Amalie that she used to write but gave it up when writing stopped being fun and when she accepted that it inspired no one. But Amalie disagreed.

Amalie was always quick to remind Emma how she saved her life. It was Emma's stories which showed her how the world was an endless stream of possibility. A place where she could be a photographer who captured the pain and suffering she endured to find peace with herself. Through Emma's example, Amalie learned the way to joy was to forgive herself for making ill-informed choices so as to reclaim and rebuild her life. It was this life lesson that inspired her to ask questions about Emma's life choices and unearth why she had chosen a career in marketing over writing.

"You don't owe me a thing. Why did my sister call you?" she inquired in her serious business tone.

"She's been trying to find you. Call her back. She tried Lillian, but she hadn't heard from you. Also, she wants my help. Do you mind? This is your job. I don't really do marketing."

"Amalie, our team needs you." Annabelle's confident voice echoed in the hall to remind Emma who the eldest was in the family. "I can see that my sister is shying away from praise. Come on in."

Annabelle invited the two of them into her office. Though small, it was a room full of light. It was a corner office that told its inhabitants where the sun rose and set. The best part was how the local bakery around the corner had so much business that Annabelle's office always smelled like fresh bread, even when the windows were closed. The aroma only heightened the warmth from the beige walls and a worn-out couch in the room. With a lack of clutter and walls adorned with inspirational posters and pictures, one left Annabelle's office, believing that tomorrow would be better than today. Yet, Emma's current mood did not appreciate the comfort nor the positive messages surrounding her.

"You've painted and organized it," Amalie squealed as she took pictures of the posters.

Annabelle grinned at Amalie then turned to Emma. "Thanks. How is your new office?"

"Lovely. You realize that Amalie can't help us until I meet the new owner." Sitting across her sister, Emma sat up straight and crossed her arms.

Even as adults, Emma always felt like Annabelle's little sister, a scaled-down version of her sister in appearance and intelligence. Emma was shorter, wider at the hips and shoulders. Where Emma was a great wordsmith and creative, her sister was also gifted in those areas, while still excelling in the scientific realm. In short, Annabelle was a renaissance woman whose hair was perfectly styled and suited to her well-proportioned face, but whose outer beauty paled in comparison to her giving nature and patience. Yet, being the youngest sister, Emma was treated more to the responsible sister who told her what to do. But, Emma couldn't hold it against Annabelle. She was too beautiful and smart for Emma to hate. In fact, she adored Annabelle. She had it all. A career she loved and thrived in and a family to go home to where she could escape the pitfalls of her job where she dealt with the worst of our human nature.

With her dark brown eyes and haired pulled back, Annabelle stared at Emma and tried to use reason to explain Amalie's presence. "We need to throw everything at your new boss. I took it upon myself to research your new eccentric millionaire." Sounding like a drill sergeant, Annabelle handed Emma her research.

"My team has provided me everything I need for the presentation."

"What's your new boss's name?"

Emma remained silent.

Shaking her head, Annabelle showed her a business card. "Great team. His name is Mr. X."

"Really? No first name? Great research team!"

"The name isn't as important as the person. My sources tell me this millionaire likes the human touch. Em, ever since you graduated from business school, for you, it's always been about the bottom line. If you have someone on your team who has enjoyed our services, then it'll show how important this campaign is to you."

Emma winced at Annabelle's words. Since childhood, Emma could not conceal her fears or joys from her.

Passing her a compact mirror, Annabelle added, "Besides, you need help. You look like a bus ran over you ten times."

"I've been working on my new boss's approval. Nice to

see you again. " She shot up to scrutinize her sister.

"Oh, for heaven's sake, I'm making a keen observation. If you returned my calls, then I could help you."

"Sorry. I wasn't sure which message I should answer. You left a hundred of them," Emma yelled so people down the hall could hear her.

"Are you okay?" Annabelle touched Emma's hand.

Emma slapped Annabelle's hand away. "What do you think? My team worked around the clock last night. They're still finishing the presentation."

Instead of standing in place, Emma wandered around Annabelle's office. She didn't want anyone around her to see her tears streaming down her face.

"Is Emma's firm helping with the fundraiser?" Amalie asked Annabelle.

"Maybe. But with my help, Emma and her team can impress Mr. X."

"Fantastic! We can work together, and you can write and—" Amalie screamed.

"No," Emma yelled. She didn't mean to raise her voice. But, she needed to remind her sister to treat her like an equal. "Anna, we're meeting his representative tomorrow. We're fine. I'll do whatever I need to do to make it happen. Besides, it'll be fun… to work with you."

"I was excited when I heard the news. It is a dream come true, you and I working together." Annabelle patted her sister on the back.

"Sometimes, we don't get what we want, only what we need, remember?" Emma embraced her sister.

Simpering, Annabelle glared at her sister. "You're using my own words against me?"

"I'll fix it."

Emma was moved by her sister's passion since

Annabelle only showed her feelings when she was really worried. Between the two sisters, Emma was the cry baby of the family. As they were growing up, Annabelle and Lilian were merciless every time Emma cried at the ending of *A Walk to Remember* or Mr. Darcy's declaration of love to Elizabeth in *Pride and Prejudice.* In this relationship, Annabelle was the strong-willed and confident sister who believed things would work out in the end. Yet as she cried, Emma wasn't sure; she couldn't ignore a sister in need. Annabelle was a sister who never sought help or reassurance from her. It hurt her to see how Annabelle was pleading for her assistance. Holding her sister tightly, she exhaled, accepting she had to be successful tomorrow and work with her sister even if it meant breaking her rules and accepting the promotion.

"Regardless, if this millionaire wants to keep me or not, I'll help you," Emma promised as she offered her pinky to her sister as a means to swearing to it.

"Don't sugarcoat the problem. We're in trouble."

"We're fine. A bump. Nothing I can't fix." Emma went into her marketing persona, trying to convince Annabelle that charming a millionaire was an easy task to accomplish.

Amalie leaned forward. "Have faith, Annabelle. As your sister has told me, the impossible is always the bleakest at the start because you fear the unknown. But, when you take the first step, light shines through the darkness," she added with her trademark childlike trust.

Emma was relieved to see her sister's shoulders relaxed. It made Emma believe that her sage wisdom could still comfort her sister. Emma returned to her seat in triumph that she had defused Annabelle's anxiety with Amalie's help.

But the peace did not last long as the door to Anna's

office banged open. A young and agitated man of a mixed-race shut the door. He pointed his gun to their heads. Emma gasped as Amalie and Annabelle raised their hands. In the blink of an eye, danger entered.

"Curtis, what are you doing?" Annabelle demanded, levelheaded, as always.

"I don't want to go back."

His voice was shaky and loud. The gun was rattling in his hands as he squarely pointed it at Annabelle's head. She didn't flinch or break eye contact with him.

"Where?" Annabelle inquired.

"Juve."

Emma remained silent, clenching her fists as she saw Annabelle turn into a superhero. She wanted to help her, but her legs couldn't move to protect her sister. Fear was real. Her sister could die before her eyes and vice versa. The thought sent her body into shock as she watched Annabelle, with her sympathetic superhero stance, face the barrel of a gun, wondering if she would be as calm and compassionate towards the assailant.

"This isn't my fault—"

"It never is, Curtis."

Breathe, Emma. God, please help.

Emma bit her lip to keep from crying, but a whimper emerged. Curtis turned to her as he kept the gun pointed towards her sister's head. She studied his eyes and noted the fear and guilt of whatever he had done and the consequences of his actions.

"This time, it isn't. The guys dared me to take Linda to the bleachers and have sex. They recorded it," he confessed to Emma as if she had the power to forgive him.

In a soft and comforting voice, Emma asked, "It wasn't your idea?"

"No."

"Did you like her?"

Curtis's mouth opened, but no sound came out. He shook his head frantically as if he realized he hurt someone he cared about.

"Uh…well…I…yes."

Brushing her tears away, Emma asked, "Then why did you do it?"

"I didn't know I liked her till we did it. I tried…I tried….to get them to erase it, but, they didn't listen…they sent —"

Annabelle reassured Curtis. "Listen, if you keep holding that gun, I can't help you. Lower it so we can talk. Don't worry. You can trust them." She pointed at Emma and Amalie.

"She liked me…and…I used her." Curtis's gun began to rattle again in his hands as he returned his attention to Annabelle.

"You took advantage of her feelings, didn't you? Did you consider her feelings and the consequences of your decision?" Annabelle's stern voice seemed to wake something up in Curtis to admit his fault.

"I get it. I was stupid. What will happen?" Curtis cried.

"Curtis, if you put the gun down, we can talk and find out."

"But I've been working so hard. I don't know….why…but you can testify that I've been trying… in case…I…might go to jail….and tell her I'm sorry….and my brother….I can't….please, I don't know what to do…can you help—" His hand lowered to his side with the barrel of the gun pointing down.

"Of course, I can." Annabelle compassionately stretched out her hand in a way that Curtis could not deny.

Watching the action unfold before her, Emma's lungs

begged for air. Her sister never lost her calm and nurturing spirit nor let fear overtake her responsibility to take care of another human being in distress. It was an ounce of compassion before law and order took over.

CHAPTER 5

Through pursed lips, Christopher pleaded, "Emma, don't do this!"

Anger filled her blood. Rage muted her soul's compassionate voice. Instead of listening to his pleas, she slapped him.

"Tell them, or I will."

"Please, I can explain."

Leering, she backed away and held her hands up to stop him from coming any closer.

"It's true. Winston, Lionel, Greg, Michelle, and I made a bet. I told them you would sleep with me... I could get you to sleep with me. I didn't know that...I'm sorry. Em, please let me explain."

Emma punched him and stomped away.

The EMTs were checking Annabelle's vitals, while Emma peered out Annabelle's office window. Outside, a crowd gathered to record Curtis being pushed into a squad card. Her stomach tingled with pain. She wondered if this is what happened to Christopher after leaving him on the stage.

Her sister's voice brought her back to the present. She didn't realize that Annabelle's supervisor Douglas had come into her office nor how her sister was acting as if she didn't have a near-death experience.

"I have to call his mother. He has a younger brother." Annabelle handed him Curtis' file.

"I'll get someone to do that for you," Douglas offered.

"How good is their case?" Emma tore herself from the window and joined her sister and Douglas.

"Enough to charge him. If they need information, they'll contact us."

He took the phone from Annabelle.

"What will happen to Curtis?" Emma tried to sound calm and indifferent, but she heard the wobble in her voice.

"The court will decide. You should both go home. Hug your kids. Hug anyone."

After a few more encouraging words, Emma and Annabelle listened to Douglas and left the Centre.

"Say hi to the kids for me, okay?" Emma hugged her sister tightly.

"I will. Will you be okay?" she inquired with sisterly love.

With narrowed eyes, Emma studied her sister's relaxed shoulders and calm expression. "Why are you so calm?"

"This isn't the first time someone came into my office with a gun."

Emma's mouth dropped in shock.

"I don't tell you everything. I didn't want anyone to worry. But, we fundraise every year, so we don't have to choose to save our client's life or have better security. We choose life. Now, do you see why I need you to impress your new boss?"

To save your life!

"Do you need a ride home? You shouldn't be alone," Annabelle asked as Emma stood in front of her with a stoic expression.

"I'll walk," Emma responded as she pushed herself to stand straight and put on her brave face for Annabelle.

"Are you sure?"

"Fresh air and people will help me relax."

Eyeing her sister, Annabelle pried, "Did you call Martin?"

"As soon as we say goodbye."

After a few more reassurances, Emma made her way home. It was a luxury to have a pleasant stroll down Toronto streets, even if the summer odour was pungent on humid days. Yet, the cool breeze off Lake Ontario kept the stench from hanging in the air too long. You could smell it, but it was not a scent that stopped you from enjoying the outdoors. It allowed city dwellers to soak in the glistening sun on store windows and forget their troubles. She almost got lost in it, but her mind couldn't forget how a gun was pointed at her. Gasping for air, the Toronto summer odour was too much for her senses to ignore.

She dialled Martin's number with shaky hands. "Martin, please call me. I'm sorry. Please, don't be angry, but I can't make it tonight. I just…witnessed a young man hold a gun to….Annabelle's head because he recorded having sex with a girl he liked…and my sister saved herself from being shot. And, she protected me…and now needs help to…raise money so when it happens again…I almost died today."

She tried to take deeper breaths, but the shallowness in each inhale shocked her system. Up and down, her legs were pulsating pebbles of pain that paralyzed her ability to move at any normal pace. Her head was spinning as her mind and body begged for rest from the memories and feelings exploding within her heart.

She found a bench to sit on in High Park, but it didn't help to temper her emotions. Rummaging through her bag, she desperately searched for a tissue. She only found a Post-it Note stack. Out of desperation, she dabbed her eyes with them. It didn't dry the downpour of water from her nor aid in shielding her from strangers' unwanted attention. She opened her purse again and found a pen. Her impulse told her to write, even though it was something she hadn't done if it wasn't work-related. Yet, the thought produced a rush of peace in her heart. It gave her shaking hands a job to control the terror racing through her blood.

"One is never good with responsibility for one's actions. We always fear embracing the consequences of our choices. Still as wise as ever?"

Seriously! Out of all the parks in Toronto, I have to run into you. Christopher!

His sarcastic timber had aged, but the tone made the hair on her skin rise to attention. Lifting her head, she nearly lost her breath at those charming dark hazel eyes, if her defence system didn't kick into high gear.

"Sorry, did I bother you?"

"You could never bother me, Christopher. I enjoy complete strangers reading over my shoulder," she growled at him as she covered her Post-it Notes.

He grinned. "Can I join you?"

"It's a free park." She pulled her hair back and sat up straight, trying to appear confident, but he didn't budge from his position. Unable to move her legs and leave the awkward standstill, she invited him to sit down rather than having him hover above her.

As she was moving over, her Post-it Notes fell to the ground, and as she tried to pick them up, his head thwarted her from the task. Wincing at the pain and swearing under her breath, she was the first to relent to the contact, which allowed him to retrieve her notes.

"I guess we're still hard-headed," he claimed, she supposed, trying to be funny, but as he read the notes she dropped, he pinched the bridge of his nose, mumbled some expletives, and evaluated her forlorn expression. "Emma, are you okay?"

"I'm fine."

"A young man pointed a gun at you?"

"Actually, my sister had a gun pointed at her but remained calm like someone diffusing a bomb. Then he asked for forgiveness from me. You haven't learned to mind your own business." Snatching the notes from him, she tucked them into her bag.

"Em, are you okay?"

He crouched in front of her and gently took her hands into his own. Surprisingly, the way he stroked his thumb against her skin and stared didn't infuriate her. Instead, the gesture and silence that followed stirred a calmness in her that she hadn't felt in a long time.

"You tell me? I've been working for two days because I have to undo my staffs' stupidness for sending this horrible representation of my work to my new boss. An eccentric millionaire, who won't even meet me so I can defend myself, sends his grim reaper to fire me and my staff. We've been working long hours the past few days, and worse, if I fail, my sister's Centre will have to place their financial future in a stranger's hands who might not even care that the Centre has proper security. A young man holds a gun to my head and wants me to forgive him for making a sex tape, then my Wonder Woman sister saves the day and tells me this is not the first time. I can't get a hold of Martin, who hasn't even bothered to call to see if I'm okay because he's busy building a future for us. Plans I thought were secure are disappearing. You accept that your failures are undoable, but when my sister and my mentee…and this young man who made a mistake decides to bring a gun…and I…could've…died…you…you realize—"

On instinct, she fell into his arms. Feeling his touch, she

wanted her doubts and fears to disappear in his embrace.

"It's okay. You're okay. It could change his life. Didn't you used to say people need to hit rock bottom before changing their life?"

She began to sob. Christopher held her closer, rubbing his hands along her back. It was an innocent gesture, but a jolt raced up her spine. Startled, she pulled away. "Sorry I ruined your shirt."

"It's just a shirt."

Trying not to laugh, she produced a reassuring smile.

"You can use shrimp fried rice, lemon chicken, and sweet and sour pork," Christopher suggested as he handed his tie to Emma to wipe her tears away.

"This is a really nice tie."

"It works better as a tissue. So how about it?"

She blinked several times, unsure what Christopher wanted from her. "What are you talking about?"

"We can talk it over while we eat some Chinese food. I remember you saying that shrimp fried rice, lemon chicken, and sweet and sour pork can cure any problem."

She laughed out loud. "I wanted you to buy my favourite meal."

Seeing him grin, her lips frowned. She didn't want to feel comfortable and concern from him. "What are you doing here?" she asked in the best business voice she could muster.

"Walking home from work."

"I thought you were in London or moving to London."

"Still deciding. I took on one more project before I decide where I belong. And… Beth thought—"

"Beth?"

"Forget it. My problems are minor, considering what happened to you today."

"I need a distraction. Is Beth your girlfriend?" She leaned back on the bench.

"Maybe."

"Maybe?"

"She's building a career for herself, and I've been helping her."

"Not into distant relationships?"

"Who's good at distant relationships?"

"Wandering eye and all?"

"We're not serious."

"Your opinion or hers?"

"I guess mine."

"You guess right."

They both smirked and coughed at the same time. Looking in opposite directions and releasing an awkward sigh, they sat silently beside each other. Emma focused on two teenagers who were sitting on a bench. From her point of view, they were having a serious discussion or argument. She couldn't tell. But the way they were staring at each other, she could see the affection between them. It was as if they were in their own world speaking a language only they understood. She knew what that felt like and hated how it was a feeling associated with the man beside her.

"How about yourself?" he asked as he faced her again.

Still assessing the conversation between the teenagers, she asked, "What about me?"

"You mentioned a Martin. The boyfriend?"

Biting her lower lip, she took out her phone and showed him a picture.

"Handsome and fit fellow. Is he in construction or something?"

"Constitutional law."

"Brilliant and built. You've found someone to meet your

standards. You seem happy."

Emma questioned the sincerity in his voice, but as she evaluated Martin's broad shoulders and perfectly groomed hair, she couldn't disagree. They seemed happy and well-off, secure in their careers, and on the brink of making their arrangement permanent. The thought made Emma's stomach turn.

"He's a good man," she claimed, tucking her phone back into her purse.

"Has he called you yet?"

Grunting and turning her whole body towards him, she defended Martin. "He will. I was meeting him to have drinks with people he needs me to meet. The bars are loud."

"They are." He nodded as if he didn't believe her. She always hated it when he did that.

"He's schmoozing."

"The breakfast-eating, Brooks-brother's type."

She fought the urge to agree with him, but the corners of her mouth did not listen to her.

"Well, there it is." He tipped her chin to study her face.

"What?"

"Your real smile."

Pulling away, she wiped the grin from her face. "When I met you, you didn't understand social cues."

"Not true —"

"You didn't even know what a musical was, and now you quote one."

Rendering him speechless for a while made her happy.

"Well, time changes a man, and sometimes you meet someone who teaches you about life. To learn new things. To hope."

He lingered a little too long on the word *hope* as he tried to maintain eye contact with her.

"Hope? When I met you, I couldn't even inspire you to believe in hope and see —"

"How each snowflake is different, like a person's fingerprints."

Her heart stopped as she recognized those words. "You remember something I said to you?"

He nodded and examined his shoes. "I thought you were wise."

His comment flattered her ego. But sadness filled her heart immediately as his betrayal made her question his motives towards her.

He turned his head and squinted his eyes. "Emma, I need to tell you something."

"Your phone," she pointed to his jacket.

"Excuse me?"

"In your jacket."

"I'm always on call. Excuse me."

As he checked his messages, Emma observed how rigid he became in his posture. His relaxed muscles tensed as the lines on his forehead became more pronounced, and that chiseled face full of confidence and charity hardened as if he was going into a war zone. His manner was a stark contrast to the towering trees above his head and the long stretch of grass behind him, which called for all visitors to embrace peace and tranquility.

"Is everything okay?" She had a desire to understand why his manner changed as soon as he finished checking his phone.

"My boss. He was reminding me that I have a job to do."

"Well, you should call him back. I should be going." She got up and collected her things.

"I can escort you home. My offer still stands. I can order Chinese. You shouldn't be alone. Besides, this can wait."

"No! I'll be fine. Martin will call soon, and I'll talk it out with him."

"He's your boyfriend. That's his duty," he implied as if he were her trusted friend. "I mean, if you were my girlfriend and you called me to say you almost died, then I would already be by your side."

Hearing him say that made her feel heard and seen. She felt loved and safe. Yet, these were not feelings she wanted to have for him mixed in with those of almost dying. Relieved with hearing the ring tone of a sweeping musical interlude, she said, "Your phone again."

Never taking his eyes off of her, he stammered, "They can leave a message…you see…well… Listen, we were friends before… everything came out and I, and we, let's put it this way—"

"We were never friends." Her tone was firm and absolute.

He cleared his throat. "You were the closest thing I've ever had to a friend. I missed —" His phone continued to interrupt their conversation. "I hear it. But considering what happened to you, you're more important." He stepped in front of her. "If I could take back what I did, I would. But I can't. I hope we can put this behind us. I'm—"

Emma's phone beeped. She reached into her purse for her phone and moved away from Christopher. Relieved, she read Martin's text.

Babe, sorry. Didn't hear the phone ring. Where are you? Call me. Martin

Raising his eyebrows, he asked. "Your knight in shining armour?"

"I should go."

"Wait."

He grabbed her elbow, and she held her breath. Turning around, she jerked her arm out of his grasp and offered her hand.

"Thank you for listening, but I need to call him."

"Least I can do," Christopher grumbled as he shook her hand.

She let go as soon as she felt the bolt of butterflies dance in her stomach again. With the events of today mixed in with his kindness, she was too tired to understand why this tidal wave of emotions drew her closer to him. She didn't understand why her heart raced with affection and trust when he listened to her when she was prepared to hate and distrust everything that came out of his mouth forever.

CHAPTER 6

Emma was pacing the boardroom like a queen ant, ordering her colony to bring sugar home. Hollering and reading over her staff's shoulder, it was the way to keep her team focused and ready for the presentation ahead. In Emma's mind, lives were at stake.

Amalie whispered to Richard, "Is she okay?"

"A nervous wreck? Absolutely! She's getting us revved up. Never seen her rule her kingdom with an iron fist?"

"Richard!" Emma's voice was piercing and assertive. "Where is the report?"

"Report on your side. Presentation ready to go. Copies for everyone. Relax. We got this."

Instead of yelling at him for his irritable professional readiness, Emma reviewed the report in front of her and found everything she needed for the meeting. Thumbing through the presentation eased her mind, but her body was starting to numb as her breakfast was ready to come up from her stomach. Inhaling and closing her eyes, she counted to ten to refocus and warm her body. But her cold, shaky hands told her it was not working.

"Emma, are you okay?" Amalie pulled Emma down to sit in her chair.

"Fine. Nervous. I didn't realize how important this Centre is to the community. Coffee, Richard? I need coffee," she hollered.

Richard didn't even glance up from his phone. "Your coffee is in front of you."

Wanting to rip the phone from his hands, she turned instead to Amalie, who pushed the coffee closer to her. She inhaled the Bavarian chocolate-flavoured coffee and let the aroma invade her senses. The caffeine brought her back to a state of calm even though she wished Richard would remember to throw a dash of cinnamon in her coffee. Richard refused, claiming that you never mix anything with chocolate. As the cup of coffee warmed her hands, she hated how he ignored her at times but was grateful for a cocky and competent assistant who anticipated her needs during times of stress.

"Did you fight with Martin again?" Amalie questioned Emma with the insight of a spy.

Her tranquil state evaporated as Amalie's noisy and astute nature reignited the anger she felt towards Martin. He insisted that she stay home, that she needed time to process what happened to her. Emma disagreed. She had a job to do so Annabelle could have a safe place to work and save lives. It escalated into a full argument where he pointed out that she needed to stop trying to solve everyone's problems.

"No, I'm worried about this presentation."

Amalie raised her left eyebrow. "You know I'm here for you as well, to listen." She moved Emma's coffee away from her shaking hands. "Remember to take a breath. You taught me that."

Emma tapped her fingers along the surface of the table as if she was playing scales. She hated it when Amalie used her own advice against her.

"So, how are Sonja's wedding plans coming along?" Amalie probed like a good friend who wanted to help.

Relieved for a change in topic, Emma replied, "I need to return a hundred messages from her. She's a demanding bride."

"And as her friend—"

"I want to do everything for her."

With wide eyes, Amalie retorted, "Shocking!"

"You okay? I mean, you were there yesterday," Emma whispered as she examined Amalie's tranquil expression.

With a shrug of her shoulders, she confided, "I've had a gun pointed at me before. It brought back memories. But, as I did then and will do now, it's the wake-up call to change something in my life, right?"

"What do you mean?"

"Remember when I slipped and had a drug overdose, and you had to come and get me at the hospital? Well, you said it was my wake-up call. You told me that near-death experiences inspire those with regret to change their life."

Or hitting rock bottom.

"You sure I told you that?"

"Yes," Amalie answered like a child who was caught stealing a cookie from the cookie jar.

"'Tight Ass' is coming. 'Tight Ass' is coming!'" Gasping for air, Richard rushed into the conference room. "Scarlett called from downstairs. She testifies that it's true; the man has a tight ass."

"Richard, go greet our visitor," Emma reminded him.

"Right."

"Why is he your assistant?" Amalie pointed as Richard left the boardroom.

"He's organized and productive."

"Nervous?"

"I have to be perfect."

As Richard rushed out to meet Mr. X's people, Emma tapped her finger on the table again, wondering if she was good enough to lead a new division and convince 'Tight Ass' how valuable her team was to her work. But doubt clouded every affirming mantra in her head, which told her that she was capable and talented to meet the demands of running a massive fundraising campaign.

God, if you're listening, I need this to work out. I need something to be right with my life.

"Emma Alamayo, Christopher Gomes Riley and his team, Kyle, Bridget, and Linda."

You got to be kidding me! Really, God? Really!

Emma blinked a thousand times to cool the anger boiling through her blood. Her deadpan expression concealed her surprise. She wished she had prayed for a kind stranger's understanding ear as opposed to having a successful meeting.

"Mr. Riley, a pleasure to meet you. You've met Richard. He's my assistant. This is Donald and Debra, my senior associates. Joanna and Jack are my creative team. Jane and Calvin, they're my event planners. This is William and Amalie. They're here to represent the Centre." She smiled like a pageant contestant telling the audience that her dream was for world peace.

"Christopher, please. It's a pleasure to meet you, Emma."

His limp handshake expressed how he was waiting for her to say something. There was nothing in his eyes that pleaded for her to remain silent about their connection. Instead, they were open and were urging her to say something about their relationship. Yet, she reasoned that lamenting or screaming would not help her to keep her job. Releasing his warm and sweaty hand, she invited him to sit.

"I'm sorry. Did you say your name is Christopher Gomes Riley?" Amalie drew Christopher's face towards her.

"Yes, why?"

"No reason. I'm hard of hearing."

"Should we get down to business?" Emma invited her

team to take their places.

Christopher turned towards the presentation and then to Emma. “You’re not presenting?”

“I decided my team needed to prove their professionalism, considering what they sent our boss.”

She sat across from him but did not attempt to make eye contact. As she reviewed her notes, she wanted to temper the goosebumps on her skin and the fury raging in her heart. When she opened her eyes, he was focusing on her. He nodded as if he was inviting her to join her team, but she turned away instead.

The lights dimmed, and her team began their presentation. Professionalism oozed out of them. Like a proud mother watching her child sing a solo in perfect pitch, the hours she had sacrificed rehearsing with them had built them into confident marketing professionals. They were proving to Christopher that they were not naive idiots but were intelligent and smart individuals. Emma noted that their presentation was seamless, as if they were Shakespearean actors speaking Elizabethan English as their mother tongue. Unfortunately, their professional perfection made it easy for her to watch Christopher.

Assessing his every move, she could not tell if Christopher was paying attention or trying to avoid making eye contact with her. As the presentation went on, his indifference to her presence as he listened and made notes annoyed her to the point that she would’ve left the room if her sister and staff didn’t need her to stay and help. But what bothered her the most was how the arrogance and confidence he exuded in his youth had matured and softened and compelled her heart towards him. It infuriated her. So much so, Amalie had to stop her from tapping her fingers on the table several times.

"Thank you. But to verify, no one here has ever led a not-for-profit campaign?" Christopher leaned forward and sized up Emma's team.

"Regardless if it's public or private, we're the best," Debra answered.

"Emma, from what they showed, did you lead those other marketing campaigns?" Christopher focused his attention on her.

"Yes, she is the unseen fuel that keeps our engines going," Richard stated with heartfelt pride.

"I oversee every project. I make sure we stay well under budget, and I keep my team on point. My team handles the research, marketing, and event planning. Final decisions are mine. I trust them to do their job." Emma sat straight up in her chair.

His eyebrows shot up. "Even after what they did?"

"A lapse in judgement. I'm sure you've made poor decisions in your youthful enthusiasm." Emma clasped her hands on the table and leaned forward.

Reaching for his water and taking a sip, he cleared his throat. "But when you call yourselves professionals, you expect perfection. Simple thing I learned, but if the people you work with show poor judgement and produce subpar work, you have to let them go. But, since they're still here, what does it say about their leader?"

Richard spoke up. "She doesn't treat anyone like a subordinate. Emma is faithful in her relationships to the point where you trust her with your life." Richard defended Emma as if he were being personally attacked.

"Your team went rogue." He started to text on his phone. "I'm surprised you gave them a second chance, considering what they sent my boss."

"And they've apologized. OUR boss gave them a

second chance, so I followed his lead."

"You didn't want to give them a second chance?" Christopher passed his phone to his assistant.

Emma's mouth went dry as she searched her mind for a response. Meeting his gaze, she replied, "I've reviewed the materials they sent. Mr. X is very generous."

He leaned forward and never broke eye contact with her. "Emma, do you believe in giving people second chances?"

She blinked continuously as her heartbeat doubled in speed. She had two ways of answering that question. If she answered no, her staff would lose their jobs, but if she said yes, that would mean they could start over.

Richard spoke up with urgency. "As we explained, we assumed Emma was testing us, and we called her bluff."

"If you sent this to her, and it was her, would you be here? Emma, who would you fire?" Christopher's voice vibrated off the framed paintings on the wall.

"You're a jackass!" Amalie blurted out as she stood up.

Stunned, Emma glared at Amalie to sit and shut up.

Amalie continued. "Sorry, this job isn't worth it if he treats you and your team like idiots. You can tell your boss, he can stick it—"

"Amalie!" Emma yelled as she stood and forced Amalie to sit.

With a softer and tight voice, Amalie boasted, "Emma goes beyond what any sane person would do for another person."

"Mr. Riley, what Amalie is trying to say is that my team and I can produce amazing work. We work tirelessly."

"I've seen the numbers. You're efficient. Mr. X wants to work with you. He loved your campaign in Europe for Coffee and Tea Bundle. Yet, your professionalism concerns me."

He tossed the package her team sent onto the board table. Its thudding sound alerted Emma's defence system. She knew she would have to explain why she gave her team a second chance when their error in judgement illustrated a lack of respect in her leadership. But to do that, she would imply that she was willing to give him a second chance for his youthful crime. Her pride refused to give him the satisfaction.

"Ms. Alamayo, my boss sent me here because you're talented and very successful. I'm not here out of compassion. Amalie, if Emma were serious about her job and this campaign, she would have a new team around this table. I have heard Emma is ruthless, but if I may be frank, the work you produce is spectacular, but it lacks something. You and your team can sell dirt and call it gold, but raising money for a cause is delicate. You have to be honest about what the money will be supporting. Mr. X invests in people first before considering the profit margin. We're holistic in our work, and our leaders become intimate with their projects and translate that passion to their team. It produces the best creativity, which produces successful financial and personal outcomes. My boss is interested in leaders who understand that their work is more than money. It's about the person. Emma, you didn't present anything. It suggests you have no commitment or passion. Do you even want to do this?"

Amalie jumped to her feet and shouted as if she were Emma's television defence lawyer, "Well, you and your boss are elitist snobs. Emma is the most passionate person I have ever met. Without the mentor program at the Centre, I wouldn't be alive. Emma saved my life. Is that personal connection enough? Plus, her sister works there."

Christopher motioned for Kyle to pass him his iPad. He

reviewed it while Emma yanked Amalie's arm to sit down again.

With her lips pursed together, Emma composed herself and studied Christopher's facial expression. His confident arrogance could light up the room, but she wasn't going to give him the satisfaction of getting under her skin. "I don't see how my personal involvement is any concern to the work we do nor how I handle my team."

"It shows true investment, Ms. Alamayo. I've learned that, without a sense of emotional investment or a sincere understanding of the company's principles, your work is lifeless. Regardless, if your campaign is a success, it won't inspire anyone to give next year. Did you consider the lives you could save today and tomorrow?"

Amalie cleared her throat. "Emma understands how to help people. She knows why the Centre is important. She almost died there." Her statement vibrated through the boardroom.

Every head turned towards Emma. Feeling the need to strangle Amalie for another outburst didn't compare to the embarrassment she felt when every eye pitied her. It made her furious. She never wanted to appear vulnerable in front of people again.

"What?" Richard yelled in his usual disbelief of danger ever happening to people.

Composed and professional, Emma responded, "I'm fine. I'm here, aren't I?"

"My team would like to hear about your experience." Christopher's voice was softer as he nodded to encourage her to share her story.

Her hands started to quiver as a dozen eyes and ears waited for her to say something. It had been a while since she had a captivated audience, an audience who wanted to hear her story, and it petrified her. She wasn't ready to discuss what happened in her sister's office nor what it meant to be Amalie's mentor. Studying the room, she searched for anything to get her out of the situation, but all she saw were blurred faces. Christopher's face was the only image that was clear. He nodded gently and held her eyes. They were as calming to her as they had always been. Sucking in her breath, she tried to find the words to tell her story. "My sister begged me to be a mentor. She told me a young girl, Amalie, needed someone like me, and I…"

Emma paused for a long time.

Amalie continued, "… regained my confidence after being in an abusive relationship and have remained sober for two years because my mentor taught me to believe in myself. If you met me three years ago, you would ignore or judge me. But not this one. She stood by me and —" Amalie stopped talking as Emma placed her hand on her shoulder.

Rising from her seat, Emma addressed both teams. "I'm a mentor because my sister needed help. Amalie needed help. I didn't realize that Amalie would become a thorn in my side. She forgets nothing I say to her as she likes to write it down and read it back to me. Second, my experience shows how the Centre needs security to protect everyone who is there. The young man who held the gun to my face was desperate. He had made a terrible mistake and was about to make a greater one if my sister didn't talk him down. Amalie and I would be dead without my sister."

Sitting down, she lowered her head. The room remained silent until Christopher coughed and reached for his water. Everyone returned their attention to him as they watched him silently. As he was reviewing his messages and texting someone back, his grin faded. "Kyle, make a note. I,

Christopher Gomes Riley, texted Mr. X approving Ms. Alamayo and her team."

She felt the heaviness on her shoulders lighten. Her job and her team were safe. "Thank you."

"On two conditions. The St. Michael's campaign must be financially and socially successful. Mr. X loves a good cause that helps build community, but he recognizes how dollars sustain good work."

"Sounds fair." She relaxed in her chair, relieved that they were talking business.

Leaning forward, he continued, "We work together."

She jumped up from her chair and scowled at him like a spy, ready to kill her target. "What?"

"It gives me and my team a better understanding of who you are. We want to see if you can work according to Mr. X's standards. It's why he sent me."

"Your boss is odd," Amalie remarked aloud.

"He always sends me to vet out his new acquisitions and people. Ms. Alamayo, can you work with my team…and me?"

"And you?" She surveyed his eyes, trying to figure out what he really wanted from her.

From an outsider's view, she never flinched or gave any indication of how her stomach was a belly full of knots. The easiest thing to say now was no. She could walk away and never see him again. Martin's political campaign and Sonja's wedding would keep her busy. She had enough money saved to be out of work for a year. But as his eye twitched, she accepted his challenge and was ready to beat him at his own game. Closing her eyes, she nodded yes.

"Good! The first order of business, lunch?"

She sat and watched him take over the room. Everyone followed his lead as they had at camp. Watching a new group of adorning fans listening and acting according to his demands made her sick.

What have I done?

CHAPTER 7

She stopped reading her notes and stretched to find that she was alone in the boardroom with Christopher. He was working quietly on the other side of the room, focused on his work. She loathed how his suit still looked unwrinkled and perfectly tailored to his body after hours of work and how he had seemingly matched the decor of the boardroom. His crisp blue shirt and grey suit were as warm as the grey walls and the blue sky outside. It made her want to gag.

"Where did everybody go?" she finally asked.

"Coffee break," he replied, raising his head to answer her.

"Oh." She resumed reading her notes.

"Do you want to talk?" His voice lost the tone of confidence and arrogance he had when he entered the boardroom.

She continued to read her notes. "About?"

"I'm sorry." His voice was cautious, with no hint of his assertiveness.

It was a tone she recognized. He always sounded like that when he wanted to apologize to her. She used to trust it, but after he lied to her yesterday, his *mea culpa* left a bitter taste in her mouth.

"For what? Not telling me the truth? I'm used to it." She started to play word link on her notes to pretend she was busy.

"Our boss sent me because he wanted to make sure your transition went smoothly. I tried to tell you yesterday, but considering your state of mind, it wasn't right."

She shrugged her shoulders half-heartedly. "This was

better? Pretending we never met. Well, you knew who you were seeing."

"Emma, you were in no condition to hear my news."

"Because you, before I learned it was you, were coming to fire my team and me. I shared that with you yesterday." She glared at him as her voice rattled the framed pictures on the wall.

"Em, your sister could've died. I could've lost...you could've died yesterday."

"At the hands of a boy, who set up a girl to have sex with him while his friends watched, Mr. Riley." She brushed the tears away.

Exhaling, Christopher moved to her side of the table. He sat in the nearest chair, waiting for her to speak. She tried to reach for her pen, but he moved it away from her. Leering at him, she crossed her arms across her chest, hoping that her stoic mask would scare him away. It didn't. He waited for her to say or do anything. The silence that followed unnerved her as it left space to remember yesterday and confront the pent-up fear and anxiety since seeing him again. Covering her face, she could no longer keep her feelings in check.

"I'm glad you said something. I've been waiting." His voice was soft and solemn as he gently removed her hands from her face and offered her a hanky.

"What are you, an old man?"

"I came prepared; I like this tie."

Shaking her head and rolling her eyes, she groaned. He smirked and placed the hanky in her hand.

"Thank you," she dabbed around her eyes.

"No problem. I knew who I was seeing and what yesterday dredged up. I planned for the worst. Why didn't you say anything about me or us?"

"No choice. You're my boss."

"We're partners. We're equal."

"But only one can fire at will."

Pinching the bridge of his nose with his fingers, he sighed deeply. "I'm sorry, but I can't change what I did."

"Past or present?"

"Both. I accept my decisions and the consequences. Tell anyone. I'm not afraid to confront my past. You have every right to tell anyone not to trust me. It'll make this arrangement easier if we start fresh. But you're right; we're not exactly partners. However, I would like for us to try and work together, regardless of our titles. Our past can influence the present, but the future is determined by what we do today."

Are you kidding me? How dare he quote me as a way to tell me what to do!

She studied his hazel eyes; the warm hue in them told her it was okay to tell people the truth. He could handle the fallout. But she didn't feel as confident knowing that it showed her weaknesses and foolishness to believe a liar and in her ideals. Sarcasm was her only defence to his sincerity. "Was that in a fortune cookie?"

"No, I learned it from someone wise." His gaze was fixed on her as if she was the only one that mattered to him.

"She sounds naïve and unrealistic." She backed away.

"But right. " He placed his hand on top of hers.

She didn't pull away as the warmth of his touch felt reassuring as it did yesterday.

Don't forget he's the villain in your story! He doesn't want people to know the truth.

Amalie and Annabelle strolled back into the conference room, arguing about ideas for the fundraiser. "What's wrong with a picnic carnival?"

"Sorry I'm late. I'm Annabelle, Emma's sister. Did we interrupt something?" Annabelle placed Emma's coffee between Emma and Christopher.

Emma snapped her hand away from Christopher and gave his hanky back to him. She returned to her notes and reached for the coffee. He hung his head low and moved so Amalie could have her seat back.

"Go home," Annabelle suggested to Emma.

"I'm fine. We've work to do, right, Mr. Riley?" Emma rolled her shoulders back and passed a file to Amalie.

Packing his things away, he replied, "Your sister is right. Let's call it a day."

"Amalie, we can't do what they did last year. It was a fiasco. Wilson's firm did such a hack job last year. Barely broke even. That's not how I work." Emma opened her iPad to show Amalie pictures from last year's gala.

"I guess we'll continue brainstorming then," Christopher muttered and sat back in his seat.

"I'll check if the Omni King Edward Vanity room is available. We've never held the gala there, plus people can stay in the hotel," Annabelle suggested.

"We can have it for free. It's a beautiful choice," Christopher added.

"Free?" Emma questioned his confidence.

"Mr. X. and the owner are friends. Choose dates so I can see what's available."

She clenched her hands into a fist; his confidence inspired her to hit a wall. The idea that he had the influence and power despite what he did to her infuriated her. It was proof to her that nice people never win. Nice people, as she experienced, get hurt. Their beliefs and ideas are used by others to win bets and become successful, while nice people are left wondering what the point is in being kind when it changes nothing.

"Emma, what's your opinion?" Amalie nudged Emma's elbow.

Emma blinked several times at Amalie, unaware that she was lost in her thoughts. "Sounds great," Emma replied, using her fake confident voice.

"See, Mr. Riley, if you ask her, she says yes," Amalie shouted and hugged Emma.

What did I just say yes to?

Beaming with pride, Christopher exclaimed, "That is what my boss likes. He enjoys the personal story. I can't wait to hear both of your experiences."

"What are we talking about?" Emma noticed everyone in the room was staring at her.

"You'll write a song. We'll use the lyrics as captions for these photos," Amalie yelled as she projected her photos on the screen. "Then, I share my experience, and you sing the theme song. Then, we can record and sell it."

"No!" Emma shouted and slammed her hand on the table.

"But you've agreed," Amalie whined like a child who heard no for the first time.

"I…no…no…I don't perform anymore."

"Can't or won't?" Christopher leaned forward to study her reaction.

"Mr. Riley, I'm a private person. Amalie's story is enough. Writing and singing something personal is self-indulgent."

"Your story is important. We've been sitting here for hours planning and trying to do something different and heartfelt. You're the difference."

"I respectfully decline." Emma controlled the volume and pitch of her voice.

"Are you saying no because I want you to do it?" Christopher asked.

She swallowed expletives down her throat and counted to ten. Her rage and discomfort had reached its limits. "I'm a professional, Mr. Riley. I've never let my personal experiences cloud my judgement."

"Hard to believe. I've seen your work. Emotions motivate you. You know, heartfelt actions inspire people," Christopher insisted as if it was an obvious observation.

Standing like a dark brown stallion rearing in the wild ready to strike another horse with their front legs, Emma argued, "Emotions are unpredictable. They can lead people to make bad choices. For example, your anger forces you to turn your back on a friend who needs your help. Then, when your feelings outweigh reason, you do something you never believed you could do."

He rose to defend his argument. "Are you sure you're not trying to protect yourself from being hurt again? A mature person learns from their mistakes and uses those lessons to influence stubborn cynics to believe that people can change. It gives them hope."

"Hope, really? Is that what makes them give more? We both know that people give more when they can get something in return. No heartwarming story can compel someone to give that much."

"My story did, and your story can do the same."

Annoyed at his calm and appealing voice, she yelled, "My story only reminds me of all the mistakes I've made and how to avoid them. Amalie's story shows one who grew from her mistakes!"

"I can do it. I can share my experience as a counselor and helping people like Amalie," Annabelle shouted and stood between them as if she was disciplining her children.

Emma scanned the room, remembering that she had a captive audience to her outburst. Under everyone's scrutiny, her knees buckled underneath her. Feeling her cheeks burn with embarrassment didn't help the situation as the silence, which followed, gave her enough time to realize she had exposed too much of herself.

"Amalie, your idea of how to present the Centre is brilliant. Christopher, let me take you on a tour of the Centre?" Annabelle suggested as she moved closer to Emma.

"Excuse me, will you?" Emma brushed past Annabelle.

Christopher lowered his voice. "Emma, are you all right?"

"I'm okay. Low on sugar. Excuse me."

The walls were closing in on her as the weight of doubt and anger attacked her soul. She had to escape the weight of fear, which was cutting short her breath and blurring her vision to see ahead.

CHAPTER 8

As the sun set, Emma's grey walls glowed with a warm orange and red hue. She loved the evenings in her office as the quiet and the yellowish-red light that streamed into her office settled her and cleared her mind from worry. She got to sit and plan what to do next with each project without the chatter of her team nor Christopher's voice ringing in her ears. Concentration was the key to her success, especially when her work became mundane and repetitive. She was creative and savvy, which made her marketing campaigns successful, but it took a lot of energy to get excited about every day.

What she loved most was rearranging her Post-it Notes on the board. With the various colours to write ideas and her plans, the organized colours on the board reminded her of the days when she used to storyboard her ideas. Using the same skills of organizing her settings and characters mixed with her research on occupations, which she learned in Writer's Craft, helped keep her team focused to produce effective marketing strategies. But instead of assessing people as characters in a story, they were people with talent who needed a leader to guide them in creating an illusion. Releasing an apathetic sigh, she hated how the product she helped to sell was the greatest fiction she ever created.

"You can go home. No need to impress me," Christopher announced as he stopped inside her door, "it's Friday night."

"Then, goodnight." She inhaled through her nostrils and exhaled through pursed lips as she continued to rearrange her Post-it Notes in the hope that he would leave her alone.

"What are you working on?"

Scowling at his question, she invited him in. "Come and see."

For two weeks, she tried to avoid working with him one on one. But every night, as he was leaving the office, he would ask her what she was working on. At first, he would suggest something from outside her door then leave. A few days later, they started brainstorming, and he would come into her office and stay till they were satisfied with the plan. Though she hated the arrangement, she detested how his presence had sparked a creativity that she had forgotten existed within her. Something in his manner always inspired her to either one-up him or make her ideas clearer and vice versa. Yes, they disagreed, but between the daily exchanges, they would find solutions and develop better ideas if she was opened to working with him. Though she would not admit it to him, working with him had made her work enjoyable.

But, these late hours wreaked havoc on her personal life. Her obsession to work kept her from a dress-fitting appointment and a hair consultation for Sonja's wedding. She had also missed several of Martin's political functions.

"May I?" Christopher moved her Post-Its around.

"Please don't move my —"

"Let me help you. I know what you want to do. Trust me."

Their hands touched. As warm as it felt, she snapped her hand away as if it was burning her skin. After their exchange in the boardroom that first day, Emma tried to avoid any form of physical contact with him.

"Fine. If you need to feel powerful, please explain it to me." She meant to sound sarcastic and make him feel uncomfortable. But, as he tilted his head and smirked, he continued to rearrange her cards as if he was immune to the lethalness of her words. Defeated, she sat on the couch to read the marketing plans for the Centre.

"So, what do you think?" He stood back to admire his work.

Flipping through her notes, she grunted, "About?"

"Richard and Rebecca working together?"

Closing the file, she strolled over to review the board. It was a brilliant idea to pair an organized person with a creative one.

Do not give him the satisfaction by telling him he is right.

She scurried back to the couch and resumed reading her notes.

"May I?" Christopher was requesting Emma's permission to sit with her.

With an assertive finger, she pointed to the empty space on the couch. He chose to sit in the chair across from her.

"Emma, let's go to the Centre tomorrow. Your team hasn't grasped the Centre's essence."

"Are we back to that? My team has captured the essence. With Amalie here, they get a good idea about the work. Satisfied?"

"No, but I assume I'm not going to convince you. Yet, if we both work together, we could find dynamic partnerships and ideas for the other projects you're working on. Two heads are better than one, right?"

She cackled as if she was a witch from *Macbeth,* "If one head agrees to be fair."

"Are you implying I'm not fair?"

She bit her lower lip. He was trying to bait her into their usual friendly banter. She wasn't going to take the bait. She continued to read her notes, but she could not resist sparring with him. "It'll be fair when our decisions reflect our discussions. If I'm here, it's a guarantee that my plans will go forward."

He howled as he responded in a husky voice, "As you wish, your high—" He stammered and tore his eyes away from her. He focused on the action occurring outside her window. "...Your... high..est... opinion always matters to me. This isn't a competition. We're here to put together a team to plan an event and establish a foundation for current and future projects. Imagine a campaign that reflects helping others and the best work we—"

"We?"

"Our work."

She squinted her eyes. "*Our* work?"

"Yes. Our. Your team. My team. Everyone's work. Our meetings can be collegial. We don't have to argue every point to come to a decision."

"It is our process," Emma murmured.

With a cocky wink, he teased, "Our process? As in we, together? Partners?"

"Well, I meant the process we take to realize I'm right," she teased with a hint of glee in her voice and a twinkle in her eye.

"Em, can *we* work together?" His voice was low and didn't have any trace of his usual self-assured tone.

With a measured response, she insinuated, "I had no choice. I agreed to work with you to help the Centre and save jobs."

Rubbing his face and rising, he mumbled, "Right, I forced you to work with me."

"Those were the conditions."

Watching him saunter over to the window and study the early night sky disturbed her in an unusual way. She didn't mean to sound blunt and uncaring, but it was the truth.

Those were the conditions he laid out, and she was reminding him. She should be happy that she pointed it out to him and had hurt his feelings, but seeing his hands tucked away in his pant pockets and his shoulders hunched over tugged at her heartstrings. It was a stance he used to take in their youth when they had fought, or when she had criticized him with her unvarnished honesty. Hating how it changed the mood in the room, she was compelled to make peace as they had a job to do.

"Take my team's proposal and present them, and I'll present your teams. We'll eliminate the worst ideas." She handed her folder to him. "Two vetoes for any idea you pass on and vice versa. The rest we debate over, then we choose. Deal?"

Releasing a pent-up breath, he nodded and took the file from her hand. "Deal."

He sat on the couch and passed his iPad to her. As they read, a professional silence settled in the room. They read and took notes. She would pass him a note, and he would respond and vice versa. Though her skin was painted in goosebumps, she found a way to conceal her unease as they worked together in silence. Focusing on the work helped keep her emotions in check and develop plans and ideas for the campaign. Not arguing with him was enjoyable, even though it made her feel like his partner at camp. It was natural to fall into this rhythm as if they were still friends.

But the constant sounds of Martin or Mr. X's ringtones always broke the silence. They reminded Emma that her relationship with Christopher was a professional working one. A relationship that she could only view through the prism of pain and regret. Those ringtones only reinforced how this was not fun. It was working together with professional boundaries clearly laid out to keep being friends and reminiscing at bay.

"Still keeping tabs on you?" she needled him after Christopher's tenth Mr. X call.

"He's the hands-on type."

"Why isn't he here, then?"

"Hates planes. But, he likes you and your work."

"So much so he dispatched a babysitter. He doesn't trust me nor the way I run my team."

"Because of what your staff sent us. I'm here because it was my choice. If you recall, I had to work here or back in London."

"So, you chose the girl?"

Christopher stopped reading and rubbed the back of his neck. "Pardon me?"

"Beth?"

"Right. Beth," he mumbled her name under his breath.

"Sounds serious."

"No, I needed a change. Reorganizing companies—"

"Firing people? I know about the flowers."

"No, I help companies rebrand themselves. I encourage CEOs and stockholders not to fire people. I'm glad you got my flowers."

"The doom and gloom message. I'm surprised your boss gave us a chance."

"Doom and gloom? I sent flowers, and you thought you were being fired?"

"Isn't that why you send flowers?"

"Rumour. Emma, I sent you yellow roses and white lilies. I was trying to tell you—" he stopped as if she was supposed to understand the significance of the flowers.

In a staredown, she didn't know what he wanted her to say to complete that sentence. She was relieved when she heard Mr. X's ringtone.

"Say hello to Mr. X, but after you're done, can you please turn your phone to vibrate so I can concentrate? I'd hate for him to be wrong about me."

The ringtone continued. Christopher ignored it. "Em, the flowers were a peace offering."

"Aren't you going to answer that?"

Reviewing his phone, he replied, "He'll leave a message."

"Answer the phone or turn it off. Work or leave. Choose."

Raising his hands in surrender, he suggested, "Okay. Let's forget the last five minutes and the constant reminders of our responsibility to others and focus on work. I'll turn off mine if you turn off yours."

She grabbed her phone off the table and switched it to vibrate. His shoulders relaxed as he switched off his phone and slid it over to her. Not one to let him win this standoff, she passed her phone to him and opened a file to read. As the silence returned, so did the peace and ease between them. Feeling comfortable again, she pulled her legs up and rested her back against the arm of the couch to read. It gave her the opportunity to keep an eye on him while enjoying the view from her window as she settled in to work.

Reading on a couch always cleared her head. Whoever picked out her couch must have known she liked to read on them and would want one to admire the view from. Even though it was a firm and professional couch, it was cozy enough to take a nap on during the day or late work sessions. She had caught Richard sleeping on it after lunch. The couch was also a place where you could sit and view the most glorious sunrises, a sight only matched by the beauty of the clear night sky with a perfectly lit CN tower that broke the darkness of the sky and the water below. Sitting on this couch was her dream, the dream where the view of the world is seemingly serene that you curl your legs under you to read a good book or write a story. Admittedly, Emma was not writing, nor was she enthralled with her work, but the coziness of the couch and the truce with Christopher made her feel safe to get the job done and believe in the possibility of raising money for a good cause.

An hour later, she flickered her eyes open. But she didn't feel scared or disoriented. Instead, she felt warm and safe in hints of cinnamon. Surveying her office, she wrapped herself in Christopher's jacket. As it had been for the last few nights, she had fallen asleep, and he had given her the space to rest by working at her desk. It had become a habit. Every night, she would fall asleep, but he would make sure she stayed warm and had space to rest.

Wrapping herself tighter in his jacket, she got lost in the intoxicating scent of cinnamon. She noticed how his cologne had changed from the harshness of AXE to the soft scent of Polo Ralph Lauren. It wasn't an overpowering musk scent but had mellowed amongst the touches of warm spicy cinnamon. It made her remember when they had sat by the lake sipping cinnamon lattes and how he always placed his sweater or jacket around her shoulders on their evening hikes.

"Em, you okay?" He raised his head.

"Sorry, I dozed off. Just cold."

"No worries." He handed her phone to her. "I believe your boyfriend texted you again. Might be important."

She reviewed her messages and frowned. "Just curious what time I'll be home."

"Hot date, then?"

"Hot meeting with his campaign team! I've cancelled a

lot of our dates. He gets worried."

Through pursed lips, he mumbled, "That's a good word for it."

"What did you say?" she asked between her yawns.

"Nothing. I'll finish up here. You should go and see the boyfriend."

"Martin understands. We have to finish and make sure we're ready with a plan for next week."

"You can trust me. I'll make sure that the campaign represents at least ninety-nine percent of my ideas." He grinned as he tided up her desk.

Rolling her eyes, she rose and approached him. "If I don't stay, you'll hire acrobatic artists to fly from the ceilings."

"I stand behind my idea. Seeing guys balance a girl on their finger, and—"

"What?" She stood close to him as she leaned against her desk, wrapped in his jacket.

"Sorry, it was a dumb idea. You were right." He stood and offered her chair back to her.

She was almost eye to eye with him, to be held imprisoned by his gaze. They hadn't stood this close since the night he almost destroyed her virtue. But as their breathing came in sync, she couldn't resist the urge to tease him nor get closer to him. "I love hearing you say that to me. Still difficult for you to say?"

"No, I trust you."

She bit her lower lip to pinch back the delight she took in teasing him. His eyes bore into her soul, making her forget, for a moment, the pain of humiliation. "Besides, what happened to making it a meaningful campaign than spectacle?"

"I tried. Someone didn't want to share her story."

"I was never a writer nor a very good singer."

Christopher scoffed. "I loved reading your stuff and hearing you sing."

She shook her head and lazily strolled over to the board, hoping that work would protect her from the uptempo beat of her heart.

"If I can't get the personal story, then spectacle is my only option. It is what you want." Christopher was teasing her.

Straightening her back, her anger flared, burning the desire to banter with him anymore. She couldn't hide the edginess of her tone as she confronted him. "Excuse me?"

"Sorry, it's late. I'm not making any sense. I should call Mr. X back." He raised his hands in surrender as she reviewed her notes again. "We have time. I'll make you a deal. Let's leave and enjoy the weekend. Come back refreshed and ready to work."

She turned, not realizing that he was standing beside her. He was reviewing the board, unaware of how her body shivered when her hand brushed his butt. Exhaling, she was relieved to see that he was focused on one of the pink Post-It notes. But as she considered the way his Adam's apple throbbed and his intense focus on the notes, there was something about his serenity that captivated her and made her wonder why he didn't acknowledge her touch.

"You okay?" He removed a blue Post-it Note from the board.

"You have a deal." Emma took the Post-it Note from his hand and reposted it on the board.

He reviewed it and conceded to her suggestion. "Miracles do happen. We can agree on more than one thing a day."

"Well, I guess this was good for us to work and—"

"Listen to each other."

He swung his head at the moment she lifted her head. Studying his eyes, she noted how they were still as mysterious and engaging. They were older and tired, but there were hints of hope. He didn't say anything as she inched closer, wondering why he had a speck of sadness in his eyes when everything she knew about him seemed perfect and ideal. What followed was a silence that crackled like a newly lit candle. It was unlike anything she had experienced with him. The closer she got to him, his eyes softened. They made her feel cherished, but the memories always came back to remind her how he had pierced her soul with his lies.

Taking off his jacket, she handed it to him. "You're right. I should go home. I need a break from you."

"Right." He accepted his jacket and stepped back.

"Sorry, I promise to bring a sweater."

"You should; you always get cold."

"Lucky for me, you remember."

She poked him on the chest and then flattened her hand briefly against him. Cupping her hand in his, he leaned in closer to her. Her face felt hot under his gaze, but its heat could not compete with the searing need to kiss him. Clearing his throat and releasing her hand, he stammered, "We're…partners. Your health and well-being are important to me…Good night. Say hi to Martin. I … hope you have a wonderful weekend with him."

Christopher stepped away and immediately left her office. She stood still, unsure what had happened between them. They were working together, and after her nap, it became weird. Shaking her head, she wondered what her heart and mind were trying to tell her. Could they be professional and work together for the common good? She didn't know, as the thorn of the past never stopped to remind her of their history. She had to call Martin back and go home to him before her feelings led her down a path that had only brought her misery and despair before.

CHAPTER 9

The weekend meant sleeping in and completing errands. But not if your name was Emma Alamayo. She could never decide what was worse, her regular workweek or her weekend social calendar. Luckily for her, running was an escape and a healthy way to deal with the stress associated with her career and personal life.

Running in the city on the weekend was bliss for her. It was quiet and less crowded. The energy of investors and entrepreneurs was non-existent as city dwellers came out to shop and eat at the mom and pop shops and market stalls in St. Lawrence Market or Chinatown. Their energy, coupled with the cool and soothing breeze from the lake, caressed her skin as they ran the path parallel to the lake. It was a sweet perk of living in the city so close to the endless blue of Lake Ontario.

"Is there a reason we're running at a Kenyan pace today?" Martin gasped for air as they returned to Emma's condo.

As she was stretching on the stone benches, she relished in Martin's exhaustion. "Sorry. Work has kept me in the office for the whole week."

"When you get a chance, can you pencil alone time with me?"

Emma closed her eyes and bent over to touch her toes. She was hoping the movement told Martin she wasn't in the mood for an argument. But as he sneered and hovered, she had to defend herself.

"And Leon and Ravi? You're lucky! Sonja is furious. I've missed my dress-fitting three times. I'm sorry for trying to do my job well. And let's not mention how I always make time to listen to your political plans before I sleep." She trudged away from him to stretch somewhere else.

"The 'Tight Ass' guy?" He touched her shoulder, but she brushed it away. "Sorry. When you're in an intense meeting, Richard says you're with him. I hate how this guy occupies your time when I'm supposed to be the number one man in your life."

She didn't answer him.

"That was a joke. Seriously? I'm on your side. And knowing you, you're putting up a good fight. I can see more wrinkles on your lovely face."

She bit the inside of her cheek to suppress lashing out. Shaking out the frustration, she explained, "It's been a rough transition. Plus, Annabelle is counting on me. Amalie. My reputation is on the line."

"Em?"

"I mean, I take my work seriously. And it means something personal... Then Sonja is on my case. I almost died and..."

She felt Martin's arms encircle her. "Listen to me. You need time to process. You're frazzled and unsure of yourself. Consider this: if you marry me, you can do something else. We can find better ways for you to use your time."

With a dispassionate sigh, she stomped away and focused on the boats sailing on the water, free from the worries of land and open to the freedom of the open water. She envied them.

"I'm joking. I'm just saying, I'll support you if you quit."

"Don't tempt me. Everyone depends on me." Her voice

was loud enough for other runners to stop and see if she was okay.

"Fine, we don't have to make decisions about our future today. We're good. Do what you have to do." He raised his hands in defeat.

"I'm sorry. You make a good point. I'll consider it, and we can talk about it at dinner."

"I don't think the Parkers want to hear our problems. But I do like the idea of spending time with you."

Martin drew her close and kissed her. She relaxed in his arms, and he deepened his kiss.

"Quality time? Is that what you're calling it?" She pulled away and taunted him.

"Don't make my words dirty. We need time together. Eating and talking like normal people. What are we doing this afternoon?"

"Planning a wedding."

"Ours? Oh, right, the Charlotte and Sonja monthly lunch date. Then tomorrow night?"

"Family dinner."

"Right. Let's plan something for next week." He kissed the top of her head and took a defeated step back.

"What are you doing now?" She inched closer to him and kissed him lightly on the lips.

Grinning like a well-fed pig, he answered, "Having quality time with my girlfriend."

CHAPTER 10

The noise and chatter of restaurant customers and employees at Sushi Inn in Yorkville was exploding. People were yelling and drinking as if everyone was part of the same party, literally sitting on top of each other with a view of city dwellers spending an enormous amount of money in the Yorkville boutiques. The atmosphere was a feast of good food and good company. But Emma was deaf and blind to it all.

"Emma? Are you listening?" Charlotte asked over the brim of her martini glass.

Charlotte was one of Emma's best friends, the first in her circle of friends to get married and have a family. Everything about her appearance and speech screamed that she was a mother of three exuberant and polite kids under the age of ten. She was a short and loud Latina, which helped to keep her children in tow and feisty when the daily routine of raising children became the centre of her life. Never one to silence or edit her inner voice, she was Emma's tether to the days of her romantic ideals.

"Sorry," Emma continued to play with her sushi and salad.

"I am too. I'm sorry for always leaving messages that sound like real emergencies. But can you blame me? You didn't make your dress fitting," Sonja added as she placed her hand on her heart then angled them like a lawyer prosecuting a criminal.

Sonja was Emma's other best friend. She was the realist and worrywart of the group. Nothing was ever perfect. Everything always needed tweaking and refinement to reach her level of perfection. In comparison to her, Emma resembled a slob. Sonja looked like a high-end fashion executive at Paris Fashion week, who would close deals before the last model walked down the runway. With her auburn hair up in a messy professional bun, she was ready to review her to-do list for her wedding.

"What can I do?" Plastering a smile, Emma buried her thoughts about work, Christopher, and almost dying. But the way her friends were studying her movements as if they were collecting information to diagnose a medical condition, she realized it would be difficult to hide anything from them.

"Go to your dress fitting. I made another appointment for you." Sonja took Emma's phone and typed in the appointment. "Do you sleep?"

"Yes." Her voice was tight enough to warn Sonja not to tease her anymore.

Charlotte got the signal and changed the subject. "So, how is Martin?"

"Upset."

"Trouble in paradise?"

Emma did not like the hint of salacious interest in Sonja's voice. "I've been working late."

"Really? You? Long hours!" Sonja's high-pitched mocking voice was beginning to irritate Emma. "Martin doesn't mind those long hours?"

"He's fine. He doesn't treat me like I'm opposing counsel. I'm his girlfriend."

"Well, at least he has an ideal husband trait, patience," Charlotte chuckled.

"I don't understand." Emma squished her eyebrows together as she studied her friends' body language to decide if they were teasing her or telling her the truth.

"You've been hot and cold since the start. It's been almost a year—"

"When you break it off," Charlotte finished Sonja's sentence.

"We're good," Emma claimed more to convince herself.

"You travelled without him," Sonja noted.

"I needed to mull over things. Martin has been hinting."

"Hinting? He has your reception venue picked out." Charlotte showed Emma a picture of the hall Edward mentioned once at a dinner party to her.

Sonja hit Charlotte on the shoulder and glared at her.

Charlotte ignored the warning and continued, "Don't worry, we'll get to your wedding stuff, but our friend left to consider getting married to Martin, has a new boss, has to work with her sister to create a campaign that impacts her employment, and she almost died. If we measure drama for drama, she wins."

Sonja howled so loudly that she interrupted the conversation of the tables beside them. "Fair enough, but I'm the one making a lifetime commitment. She doesn't know if she wants to marry Martin."

"Well, you can't be like me and marry the ideal man, like my Owen. My best friend."

Sonja and Emma burst into laughter.

"Okay, he doesn't resemble those guys we used to dream about or have any exceptional gift or talent like them, but he makes my coffee the way I like it and gives me a break from the kids when I need it. I love him."

"Let me take out my Kleenex." Sonja started to over-exaggerate her movements as she mimicked the sorrow sports fans feel when their teams lose the championship. Emma had to stifle her laugh.

"Don't worry; your day is coming when you'll realize

that being married to someone who understands you is the best part."

"True. But my future husband resembles George Clooney, so I'm good either way," Sonja exaggerated with Disney-like hopeful eyes.

Charlotte and Emma howled like wolves, almost knocking over their drinks.

"Okay, I get it. He doesn't live up to the ideal husband image, but when he holds me in his arms, I want to spend my whole life with him," Sonja boasted wistfully.

"So naïve! Tell me what you believe when you have kids," Charlotte shot back as she swallowed the last drop of her martini.

"Marriage is wonderful, right?" Sonja murmured.

"Oh, it's great. Yet, when your screaming kid camp is running around your house, you'll wonder where your life went. You'll gawk at your husband and realize he isn't your hero. Trust me, when you find time together, you're not celebrating your blissful life; you're wondering if you're invisible."

As her friends discussed marriage, Emma's stomach hurt from laughing so much. She loved how her friends had ideal lives where everything seemed to be falling into place for them. Both had careers and love. It made her wonder if she could also have the same life with Martin. To the outsider's view, he was an action hero with the voice of a romantic leading man. He was perfect for her, but she still couldn't understand why she wasn't ready to marry him.

"Are you daydreaming about Martin again?" Charlotte pushed Emma's bento box towards her.

Emma cleared her throat. "Guilty."

Hissing like a snake ready to attack her prey, Charlotte asked, "Are you going to marry him?"

"I'll tell you if we change the topic." She grinned as she successfully skirted away from Charlotte's probing eyes.

"Well, I've been sitting on this forever, but I have news." Charlotte yanked out her phone, "Do you remember Christopher Gomes Riley?"

Emma grabbed her drink and downed it.

"The jerk who used Emma. Yes, how could I forget?" Sonja rolled her eyes to the sky.

"So, I've been following this new inspirational writer, Beth Williams. She explains how to change your life from the inside to find your life. Bloggers say she'll be moving to Toronto or London to set up a retreat house and a centre to help others find their purpose in life. I'm an avid follower. I was on her site when she posted her relationship with this guy."

Charlotte swiped through her phone to show a picture of Beth and Christopher. The picture wasn't anything special. It was your typical staged picture of a couple gazing into each other's eyes as the sun behind them set. Some would say it resembled an engagement picture. Emma ordered a Long Island ice tea as she discerned the meaning of the happy couple's body language.

Charlotte shook her head in disbelief. "Can you imagine? The guy who took bribes to sleep with women is dating the most virtuous Christian woman today. Astounding, isn't it? I've been dying to tell you."

"It's been fifteen years, Charlotte." Emma passed the phone back to her then stuffed a shrimp tempura into her mouth.

"Yes, but well, when it comes to you and Christopher—" Charlotte raised her eyebrows at Emma.

"What?" Emma hated when Charlotte's idealistic romantic persona appeared.

"Well, seeing how we're mature women, we always assumed you had a crush on him, " Charlotte responded as she examined the tips of her light brown hair.

"So when you found out about the bet, well, it became a mute topic," Sonja added as she nudged Charlotte's hand away from her hair.

"What's the mute topic?" Emma squinted her eyes at them.

"Well, Christopher was handsome. It was obvious you liked him." Charlotte patted Emma's hand.

She spat out her food. "I never liked him. His welfare was my concern as I have for any human being,"

Charlotte and Sonja exchanged glances then pursed their lips together. She hated how they didn't believe her.

Lilting her voice as if she was an infatuated teenager explaining her latest crush, Charlotte gushed, "I'm a romantic, what can I say? Ever wonder what would happen if you ran into him again? I always imagined you being delayed and seeing him in an airport. You want to ignore him, but you need to know if there was anything ever there."

Yelling for the whole restaurant to hear, Sonja brought Charlotte back to reality. "Charlotte! Seriously, you need to stop reading those romance novels! I told her she was dreaming. He hurt and used you. He was a jerk. Who he is now can't erase what he did to you."

Emma blinked several times as she chewed on their opinions about Christopher, afraid to see their reaction when she told them about her new working arrangements. "Both of you thought I had feelings for him?"

"Who wouldn't? He was gorgeous and smart. I always thought that your bickering was concealing your true feelings," Charlotte surmised confidently.

Emma pushed her food from her. As she listened to her friends talk about Christopher, she bit her lip. No matter what life experience brought her, she could count on Sonja being the eternal pragmatist and Charlotte, the idealistic romantic. She used to be like Charlotte, where she believed in finding the one perfect kiss to wake you from your sleep. But after Christopher, she adopted Sonja's views on love being this journey of finding a compatible partner, a partner who wanted to build a future and a home.

Pointing at Emma, Charlotte wondered aloud, "I've also imagined him strutting into your office, and you were rendered speechless?"

Emma stuffed a sushi in her mouth. If she mentioned how they met at the airport, how she cried on his shoulder in the park, or the time they were spending together alone in her office, Charlotte would be in heaven. But Sonja would want details and help find a way to get rid of him.

"Then he would see that you aren't this damaged woman, but a successful independent one." As soon as the words left Charlotte's mouth, Sonja covered them.

"Damaged?" Emma's question was barely audible as the weight of *damaged* hung on her like one hundred pounds around her neck.

Charlotte took a sip of her drink. "Well, ever since Christopher, you're cautious, especially in your relationships."

"I've dated."

"And we've seen great guy after great guy come and go. I, we, always theorized you were too shy to trust any guy."

Emma straightened. "Great guy after great guy? I'm glad we're being honest."

"But, Martin is proof that waiting for the one leads to someone amazing. And he's… an intelligent and…nice guy," Sonja babbled with compassion.

Emma tapped her finger on the table. Her friends were being annoyingly polite. "You don't like him?"

"As your friends, we want the best for you." Charlotte stopped Emma's hand from tapping on the table. "We're concerned about your happiness. Christopher hurt you in such a way that it changed you."

"Not true. I'm so happy with Martin that I can work with Christopher. We've been working with each other for at least a month."

Dropping their forks, Charlotte and Sonja stopped chewing their food.

"WHAT?" Charlotte yelled. "Does your staff know? Your sister?"

"We're like strangers." Emma smirked.

"So no attraction?" Charlotte made a bridge with her hands and placed it under her chin.

"Trust me. Other than planning the campaign and learning how to manage multiple charity projects, we don't talk. I need him to help my sister, to keep my job, and that's it."

Moving her seat closer, Sonja reminded her, "Don't forget what he did to you. He hurt you. You can't trust him."

"But what if she has forgiven him, she can trust him again. Have you forgiven him?" She nodded as if she wanted Emma to make her dreams come true.

Gulping her drink, Emma assessed her friends' reactions. One wanted her to affirm their statement, while the other wanted an answer to her question. It was a no-win situation for her.

"Trust me. I don't trust him. Nor have I forgiven him." Pulling out her maid of honour notebook, she began to flip through it. "Don't we have a wedding to plan?"

She passed her notebook over to Sonja with the same determination she used for work. Her friends sighed and changed the topic. Pleased with herself, Emma was determined to complete a to-do-list for a wedding, and she was going to force her friends to follow her lead.

CHAPTER 11

As Emma rummaged through boxes in her childhood bedroom, Martin bounced on her bed and watched.

"You grew up here?" Martin scanned her well-maintained bedroom, complete with a wall of awards, certificates, and diplomas.

"You've been up here," she mumbled as she continued to unpack boxes.

Martin didn't bother contradicting her. She resumed searching through her boxes in hopes of finding something to prove that Sonja and Charlotte were wrong about her.

"What are you searching for?" Martin sauntered over to her bookshelves. He began to reorder them in alphabetical order.

"I'm trying to find a book."

Martin moaned. "So, it can sit in your living room with your other books? My offer still stands, let me hire someone to organize your place. Leon is concerned."

"And put my stuff in places I can't find later. Don't worry; it's Amalie's pet project."

"She can never finish a project. Is this a shrine to you?" He inquired, examining the trophies on her shelves and the plethora of awards on her walls.

"Funny."

"Do you have an award for everything? Best short story. Best novel. Favourite poem. Best original song. When you said you used to write, I didn't think it would be this."

"Pay no attention to those awards. They were local contests. Lillian submitted my work."

"Can I tell Leon? It's interesting. No running awards?"

"I didn't run till I was in my twenties."

"No aspiration to be a writer? Nothing political which could damage my image?" He analyzed the framed poems on her wall. "Did you write this?"

"You tell me," she replied as she struggled to remove a box from the closet.

"Does this sound familiar? We fear. We never embrace it. We make choices but never handle the consequences. But once we let fear go, we embrace it. No longer is the consequence unbearable, but become acceptable. We must live another day despite what we cannot control."

Emma stopped her search as she listened attentively to Martin's monotone reading of her poem. The poem was no Chaucer or Shakespeare, but it encapsulated her youthful feelings when her cousin Marty was fighting cancer.

"Didn't realize you were a poet." He returned the poem to its place.

"It's nothing." Tucking her hair behind her ear, she continued to pull more books from boxes.

"It's well-written."

"For a teenager."

"This Marty?"

Emma stopped searching and examined the picture Martin found. He was flipping through a scrapbook.

"Yeah. That's when she was undergoing chemo."

"How old was she?"

"Seventeen."

"And when was this taken?"

Sitting beside him on her bed, she leaned over his shoulder and was overcome by her emotions. The picture of her, Annabelle, and Lilian at one of her high school productions made her sad and long for the girl who used to live happily in that world.

"High school. I wrote and starred in a play."

"Interesting."

She pinched her nose as she faced Martin. "I haven't mentioned it?"

"No. And this?" Martin flipped to another page. It was filled with pictures of her and her drama friends. "Another play? Who did you play?"

"Sarah."

"Ex-boyfriend?" He pointed to a handsome, dark, and brooding Johnny Depp lookalike.

"No. Public enemy number one. He was Sky Masterson."

"Was that his name?"

Snorting, Emma remembered Martin's IQ in musical history was nearly zero. Her love and knowledge of musicals was something she didn't share with him. It was a world she wished would never be rediscovered by anyone new to her life.

"His name was William Baxter. Sky was the character's name."

"Were you close?"

It was an obvious observation as she sat on William's lap with a huge grin. But pictures lie when you understand the context behind the mask of an actor. Her smile concealed her sadness. Her cousin Marty was at the hospital receiving her fourth round of chemotherapy. She wanted to be by her side, but Marty insisted that she have fun. And like a good actress, she followed the mantra, *the show must go on.*

"I'll understand if you dated him."

"He preferred someone like you."

"At least someone does."

"Wow." She stood up and crossed her arms across her chest.

"That didn't come out right." He reached for her hand.

She refused to take it. "What did you mean?"

"Sorry. Your past is like a mystery that I want to unravel."

She wasn't happy with his answer. Her glare was intense and unemotional.

"Em, it's been two weeks since you returned. We haven't talked. What am I supposed to believe?"

She didn't like it when Martin raised his voice to her, nor when that same tone sounded like he was accusing her of something. But, she reminded herself that this was supposed to be the love of her life. She must practice patience and understanding.

"I'm sorry," she murmured as she took Martin's hand and sat on his lap. Wrapping her arms around his neck, she kissed him.

"Well, it's a start. What were we talking about?"

"My past."

"Right. Sorry. My girl sits and kisses me on a bed, and my body responds."

"My parents are downstairs. Don't forget how you met my parents."

"It was innocent."

He stroked her inner thighs and nuzzled the nape of her neck. It was becoming difficult to resist the temptation of his lips.

"You opened my door in a towel," she groaned without the desire to stop him.

Martin relented and kissed her forehead. "True. I should behave, but you smell so nice. I like time with my girlfriend."

"You love getting caught. This will not impress my parents."

"Hmm?" He traced his finger along the contours of her mouth.

"Martin, listen, I'm sorry for this week, but we need to talk and—"

He pressed his lips against hers until she opened for him to explore the inside of her mouth. She wasn't sure how it happened, but he always found a way to pin her underneath him. Before she realized it, she forgot why she was in her room. Swept away in his desires, he erased the doubt and fear she was feeling. His sheer rawness drew her into his world. She felt her back arch to his touch. His hands found the skin under her shirt, and his lips found the skin below her neck. The pace quickened between them. She bit her lower lip to silence her groans.

"Auntie Emma, where are you?" Annabelle's five-year-old son, Simon, yelled from downstairs.

She became alert to her surroundings, but Martin sealed her mouth with a kiss.

"Auntie Emma, we need you." Simon's voice grew louder as his tiny feet raced up the stairs. "Auntie Emma!"

She heard the shrieking child's voice again. It brought her back to reality.

"You said Simon had impeccable timing."

He grumbled in defeat. "I've said many things regarding that kid. How long are we staying?"

"Your fly."

As she fixed her outfit, she listened to how close Simon was to her room. She could hear him opening the bedroom doors and yelling her name.

"You worked fast. But, I might have trouble zipping up." He elicited another kiss from her.

"Martin!" She pushed him away and investigated his pants.

"What can I say? You inspire me." He grabbed her again and started nibbling her neck.

"This is how we got in trouble. Simon will notice." There wasn't much authority or urgency behind her words.

"Auntie Emma, where are you?" Simon's voice now boomed like a Bose speaker.

"I'm in my bedroom."

"Don't move," he whispered into her ear.

"There you are. Momma's been searching for you, and I've been sent to get you. Why is the bed messy? Lola said not to mess up any of the rooms. What were you guys doing in here?"

Simon inspected the room like the Royal Canadian Mounted Police. The rumpled flowered comforter and wrinkled clothes were a dead giveaway to anyone, other than a child, to explain what was happening between Martin and Emma. But Simon didn't notice things like that, especially when his father sent him on a mission to find Martin.

"Just chatting," Emma blurted.

Martin chuckled as he released her.

"That's not funny," Simon proclaimed.

He jumped onto the bed to cross-examine Martin. He was serious as he gripped Martin's face between his two tiny hands.

"My dad said he needs you to be the fourth. Come."

"I'm coming, okay, bud?"

"Now! I don't want my daddy to be angry at me."

"How can I argue with that reasoning?"

Martin followed Simon out. But before they crossed the threshold, he rushed back to kiss Emma.

"Why are you kissing my Auntie Emma?" Simon stomped his foot.

"Well, Simon, we're boyfriend and girlfriend. It's what people do when they say goodbye."

"But why?" He whined in his high-pitched voice.

"To show her that I love her."

"See you later is faster."

Simon tugged at Martin's arm. As he left, Martin winked and mouthed his desires to her. She waved goodbye, letting the physical desire exit the door with him. She returned to her search. Determined to find these journals, she lifted her chin and rolled her sleeves to rediscover her past.

Ever since her lunch with Charlotte and Sonja, Emma wondered if they were right. After Christopher betrayed her, was she afraid to commit to anyone or anything? She wanted to say no, but her instincts implored her to seek the answers in her journals.

Growing up, she loved writing. It cleared her mind from the chaotic thoughts and doubts that festered. With her mind clear, her restless heart found a way to silence her fears. Her English teacher, Mrs. Enortep, was right; journaling was a way to sort out the multitude of thoughts to help make decisions in the present. In the future, it would be the untainted record of her experiences to aid in making wise decisions. She needed to hear her youthful voice to make a definitive decision for her future.

"Auntie Emma, my mom wants to talk to you." Simon ran into her bedroom and latched himself around her neck.

"Tell your mommy that your Auntie Emma is searching for something."

"But she wants to talk about the fundraiser."

As she admired her adorable nephew with his shaggy

brown hair and light beige tone, she soaked in his exuberant curiosity. There was an innocence of a child she wished she never forgot in her teenage years or lost in adulthood. But so is the price of growing up. You have a long browser history that reminds you of all your searches that never led you to the right site for answers. In life, your heart becomes so damaged from the pain that you are never quite the same person after that experience.

Sighing, she enlisted Simon's help in finding her journals. Simon ransacked through the boxes. He hauled out ten novels, and after everyone, he repeatedly questioned if this was the journal she wanted to find. Simon wasn't helping in the quest.

After a few minutes of searching, Simon questioned Emma. "Why is this marked in red? What does this say?"

She reviewed the overmarked and ill-written essay.

"It claims I have misused the syntax."

"What does that mean?"

"It means your Auntie Emma was never the writer she believed she was."

"Why doesn't it say that?"

Chuckling, she reread and studied the comments. In a flash, she conceded that Simon was right. Through his unbiased eyes, like any child's mind, it sees the joy before the terror. With the clarity of a wise monk, he interpreted the statement as a criticism of her grammar, which can be taught and refined over time, and not a judgement on her as a writer.

"I have no idea."

"Mommy says, you need to stop projecting your fears on others and learn from your mistakes."

Hugging her nephew tightly, she thanked him for his inquisitive sense and sharp wit. The kid had ways of inspiring and infuriating her. He reminded Emma of what she used to be like at that age.

"Is this it?" He showed her the cover of a book that had a portrait of a plain-looking, nineteenth-century woman.

"No. It's Jane—"

"I can read. It says Jane…" He studied the title and tried to sound it out. "E-y-Eye-r"

"It's Eyre." Her voice was light, as she did not want to discourage his joy of discovery and reading.

"That's not air. Air is, A-I-R."

"This is someone's name."

Simon wondered aloud, "What's it about?"

"Jane is a woman learning how to be fiercely independent. She is seeking a happy life. She believes Mr. Rochester is her soulmate. But, he breaks her heart."

"Is there a happy ending?"

"Yes."

"How was it a happy ending?"

"She learned how to forgive Mr. Rochester."

"What did he do?"

"He lied to her."

"What was the lie?"

"That he was free to love her."

"How did she forgive him?"

Shell-shocked by Simon's question, Emma could not remember the answer. She had read the story numerous times, but at the moment, she couldn't remember how Jane forgave Rochester.

"Are there pictures?"

Simon flipped through the pages. His frown could not hide the disappointment of seeing only words. "NO!" Simon screamed.

"What's the matter?"

"Someone wrote in your book. If Ms. Ocampo saw this, you would be in trouble."

Emma picked up the book he dropped. Studying the words in the margin, she remembered who wrote them. It killed her to remember how she taught Christopher to read with a pencil to keep track of his thoughts and questions so they could discuss them later.

Is this what you mean when you say God is always with you?

"Are you okay, Auntie? You have water in your eyes."

"I'm okay."

As Simon continued to dig, Emma focused her attention on Simon. She observed how Simon's exuberance radiated as he searched. No hesitation or thought to ask why he was searching for a book. He was fearless in digging with no fear of disappointment or failure. Admiring his tenacity, she longed to be that brave and hopeful.

"Auntie Emma, what does this say?" Simon had picked up another copy of *Jane Eyre.*

"Ugh! Someone wrote in this book too."

I'm guessing, something you believe? You highlighted and underlined it.

'We know that God is everywhere; but certainly, we feel His presence most when His works are on the grandest scale spread before us; and it is in the unclouded night-sky, where His worlds wheel their silent course, that we read clearest His infinitude, His omnipotence, His omnipresence.'

Is this how you see God?

Reading the quotation, Emma remembered how Jane forgave Rochester. She loved him enough to have mercy on him as she had been taught about God's mercy in her childhood. In short, one could argue *Jane Eyre* is learning that love without mercy is not love.

"Did you write it?" Simon leaned on her shoulder.

"Nope. I highlighted the words, but I did not write those questions."

"Then who wrote it?"

She read another highlighted passage. She didn't want to answer the question.

'It does good to no woman to be flattered [by a man] who does not intend to marry her; and it is madness in all women to let a secret love kindle within them, which, if unreturned and unknown, must devour the life that feeds it; and, if discovered and responded to, must lead, ignis-fatuus-like, into miry wilds whence there is no extrication.'

Is this what you were trying to tell me what love is? Confused. But your passion for this story must mean something to you. Can't wait to talk to you about it.

"Are you okay, Auntie? Your eyes are wet again."

"Let's take a break. Here, let me read you the story of the *Paper Bag Princess.*

CHAPTER 12

Sitting at the dining table of her childhood, memories of family gatherings, and shared stories engulfed Emma in a cloud of love. With some new varnish on the chairs and new cushions on the seats, her parents' dining room was as inviting as it was when she used to do her homework or eat late-night snacks with her sisters. The Last Supper still hung on the focal wall of the room and stood out against the eggshell white walls. The company around the table complimented the warmth of the simple but stylish room. Even Lillian's face being projected via FaceTime from a laptop was picturesque in the room. Yet, Emma never felt more at home and lonely.

As Annabelle served the birthday cake, Emma could feel her family's love for her mom. Beatrice was a kind-hearted woman who thanked God every day for the lives of her children. With her salt-and-pepper wavy hair, she didn't appear to be a day over fifty. Annabelle was the carbon copy of her mom, while Lillian resembled her father. As the third daughter, Emma was a combination of her parents' features. Even though they physically appeared different, they were their mother's daughters in confidence and intelligence, but also temperament. Emma was aware that her mom prayed for daughters to learn how to control their temper so as not to stand in the way of happiness, opportunity, or reconciliation. But Emma appreciated how her mom prayed the most for her. She could never convince her mom that she was happy with her life.

For a long time, Emma felt Beatrice's concerned and disapproving dark brown eyes on her. Although she excelled in her business studies, Beatrice always grilled Emma about her happiness. After changing her major, Beatrice asked Emma if sacrificing her love of art for a guarantee was worth it. It was a conversation she tried to avoid, but her mom always found ways to talk about it even as she became successful.

"Mommy, Daddy, guess what?" Simon jumped into Annabelle's arms.

"What?"

"Auntie Emma and Martin kiss when they say goodbye."

The family around the table stopped conversing with each other and stared at both of them.

"Do you know why?" Simon pressed his mother for an answer.

"No. Why?" Annabelle turned her attention back to her son.

"Martin said it's because they love each other. See you later."

Simon jumped out of his mother's arm and gave her a kiss on the cheek before running into the kitchen.

"Well, he cares for you, not so much me. But my guess, you kissed each other differently. If the way you play poker is any sign. You are a competitive son of—" Jerry yelled before Beatrice cut him off.

"Manners."

Half-smiling at her mother, Emma knew her mom didn't admire her son-in-law's sailor's mouth at the dinner table. However, like the whole family, they loved everything else about him.

"Sorry, Mom. Martin forgets he's not family yet and should remember to be nice to its members. We'll choose who Emma will marry."

Emma dropped her fork. The clanging sound drew

everyone's attention to her. Composing herself, she picked up her fork and used it to point at her overzealous brother-in-law.

"Let me guess, Jerry, he cleaned you out, again? When will you learn never to play with a lawyer? Besides, when I do anything, it's my decision." She reached for Martin's hand and kissed him on the cheek. He brought her hand to kiss it, like a well-seasoned politician who exuded confidence.

"Emma, everyone has influence over you. I was the first to publish your work." Lillian's voice bellowed through the speakers.

"I persuaded you to study calculus, biology, and chemistry when you were in high school," Annabelle declared as if she was announcing her candidacy for public office.

"And, I influenced you where to buy your condo," Jerry added.

"Of course you did, but you're my real estate agent."

Everyone at the table laughed again.

"Enough. Let's change the topic." Beatrice banged her cup down. It silenced the room.

Emma's mom was your typical Filipino mother-hen. Sweet and charming to the outside world, but within the Alamayo household, the woman controlled the dynamic of the family. On one day, Beatrice laughed and listened to your story with sympathy and compassion, but on other days, the tone would shift into passive-aggressive compliments and judgements. As a child, it was a maze of emotions, but once you learned your mother spoke and acted out of love for your health and well-being, you appreciated it, though their criticism or advice always stung in the moment.

"It's okay, Mom." Emma unclenched her fists.

"Understand, Martin, we protect Emma. She was a different young lady before you," Beatrice explained as she patted Emma's hand.

"She was like a fly. Jumping from one thing to another," Annabelle added as she chuckled with fondness.

"Or how she always goes all in and destroys everything in her path. Yet, she was amazing in her youth. There was nothing she didn't read to become an expert in it," Lillian remarked with admiration through FaceTime.

Emma shifted in her chair and let Martin's hand go.

"Oh, do you remember the endless hours she made us attend her concerts or poetry readings?" Annabelle refilled her glass with water. "It was better than hearing her practice, scale after scale after scale."

Annabelle and Lillian laughed.

"Why did she give it up?" Martin asked.

"I grew up. Reality showed me who I could and couldn't be," Emma replied in her clear and professional marketing voice.

"From what I've seen and heard today, it sounds like you enjoyed it." Martin slung his arm behind Emma's chair. She leaned forward away from him.

"She did," Beatrice answered with a regretful joy.

"But life happens. And sometimes, life helps you place everything into perspective. Plus, I sell dreams better than I can achieve them." Emma got up and started to clear the plates from the table.

"I've never heard you sing. Do you remember when we went to a karaoke bar with my colleagues? You claimed you were the only Filipino who didn't sing."

She glanced up from her task and noticed how stiff and rigged Martin's back and shoulders had become. As he rubbed his chin with a rough intensity, she wished she had told him the truth. For her, their relationship was always open and honest, but as she cleared more plates and glasses, she had shattered that image for him.

"Emma doesn't sing karaoke," Annabelle declared in a high-pitched and snotty English accent.

"She's a singing snob," Lillian shouted in a parody of Annabelle's voice.

"Do you sing anymore? Maybe Leon and his team can use it for my campaign." Martin was speaking in an even and measured tone.

"No. The past belongs in the past."

The sound of Simon and Summer barrelling through the dining room broke the tension. Exhaling in relief, she made room for their small little bodies to take centre stage in the dining room. Without much care for etiquette, the kids made a grand presentation for each gift and paraded it for their whole family to admire. It amused Beatrice, but Emma could feel her mom's eyes on her as she finished clearing the table. Even though her niece and nephew dazzled the family with off-pitched singing and flimsy dancing, which ended the conversation at the table, the fear set in that she would have to explain and confront her past sooner rather than later.

CHAPTER 13

"Seriously, Emma, it's five in the morning," Martin mumbled.

"Go back to sleep. I have a ton—"

"... of work. Whatever."

As she contemplated her morning exchange with Martin, she gazed out her office window, watching planes leave and land at the airport. She wondered if the travellers were going for pleasure or business. Regardless, she envied them. They got to escape reality for a few hours.

Hearing Martin's disappointed voice rumble in her ears and reliving the fight that followed during breakfast occupied her thoughts. His tone spoke volumes. Though he never mentioned it directly, he was still upset to find out that she sang and wanted a better explanation for working late than needing to save her job. Even the light of a new day could not dispel the bitterness in their exchange nor the fear tingling in her skin.

Sitting in her office offered her no peace. It was filled with plans for the St. Michael's campaign and three other pending fundraising projects. No matter how hard she worked, as soon as she returned, her work had multiplied overnight and created a mess in her space. Turning her attention, she watched another plane ascending and prayed for her work to disappear with it. But as she admired the beauty of her view, she had to acknowledge how blessed she was. She had a job, a boyfriend with aspirations for their future, and a friend who relied on her to organize a beautiful wedding. She was needed and loved.

Why isn't it enough?

Christopher cleared his voice behind her. "I love your

view. Seeing the planes whisking people away from reality. You wish you could be on that plane, right? Escaping your life for a couple of hours seems nice. Rough morning?" He stood outside of her office.

Composing herself, she returned to her desk and began working. She was in no mood to entertain Christopher's daily morning enthusiasm. But the hint of cinnamon always persuaded her to invite him. It never failed. He would wait at her door for an invitation, which she would always offer, then he would come in and eat his breakfast on the couch while she worked at her desk. For a brief moment, she was able to ignore him. She even relished in her ability to do it, but the sweet smell of food weakened her resolve to reject his company. It was like a chess match. No reaction until someone made a move. Unfortunately for Emma, Christopher had learned to have the patience of Job and had found a way to always corner her Queen.

"Do you need something?" she asked as the aroma of coffee and cinnamon was making her mouth water.

"Just wanted to review the day ahead with you. Breakfast?" He offered as he waved the bags in his hands.

She shook her head, determined to stay tight-lipped. If she focused on her work, then she wouldn't have to review the day's agenda with him and talk about other things. She was trying not to cross that line with him again. But lately, work conversations led to small talk, which led to a *tête-à-tête* about their personal life, that would always take her back to that moment of betrayal and their last evening session together. They were memories that consumed her heart with grief and confusion, and right now, she didn't need to add another layer to her morning fight with Martin. But her stomach always betrayed her.

"Is that cinnamon I smell?" She stopped typing and

examined the brown bag Christopher left on her desk.

"Could be."

As he sat on the couch, he took out his breakfast sandwich and another cinnamon bun box from his brown bag. "Thought we could talk face to face as we have an informal breakfast meeting treat."

"You always say that, and we end up talking about other things. Understand, the campaign and gala are taking shape. Our teams are working well together. Leave the agenda here, and I'll review it and call you if I have any concerns. We really have nothing to discuss." She tore her eyes away from the cinnamon bun and focused on her emails.

"We've been working well together, but—"

"Maybe Mr. X wants to hear my opinion in my own voice?"

"No. He likes daily reports from me only."

"Of course. A daily report every ten minutes for the micro-manager boss."

"As opposed to an overbearing boyfriend."

She straightened her back and typed loudly. She heard him clearing his throat, then his footsteps as he approached her desk and sat in a chair in front of it.

"Emma, I want to talk about last Friday."

"I have no idea what you're talking about."

How your touch makes me feel like a preteen girl who realized her crush liked her?

"Okay, then explain why we fight every time our teams are around, and when we're working one on one, we snipe at each other, then spend hours in silence before we act like colleagues to find some compromise. Then, there are moments where I have no doubt that we can talk like…friends?"

Emma rolled her eyes. "Our working relationship is fine. We have heated discussions but still produce some lovely work, like signing new sponsors to the campaign, how we designed these lovely gold napkins, even though the black napkins would add a little bit more class and sophistication to the event. This—"

"This is chaos." He pointed to the display board and proposals scattered around her office. "Besides, the black napkins darken the space as opposed to the gold napkins, which gives you a sense of hope."

Waving her hands, she responded, "Well, without this organized chaos, we would never have found that compromise for napkins. See, this works."

"True, if you enjoy taking a whole day to agree on napkins. You do realize that when one person offers breakfast, it means eating to discuss what they did last night. It doesn't always have to be about business."

Lowering her head, she stopped typing and faced him. She accepted the cinnamon bun and coffee, trying to appear unfazed by his comment.

"What did you eat last night?" she asked.

"Okay. Small talk it is. Chinese. Thank you for asking. Are you enjoying your breakfast this morning?"

"I was until my partner wanted to pry into my life."

As she savoured sugar and cinnamon on her lips, she tried to conceal her enjoyment. She hated how Christopher appeared pleased with himself.

"One milk. Touch of cinnamon. A peace offering," he offered as he ate his breakfast sandwich.

"Nice of you to remember. I hope this civil conversation pleases you."

"Right, a minute of civility. We need to tell our teams how we used to work together."

Leaning her head back, she sneered, "So much for talking about other things. I thought we agreed not to because our current arrangement is working. If you haven't noticed, your charm persuades Annabelle and Amalie to side with you."

"No, you decided. Besides, this isn't about sides. We're working for a good cause. When I implied that you didn't have a personal stake, I judged you unfairly. I'm sorry. But, if you can share what happened between us, then maybe what happened last Friday won't happen again, and we could trust each other—"

"Why do you care if I trust you?"

He swallowed the food in his mouth and wiped it with a napkin.

"I'm sorry. I didn't hear your answer, Mr. Riley."

"Well,…I…Mr. X trusts me, and…if we can then…we could really do something amazing. I don't want to disappoint… him."

"Is that all?"

He scratched his left eyebrow. "You don't believe me?"

"Seems you don't want to answer my question."

They glared at each other as Emma bit her lower lip, trying to temper the sudden heat in her cheeks. "Let's get back to work." She returned to answering her emails.

"I'm surprised you haven't told your sister," he uttered.

"She's acquainted with the details. I never told her your name."

"Too hard to say?"

She stopped typing and focused on any word on her screen. "Mr. Riley, thank you for breakfast, but I have work to do."

"Wouldn't it be better if we tell people than having people speculate and gossip about why we fight?"

"We're their bosses who have been put in charge of managing them. They will always make up stories. Regardless of how I feel about you, my sister is counting on me. We can trust each other as professionals. The truth would complicate things. Besides, I have a staff who needs me to succeed because of their foolish decision. They know it's their second chance."

"Can I get a second chance?"

"A second chance at what?"

He rubbed the back of his neck and skimmed his fingers across his trimmed stubble under his chin. Releasing a pent-up breath, he replied, "If we're being professional and I'm asking as a professional, as your business partner in all of this, trust me enough to share our experience, so it doesn't get in the way of our work—"

"I'm not comfortable discussing what happened between us. This is my workplace, and I have an image here of excellence and professionalism that I'd rather not tarnish. Why do you want to tell people what you did to me?" Her voice was barely a whisper, but you could hear the pain as if he betrayed her minutes ago.

"It's the truth."

"How I was naive to believe you?"

"No, so they understand that people like me need places like the Centre to help them, so they don't hurt people like you…again."

"You didn't hurt me. I became stronger. I'm a tough negotiator because of you, and I don't rely on my feelings to dictate my decisions."

"Another reason why people need to hear your story. I remember when you weren't afraid to talk about anything, especially when it came to your feelings or telling people the truth."

Labouring to breathe, she closed her eyes. She took a moment to find the words. Opening her eyes, she said, "The truth can be twisted and manipulated where someone's good intention turns the other into a victim."

"If I caused this—"

"Don't flatter yourself. I'm not comfortable sharing anything about my life with people, especially my coworkers. If this is some elaborate plan to get me to write my story or a song, I'm sure Mr. X can call a professional to write something better."

She pulled her hair up into a bun. It was a nervous tick when she wanted to feel in control of the situation or preparing to have a battle of wits with him. Christopher waited for her to finish.

"I told him you could write one," he asserted.

"Does he know about our past?" She crossed her arms across her chest.

"Everything."

Leaning forward, she studied his eyes for verification. He didn't flinch. As she examined them, his eyes were as open and clear to read, ready to answer any question she wanted to ask him.

"And he still sent you?"

"He's a forgiving and understanding man. He accepts me for who I am."

"You're not Mr. X?"

"No, he's a real person. But, he believes our past is an opportunity for success."

"Is Mr. X. Oprah Winfrey?" she questioned sarcastically.

Grinning, he answered, "No. But…your story will change the dynamic in the office, and if you share it in public, imagine who we could help."

He had a point, and she hated it. The longer they worked

together, she was more inclined to listen to his suggestions. Even arguing with him became like a game for her, but the more she relaxed and enjoyed herself in his company, the tidal wave of agonizing emotions and memories invaded her soul. She pleaded in a soft tone that she didn't realize existed in her. "I don't agree. Amalie will do a great job. I need you to trust me."

Placing his right hand on his heart and nodding, he conceded, "As you wish. Nice to see that my charm has no effect on you."

"It never did."

She wickedly smiled, proud that she had won this round. But she didn't relish in her victory. Something in his eyes unsettled her as if she had wounded him to the point where she regretted not finding a compromise.

Emma cleared her throat. "The work we're doing is great. I agree. We're still scratching the surface. I'll do my best to work with you and listen, if you have a good idea. There is no need to let our past affect our present working relationship, nor should your desire to tell others."

"Okay." Tossing his hands up, he rose to his feet.

"Wait. I agree. As colleagues, we can talk about things unrelated to work when we need to take a break from discussing business. I would like to talk about other stuff," she added as she stood and handed her containers to him.

"This hasn't been easy for me either…sorry…what I mean is… Beth suggested it might help us if we had small talk that wasn't work-related. Martin must love your long hours."

She sighed with an expression he understood.

"You don't have to work late. He must miss you."

"He understands that I need to impress my new boss."

"You don't need to prove anything to me."

"I was referring to Mr. X."

Nodding as if he knew what she was talking about, he clarified, "Right. Perhaps, you need me to prove something to you?"

She blinked and gawked at him. Unsure what her heart and mind wanted to do, she didn't have a quick-witted response. She was relieved to hear Martin's ringtone echo in her room. But she wasn't compelled to answer it as much as she wanted to respond to Christopher's question.

"Tell Martin hello," he suggested as he picked up the remainder of his things and headed towards the door.

"I'm sorry. I need to take this call; we had a fight and—"

"I get it. I'd be annoyed if my girlfriend chose work over me. When you're trying to build a life with someone, you make sure you call them every day, so they don't forget you're a human being with feelings. You should take the day off and surprise him."

"I'll consider it, if you tell Mr. X how you failed." Her voice was light again as her piercing sarcasm returned.

"Don't have to. He predicted you would say no. I only hoped you'd say yes."

CHAPTER 14

It was the end of another workday when Richard and Grace came running into Emma's office.

" 'Tight ass' and his squad have left!" Richard's shrilly voice broke Emma's concentration.

"And?" Emma stopped reading her notes and scowled at them.

"It's been a long day," Grace whined at Richard's side in front of Emma's desk.

"And still, we have a pile of work to finish." Richard pleaded like a child who didn't want to shop with his parents anymore, "Emma, let us go home. Please, we need to drink. We guarantee we'll arrive early tomorrow. Refreshed and ready to work."

She raised her eyebrows. "After a night of drinking? I can't seem to envision that happening."

"Emma, we promise. We need to rejoin the living world," Grace pleaded as if she was competing with Richard for whiniest child.

"We have other responsibilities," Emma explained as she felt her temper rising.

"And that's why I'm here to make sure she leaves tonight. Thanks for the call, Richard." Strutting into the room, Martin's booming voice was commanding and assertive as he walked in with a food basket in his arms.

Emma's eyes widened as she saw the overflowing basket with a bottle of wine, a baguette bread, and a platter of fruit. "What are you doing here? It's Wednesday. Don't you have drinks with the partners?"

"Not tonight. Figured you had a rough day and needed a break."

"We'll leave you two alone. I love a man who brings a food basket. If there is prosciutto and crackers in there, Emma, you need to marry this man right now!" Richard yelled as he quickly left the room.

Grace raced after him and closed the door behind her. Emma grinned and approached Martin with a heavy heart. Ignoring him all day was intentional. But she had a plan to fix it. Grinning like a cat after his prey, she kissed him.

"Don't assume kissing me will make me forget this morning or the fact you haven't called me back today."

She nibbled on his ear.

"Or how you skipped out on our lunch date today. You don't play fair."

"Do you forgive me?" Emma kissed him again.

"Evil woman."

"I'm sorry. Work has been stressful, and I'm taking it out on you." She took the food basket from his hands and dropped it on the nearest chair.

"What was I saying?" He asked as she traced her fingers up his forearm.

"I forgot," she squealed and yanked him back to her.

He propped her on her desk and wrapped her legs around him. She began to unbutton his shirt.

"Aha! I can't believe I'm saying this—" He leaned his forehead against hers and dropped his hands to her side. "Before you assume I don't, I do, but I bought tickets."

"For what?"

"Shakespeare in the Park."

"We can catch the show another day." She pressed his mouth to hers.

"I understand, but we need to have a date. We can't always do this."

"Why not?"

"I have no idea. But—"

She untucked his shirt and unbuckled his belt.

He groaned as he drew himself away from her. "I want foreplay. I'm not saying we can't return to this, which by the end of the night, guarantee, but I prefer to have a night where I get to experience something you love."

Emma searched his intense dark brown eyes. His expression was very familiar to her. He had a plan and was not going to be persuaded from it. And if she was being honest with herself, watching the play sounded more appealing. Jumping off her desk, she buttoned her shirt and made her way out of her office. "But know, there is no guarantee this will happen tonight if you don't earn it."

***

The summer night air was crisp. Sitting under the stars in High Park was like being in the middle of the forest in *Midsummer Night's Dream.* In the air was a sense of love veiled in mystery and mischief. As Emma sat with Martin on a blanket, she became lost in the intoxicating atmosphere and the sounds of audience anticipation. It helped to temper the mix of emotions swirling in her heart as she snuggled in Martin's arms. A night with her boyfriend almost helped her to forget about the tension between them and the growing ease and trust she had when she worked with Christopher.

"You were right. We needed this." She poured herself another glass of wine.

"Well, if you had told me that you loved the theatre, I'd take you every night. You live across the street."

She half laughed as she glanced at her condo building in the distance. She never realized how close she lived to a world she abandoned. Her muscles tensed.

"Did I say something?" Martin kissed her shoulder.

"Hmm? Sorry, I was absorbing the energy. We should do this more often." She kissed him lightly on the lips.

"Foreplay or going to the theatre?"

"This is your foreplay? You've been a lucky man." She took another sip of her drink.

"I can't disagree."

Martin began kissing the hollows of her neck as his arms drew her closer to him. Feeling how aroused he had become to her touch, she placed his hands on her thighs and let them explore upwards. She knew it was inappropriate, but it helped her forget how she had neglected her duties as Martin's girlfriend, the unease she was feeling in her relationship with Christopher, and how she barely got through Sonja's wedding to-do-list.

"Emma?"

You got to be kidding me!

Pulling away from Martin, she turned and saw Christopher looking down at her. He was holding the hand of an attractive female.

"Christopher?"

"You know each other?" Martin's voice was high-pitched and surprised.

"Yes," Emma released herself from Martin's embrace and got to her feet. Flattening her clothes, she winced as Martin placed his hand in hers.

"Martin, Christopher. He's my—"

"...partner. I'm helping her transition into her new role, especially supporting her on the St. Michael's Centre campaign—"

"Where Annabelle works," Emma commented quickly.

"I represent Mr. X's interest. You must be the boyfriend? It's nice to meet the ringtone. This is Beth."

Placing her most professional friendly persona on, Emma hoped it concealed her gut reaction towards Beth. Beth was stunning. Her online picture didn't do her justice. Her auburn hair was perfectly layered as if she was the model on the package of a hair colour product. The worst part, she was barely wearing any make-up, but with high cheekbones that would make models green with envy, who would need it? But what Emma detested most was how her eyes glowed when she held Christopher's hand. She radiated the belief that everything in the world was a cascade of possibility and joy. For Emma, she felt like Jane Eyre meeting Miss Ingram for the first time. The only problem was, Beth was not Miss Ingram. She wasn't a decoy girlfriend; she was a smart and virtuous woman in love with the man who had become an intimate colleague.

"I guess for argument's sake, I'm the girlfriend." Beth's sweet voice inspired Emma to give up sugar.

"Here to watch the show?" Emma inquired.

Beth responded with the excitement of a child at Christmas, "Yes, spontaneous idea on my part. You've been working so hard. I told Christopher Mr. X demands too much from him. I called him today and mentioned I was free tonight, so we needed to go out. I see you benefited from my suggestion."

"Excuse me for a second." Christopher walked a few meters away to answer his phone.

"Never get used to that, right? He's devoted to Mr. X. But I do it too. We're always working, even on date night."

Remembering that Martin was beside her, Emma added, "That's right. Martin, Beth is a writer."

"Inspirational-speaker-turned writer," Beth added with her white pearly teeth.

It was a bright smile, which made Emma respond with a warm and inviting smirk. But it wasn't from a place of jealousy. Instead, it came from fear. She noticed how they didn't bring anything to sit on. The thought that they might join them sent goosebumps racing up her arm.

"If I don't tell him to hang up his phone, this becomes a working date." Smiling like a newscaster providing hope during a tragic time, she strolled towards Christopher.

Emma released a huge breath as Martin leaned over and whispered into her ear, "They're interesting. Christopher? The big ogre and arrogant little prick. Is he the one who's forcing you to break your dates with me? He doesn't seem as tyrannical or old as you described."

Clearing her throat, she stepped away from him and stretched her arms. His tone and manner were on the verge of bursting with aggression. Right now, she didn't want to control his temper, especially when her legs could barely hold her up.

"Aren't we supposed to be focusing on us?" She turned to him with the intent of kissing him again.

He stepped back as if he was calculating how much space they had on their blanket. "They don't have a blanket."

"Bad planning."

"You don't want them to join us?"

"I desire to devote my time to you." She kissed him, hoping she could distract him.

"I'm trying to be friendly. He represents a millionaire who can help your career and Annabelle's Centre." He broke the kiss and glanced over her shoulder to see if Christopher was nearby. "I might persuade him to donate to my campaign."

Emma grabbed her wine and drank it as she saw Martin's

ambition replan the evening. She cooed and let him dream. It was better than having him pry into her relationship with Christopher.

"I don't enjoy sharing you." He tilted her head to kiss her again.

"Just to be clear, is this another foreplay move?"

"Yes."

"Am I with the political candidate Martin Torcoke or the man who physically shows the world I belong to him?"

"What can I say? Old habits die hard." Martin kissed her again in a way to claim her attention.

Christopher cleared his throat. "Oh, sorry—" He backed into Beth.

Beth pointed to the blanket. "I'm sorry, but the show is starting, and I didn't plan this romantic date well. Do you mind if we sit here? You can make out through the whole thing. We don't want your food, just a place to sit," she begged as she nudged Christopher to engage in the conversation.

Emma glanced at Martin to gauge his reaction. It was neutral, but his eyes told her he was ready to pounce on the opportunity to question Christopher.

"Why not? It's always good to meet new people and get to know them, right, Emma?" He smirked as if he won the prize for not appearing needy. Emma rolled her eyes.

Howling with the innocence of a child, Beth exclaimed, "They used to work together."

Emma frowned as she saw the corners of Martin's lips dip into a neutral state. It was an expression that politicians master to conceal their knee-jerk reaction to bombshell news of impropriety.

"Beth, I told you, it's not common knowledge." Christopher glared at her.

"Your teams have no idea that you used to work together?" Beth flicked her finger between Christopher and Emma. "Hiding, are we? What have I told you, Christopher? Concealing the truth only creates distrust. Studies have shown that—"

Mr. X's ringtone roared in their circle. Emma never felt more relieved to hear it.

"Let me guess?" Her sweet voice had touches of salt in it when she growled at Christopher.

"Duty calls," Christopher apologized and sprinted away.

With a nod of understanding towards Beth, Emma informed her that she understood Christopher's devotion to Mr. X. Lucky for Emma, Beth's phone rang. She stepped away to take her call.

"You never mentioned you worked with your new partner before?" Martin whispered, his voice dripping with derision.

A thousand thoughts ran through her mind. One was to tell Martin the truth. Then at least she wouldn't feel the onslaught of fear and unease of her past coming out. But, something inside her told her to discern if telling the truth was wise when Martin already learned that all her nights were spent with a handsome acquaintance from her past.

Through gritted teeth, Emma responded, "Well, it wasn't important. It was a long time ago."

"Ex-boyfriend?"

Gazing down at her, she felt like he was cross-examining her in the court of law.

Emma bit her lower lip. "We worked together. That's it," she kissed him before he could ask any more questions. Emma was grateful for the distraction.

Beth coughed loudly upon returning. "I'm sorry. We ruined your date. You were having a good time before we interrupted you. Once he gets back, we'll find somewhere else to go. Excuse me." Beth got up to answer her phone again while Christopher returned from the other direction.

"Where did Beth go?" Christopher asked.

"She had a phone call," Martin replied as Emma moved closer to him.

"So, tell me everything about Emma." Martin graciously invited Christopher to sit with them as any lethal lawyer would do before pouncing on a hostile witness.

Loosening his tie and rolling his sleeves, Christopher accepted the invitation. Like old friends, they drank wine and ate food. Emma watched in silence, wanting this live-action-horror movie to end.

"You planned tonight out well," Christopher commented as he examined the contents of his wine.

"Martin planned this whole evening." Emma glanced up at him in admiration.

"Nice to see that her highness is well-pleased."

"Highness?" Martin growled.

Emma cleared her throat. "It was my nickname. I'm not an outdoor person. But you know that?" She brushed her fingers across Martin's arm to ease the growing tension in his arms.

"Your nickname? No. But the name is cute. I prefer Ice Queen."

Christopher chuckled, "Yes, I've heard it around the office. But, they don't mean the same thing. I wonder where Beth is?" He gulped his wine and scanned the park.

Martin ignored Christopher's question and poured him another glass. "Don't worry; I brought another bottle."

Raising an eyebrow, Christopher examined the colour and inhaled the aroma of the wine. He scratched his nose before taking a sip.

"It's a white Chardonnay. It's Emma's favourite," Martin claimed with the confidence of a boyfriend.

"Sorry, I enjoy a Rose Zinfandel. Emma used to love them. She introduced them to me."

Spitting out her drink, she blurted, "I don't like them anymore."

Martin glared at her as if she gave too much information to the opposing counsel. Christopher grabbed a napkin and wiped some of the wine off of him as if he enjoyed being drenched in used wine. Smirking, she stuffed grapes into her mouth.

"What do you exactly do for Mr. X?" Martin straightened his back and puffed up his chest.

Emma counted to ten. She hated when Martin went into lawyer-mode. It was obvious that his curiosity had faded, and he opted to attack with an aggression that trial lawyers honed throughout the years. He was ready for a good-old-fashioned testosterone challenge with Christopher. This was not new to Emma. Every time a man of confidence or intelligence came near her, Martin became an unreasonable and possessive man.

"I'm his trusted advisor. He calls me when he wants me to vet a company or assess a team or person to see if they fit into his organization."

"Has Emma's team met your standards? Do you regularly work closely with those you're vetting?"

"Not usually."

"Are you saying Emma's team needed support?"

"No, the team she's built is excellent. Yet, we found she needed a partner to listen and challenge her. Give her a different perspective and support to follow her instincts."

"Does anyone want some fruit?" Squeaking out the question, Emma offered food to both of them. Anything to deescalate the situation.

"You assume a successful and well-trusted associate might have other projects than helping a not-for-profit one?" he growled as Emma immediately squeezed his hand.

"I do, but Mr. X has a particular interest in this Centre's work."

"So, Mr. X wants you here? Sounds odd. You seem to be like a money-making type of man."

"Not everything is about making a profit."

"True. Creating a positive image never hurts anyone, especially if it helps his business, right?" Martin's remark was making Emma shiver in fear.

"Only if you're a cynic. Fortunately, for Emma and her team, they're part of a company that tries to help people discover their potential, then making them fit into someone's ideals."

She held Martin's arm tighter as she saw the vein pulsate on the side of his neck.

"Why don't we…I mean…Martin, why don't you tell Christopher about your upcoming campaign? How we plan to…well…the….campaign?"

"Did I interrupt anything?" Beth returned and casually sat beside Christopher.

"No, we are getting acquainted," Martin gritted through his teeth as he broke free from Emma's grip.

"He was asking why I'm here," Christopher added as he took the bottle of wine and poured Beth a glass.

"It's fascinating work. Christopher buys or reconstructs companies for Mr. X. It's nice this project has a personal connection. He makes sure Mr. X's money really helps others. It's inspiring. That's why he makes sure Mr. X is always in the loop."

"To a good Samaritan," Martin held his glass up to toast Christopher.

"Yes," Beth picked up a glass and clinked Martin's glass.

"You give me too much credit. Let's toast to the person who taught me how one goal keeps you focused, but having multiple results centred on the same cause changes the world." Christopher raised his glass for everyone to toast again.

He nodded at Emma to raise her glass. As they clinked glasses, she wondered if the toast was for her. But as he reached for Beth's hand with a gentle touch, she pushed the thought away.

"Inspiring, isn't he? My staff loves him. Harry, my secretary, says we're a match made in heaven."

"So, Martin, how is the law? Constitutional law, right?" Christopher pointed his glass towards Martin.

Martin turned towards Emma. "What else have you told Christopher about me?"

Before Emma could answer, the actor's voice on stage bellowed through the park. She half-grinned at Martin and popped a strawberry into her mouth. She settled into Martin's arms, grateful that the show was starting. She didn't enjoy watching Martin's typical type-A testosterone-filled Neanderthal personality emerge, especially beside a confident and civil Christopher.

As she sat there trying to enjoy the play, her eyes glanced over to Christopher and Beth. He held her hand and whispered into her ear. She laughed at his jokes and snuggled close to him. Emma wanted to hurl.

Drawing Martin's arms securely around her, she wanted to ignore the love story between Christopher and Beth and focus on the one between Orsino and Viola. But the swirling pain in her stomach and the influx of melancholy descending on her could not be tempered by Martin's touch or in the spectacle before her eyes.

"Hey, you okay? You're crying," Martin whispered into her ear.

"Allergies," she responded.

"You're quiet."

"I was reflecting on how much I enjoy watching you interrogate people."

"I understand why you've been working so hard. We should invite them back to your place for drinks."

She squirmed in his arms. "Didn't you have other plans?"

"This is an opportunity."

"For what?"

"Research for Leon. He wants to make sure we have no skeletons in our closet. I want to make sure you're not hiding anything else from me. Besides, he represents a very wealthy man. He could be good for our future. Plus, he understands what pleases and displeases your highness." Martin kissed her lightly on the lips.

She pulled away and returned her attention to the stage. Forcing herself to relax, as the fear engulfed her, she didn't want to argue with him. It was clear to her this was what he wanted, and she could only hope that Christopher would say no.

CHAPTER 15

Emma admired the glowing building lights and listened to the summer breeze rustle through the trees as a way to keep her frustration at bay. The sights and sounds did help to distract her, but every time she heard Martin and Christopher talking to each other, she wanted to push one of them into the streets. She was appalled at Christopher for accepting Martin's invitation for drinks at her condo. Worse, she hated how Martin kept questioning Christopher, who didn't seem like he wanted to hide anything about their relationship. She feared that Martin would ask the right question, and Christopher would not hesitate to tell him the whole story. Emma was grateful for every Mr. X call that stopped Martin's line of questioning.

Casually peeking behind Martin's shoulder, she observed how the usual calm and confident Christopher had faded as he talked to Mr. X. on the phone today. He wasn't frantic or manic, but he lost that attentive energy he had a week ago. It made her wonder if her team was in trouble.

"Oh, don't mind him. If Mr. X doesn't hear from him, he calls at once." Beth continued to walk alongside Emma and Martin.

"You sure?" Martin turned to see what Emma and Beth were looking at.

"I've met no one more dedicated to his job, minus me. It's why this relationship works. But, I leave my work at the office. He works as if he's doing penance or something. Do you remember him being obsessively committed to work?"

"Yes, he worked hard. Still does. But I only worked

with him for that one summer, barely two months," Emma mumbled.

Squinting her eyes at Emma, Beth insisted, "He mentioned it was his best summer."

"I couldn't imagine why."

"He claimed the trees were glorious. When you stood at the edge of the lake, the water rushed over your feet, and the world made sense."

Emma mumbled to herself, "You don't need a textbook to understand creation. Stand in it, and it'll teach you—"

"What did you say?" Martin inquired.

"Nothing."

"Beth, Emma mentioned you were a Christian writer. What does that mean?" Martin probed as if he was sitting on a government inquiry committee.

"I help people find joy in their daily life, in God. I offer words of wisdom that I've picked up from my grandmother. My series is called *A Return to Common Sense.* It started as a blog when my grandmother died, and people loved it. As my friend Ashlyn showed me, once you have a brand, people want to buy books from you. So, I wrote other books about people who imparted their wisdom. I've published *Common Sense from my Grandmother's Table for Gratitude in Life*, *Common Sense from My Uncle Will to Understand Unemployment.* I'm working on *Common Sense From My Mother to Raise Your Teenage Daughter.*"

"Sounds fascinating. We're here," Emma declared with relief.

Christopher was blocks away.

"You must be used to that." Beth whispered into Emma's ear.

"Used to what?" Emma shifted her eyes away from Christopher.

"Having your conversations cut off when Mr. X calls."

"I guess. He misses a couple when we're arguing about something."

"They must be heated for him to ignore Mr. X. He'll be there for a while. We better go inside. I need to use the washroom. Martin, can you wait for Christopher? Sometimes I get so far ahead, he forgets we were on a date and goes home."

"Sure, go ahead."

***

"Are you moving out?" Beth examined the stacked boxes against Emma's walls.

"With my schedule, I've been unpacking here and there," Emma replied as she prepared refreshments in the kitchen

"Nice view," Christopher commented with a hint of a smile.

"Thank you."

Emma watched Christopher from her kitchen island. It was a good vantage point for her to observe Christopher, even though it unnerved her to see him in her place. As he reviewed the books on her shelves and the barren walls, she could hear him judging her in his mind.

"Thank you for inviting us. It's so nice to be around people who aren't discussing kids and married life. They can't come out on a random weekday for drinks." Beth accepted the glass of wine from Emma.

"Sorry for the disorder," Emma explained as she pointed to her unmarked and disorganized boxes as well as Martin's campaign material.

"Please, if I didn't have three assistants, my life would be in disarray."

Resting her chin in her head, Emma wondered if Beth had a self-edit button or was the type of person who was not afraid to say anything. Over the course of an hour, Beth's honesty made it easier for Emma to like her, though she prayed that Beth would stop prying into her life.

"Are you an avid read reader?" Beth asked.

Before Emma had a chance to respond, Martin said, "She likes her books. What is he doing?" Martin pointed at Christopher.

Emma glanced over at Christopher before Martin tugged at her arm so she could sit on his lap.

Leaning forward, Beth confessed, "Terrible habit. Loves analyzing what people are reading. It gives him an insight into the person's mind."

Emma choked on her drink.

"What happens if they don't read?" Martin wiped the droplets of Emma's drink off of him.

"It suggests a lack of imagination."

Christopher and Emma answered the question simultaneously. Emma downed her drink.

"Have her reading habits changed?" Beth inquired.

"She's missing *Pride and Prejudice* and *Jane Eyre*, but it seems she has a new love for the modern classics."

Discovering that her favourite books were missing was a revelation to Emma.

She glanced over to check out what Christopher was doing now. She hated how he moved his fingers over the books' spines as if he was searching for a secret passage. Beth's lips pursed together as if she was sucking a lemon and turned her attention back to Martin and Emma. "He tries to read. Doesn't have shelves of books. Keeps everything on his trusted tablet. Find anything interesting?"

Smirking, Christopher responded, "She reads more crime fiction."

"Those are mine. We read them together to see who can figure out who the murderer is first," Martin chimed in as if he was the only person in a class with the answer to the teacher's question.

"That's so cute. Christopher and I tried to read the same material. But, he's been focused on the classics while I preoccupy my mind with human psychology. We must sound boring. Chris, did you find anything else interesting?" Beth asked.

"Just a small rock and a picture of Lake Tawekenanda."

God, please don't have either of them talk about that rock.

"Right. The rock with sentimental value to her, but to another person, just a rock," Martin shouted as he kissed Emma's forehead.

Christopher scratched his left eyebrow and mumbled, "Or whose lines tell a story of every person who held it in their hands."

Emma darted her eyes away from Christopher as she felt Martin's grip tighten around her. He nudged Emma to pour him another glass.

Martin took and sip of his wine and asked, "Christopher, do you have any thoughts about the play? Before we were interrupted by your boss, you mentioned how the play was entertaining, but you didn't appreciate it?"

Christopher sat in the other Poang chair across Emma and Martin. "It was true to Shakespeare's text, but it was a safe interpretation."

Beth added, "When he's in London, he goes to the theater when work permits. You can't find many guys interested in attending a show."

"You have to be present to feel the emotions. That's what thrilled Emma about live theatre. Emma, did you enjoy the play?" Christopher leaned forward towards Emma and Martin.

"It was entertaining. I'll get the appetizers." She jumped off Martin's lap and made her way to the kitchen to remove the appetizers from the oven. As they cooled, she searched for a cracker to chew or a bottle of tequila to chug.

With pride in his voice, Martin explained, "She's always the hostess. I have to admit, I've an ulterior motive for inviting you here." He made eye contact with Christopher as if they were preparing to box each other in the ring.

"What did Emma used to be like? I went to her folks' house for dinner and discovered she used to immerse herself in the arts."

"How long have you two been dating?" Beth joined their conversation.

"Over a year. She's selective in what she shares," Martin replied.

Emma entered the room with appetizers and placed them on the coffee table. "I want you to fall in love with the present me than what I used to be. Besides, isn't that Leon's job?"

"I fell in love with you the moment I met you. But, we have an opportunity here. He has stories about your youth. Sonja and Charlotte never reminisce when I'm in the room, and your family sparingly share stories." Martin reached for Emma's hand and encouraged her to sit on his lap again.

"She loved to write, and on a rare occasion, she composed songs and shared them," Christopher commented without a trace of emotion.

It surprised Emma how offended she was by his comment. "Irrelevant poems. They were in my room, remember?"

"Was it the first prize award? Or the one published in the

magazine?" Martin questioned her like a hostile witness on the stand.

"Do you still write?" Beth inquired.

Emma shook her head and downed her wine again. "No, I lost interest."

"Fifteen years ago," Christopher mumbled.

Emma spat her wine into her glass. "Who said it's been fifteen years?"

"I'm guessing."

"Love and talent are two distinct things, Mr. Riley. They were words on paper subpar to being professional. I realized after my first year of university that writing was a dream."

"Who said?" Christopher questioned as if he was determined to unearth the truth.

"I had professors who claimed my syntax was poor and ill-formed. I accepted the hint and switched."

"To marketing and business? Do you prefer running numbers and selling things than writing?" Christopher crossed his hands in front of him.

"That's not why I stopped. I—"

"Tired of rejection?" His voice rose as high as his eyebrows.

"No! I had to concentrate on a stable future rather than investing in an unattainable dream. Writing advertisements was sufficient to quell my appetite to create fiction."

In a bold and assertive voice, Christopher stated, "But you had dreams to inspire people to greater things as opposed to buying happiness."

Emma glared at Christopher, forgetting Martin and Beth were in the room. An eerie silence enveloped the space.

"Ahem, did you hear her sing or read what she wrote?" Beth touched Christopher's arm.

Christopher tore his eyes from Emma. "It's vague, but, yeah, I remember." He shoved an appetizer into his mouth.

"What was the last thing you heard her sing?" Beth begged Christopher to share his memory.

Wiping his mouth, without flinching, he answered, " 'Cry.' It was a Kelly Clarkson cover."

"Anyone need a refill?" Emma jumped to her feet and rushed to the kitchen.

"Was she a good singer?" Martin asked as he sipped his wine.

"She has the voice of an angel. But when she sang 'Cry,' it was as if an angel had lost a soul for God. It was if someone… broke the princess's heart."

"Princess? Is that some nickname?" Beth stared at Emma and Christopher.

Christopher stuffed another appetizer into his mouth.

"Yeah, the campers gave it to me. I used to have long hair… like a Disney princess," Emma answered. She leered at Christopher to not contradict her. He shook his head and nodded in agreement. Relieved, she sat on Martin's lap again.

"You're so cute together. Are you engaged?" Beth glanced over at Emma's hand.

"No, her highness isn't ready. We're moving towards marriage, but we're focused on my political career," Martin responded as he kissed Emma's left hand.

"I'm not an expert, but you and Martin make a great couple. I'd vote for you. My grandmother taught me that when two people match in nature, then they'll live happily ever after."

"That must mean you're the Perfect Prince," Christopher added as he downed his glass of wine.

Feeling the air leave her lungs, she wiggled free from Martin's tight embrace.

Beth grinned as if a brilliant idea came to her. "Maybe you should sing again. It's rare for Christopher to praise anyone."

Christopher smirked and almost spit out his food. "Interesting suggestion, because we've been trying to get her to do it for the gala."

"Right. The personal touch. The signature to all your projects," Beth stated as if she was giving it her stamp of approval.

"But, we agreed for Amalie to share her story through her pictures. Showboating my lack of talent deters from our purpose."

"It's a fundraiser. When raising funds, you have to pull out all the stops."

Smirking with the grace of a queen, she reasoned, "Yes, my job is to raise the funds, not sing."

"Time is as valuable as one's cheque. Sharing something of yourself may help someone beyond a dollar sign."

"Yet, sharing my story will not inspire people to give more money."

"I appreciate your opinion, but you're wrong."

Exasperated, Emma jumped up, "Here we go again! I'm tired of telling you and Amalie no. But then again, both of you have that secret project that you refuse to share any details. You're going to make me do something I don't want to do."

"Do you want to help?" Christopher stood to stand toe to toe with her.

"How can I? You and Amalie want me to talk about my life," she shouted.

"Your story could help someone. It helped Amalie. It helped—"

"Your phone," Beth yelled over them.

Christopher's phone had rung five times without the two of them noticing.

"What?" Christopher turned to Beth.

"Mr. X," Emma whispered as she rubbed the back of her neck.

"Excuse me." Christopher went outside on the terrace to take the call.

Emma watched him pace and shout, noting how his personality changed again. There was jerkiness in his movement as his shoulders sagged. It tugged at something in her that made her want to weep.

"I can see why you've been working overtime. Is it like that every day between you two?" Martin squeezed Emma's shoulder.

"No, but recently it explodes into that."

"Interesting, I've never seen him like that," Beth laughed and placed an appetizer in her mouth.

CHAPTER 16

Emma assumed that she was dreaming when she heard a frantic knock at 4:30 a.m. But her hangover lodged a rock into her brain to confirm the noise outside her condo door was real.

"Emma, I'm sorry to disturb you, but is it here?" Christopher spoke quickly as she peeked through her keyhole.

As she opened the door, his aftershave wafted through the air and continued to spread through her place. It woke her up. Her heart galloped, and her skin tingled with electricity. Shaking off the sudden spark racing through her body, she focused on his disoriented state to ground her in reality.

"I'll be quick, I promise. I didn't bother you or Martin, did I?"

"He's not here."

"Really?"

"Why are you here?" She rubbed her eyes.

"My phone."

"Beth doesn't have it?"

"No."

Despite her natural irritation for being up early, she was empathic to his frantic state and helped him search for his phone.

"I have to find it. Do you mind? It might be in a box. How long have you lived here? I can help organize your stuff while I'm here."

"Your phone is more important than my boxes."

"Good point."

"Do you want to try calling yourself?"

Emma grabbed her phone and speed dialled his number. They both stood in silence, hoping to hear it.

"Battery is dead." He groaned.

Noting Christopher's anxiety jumping to the next level, she touched his arm. "We'll find it."

Making eye contact with him, she took a deep breath in with him. After a few moments, their breaths were in sync, and it was the only sound you could hear in the room. Realizing they were alone, Emma released his arm. Christopher stepped back and wandered over to the shelves. He picked up the picture of Lake Tawekenanda.

"Do you remember when you took this picture?" Christopher held the picture up for her.

She rolled her eyes.

"I remember when you took this picture. We were watching the sunrise after an early morning rain shower. You were wearing my jacket as usual, and I was sitting on a rock, watching how calm you became in the sun's amber hue." He handed her the picture.

"Aren't we supposed to be searching for your phone? Amber hue, really?" She took the picture from his hand and placed it on the bookshelf.

"Do you still get up at sunrise?" He pointed to the picturesque sunrise outside her window.

"My body is moving at sunrise, but I'm not admiring the sun."

"That's a pity."

"Life happens."

"Marketing maven and all?" He laughed as she stifled herself from joining him.

Realizing that they were staring at each other, Emma tore her eyes away from him. She didn't want to show how she appreciated his observation.

"Do you and Martin make time to watch a sunrise together and talk?"

"We're searching for your phone."

"We can talk while we search. I thought we agreed that we can have conversations outside the realm of business."

She searched between her furniture, refusing to respond.

"You've changed."

"I'm still in my pyjamas."

He mumbled as he searched in a box, "That's not what I meant."

She almost stopped searching, but as she reviewed his unkempt appearance, she had compassion for him. Something in him was starting to penetrate the walls of her heart that their past and even his moodiness could not deter her from helping him.

"I'm screwed. That's it. Outdone by my stupid—" He yelled, slamming his head into the couch. A few more profane words spewed from his mouth.

She crouched beside him and touched his shoulder. "You okay?"

Flinching at her touch, he muttered, "Yeah."

"Figures. You have a hard head."

"Really, sarcasm? If I don't find my phone, I'm ruined. Are you drinking coffee?"

"It brews at this hour? If I recall, you drink yours black."

She examined the bruise forming on his forehead. As she was checking for any damage, she could have sworn she heard him draw in a breath.

"You smell like strawberries."

"You might have a slight concussion."

Upturning his hazel eyes to meet her, as it had done in

the past, held her in a trance. "I don't feel any pain."

"Sip your coffee. You'll have a bruise to remember this morning. But no cut." Handing him his cup, she tried to hide how she blushed under his gaze.

"Thanks. I must sound like an idiot."

"Compared to what? Sorry." There was a wicked twinkle in her eye, but it was apologetic.

"I'm screwed."

"Yes, what will you do if you can't call Mr. X?"

"It's weird. I get it. But despite him being eccentric and demanding, he gave me a second chance when my record showed I didn't deserve it."

Squeezing his hand, she couldn't abandon him in his search, "We'll find it. I owe him something. He saved us last night from saying things."

"I'm sorry, I was out of line."

With a hint of glee in her voice, she declared, "You enjoy bringing up arguments I've won."

"Or he calls when you run out of reasons to say no."

Emma placed her cup back on the coffee table and scanned her condo, trying to remember what happened last night. They were arguing when the phone rang. Rising, she stepped out to her terrace and found the phone bathing in the sun's rays.

"This it?" Emma held the phone in her hand.

In exuberance, Christopher jumped from the floor. He lifted Emma from the ground and hugged her. "You're a genius." He returned her to the ground.

As he gazed into her dark brown eyes, her heart raced, but she wasn't scared. It felt safe. Feeling safe made her nervous. She stepped back, and he dropped his hands and began to check his phone.

"Is the battery dead?" Emma wondered as she tossed

some of Martin's campaign posters into a box.

"Brought my charger. Do you mind?"

"Go ahead."

He plugged his phone and checked his messages while Emma refilled her cup.

"Anything?" She scrutinized his mood over the brim of her coffee.

"No, I guess he didn't need a report."

Emma nodded. "Perhaps he's telling you to relax."

"You might be right. But he's the one who signs the cheques."

Opening her cupboards and drawers, he started to pull out the bowls, pans and utensils. With ease, Christopher organized a cooking area.

"What are you doing?" She squinted her eyes as she analyzed what he pulled from her cupboards.

Glancing up from his work station, he said, "Making breakfast. We're awake, and you helped me find my phone, and for last night, I owe you breakfast. Since we're here and home cooking is better than store-bought, unless you prefer to sleep again?"

Like a happy puppy, she sat on a kitchen stool. "What's for breakfast? When did you learn how to cook? The last time we cooked together, you couldn't tell the difference between a stove and an oven."

"A week after I left the camp. My parents took an interest in my life and sent me to work at a soup kitchen. I met Mr. X there. He taught me. Since then, it's something I do in my spare time."

"Which explains your loyalty to him."

"Yeah. I guess you're not into cooking?"

Emma scoffed. "We've been busy. We heat from a box or eat out."

He opened the fridge and peered in. "How old is this ham?"

"At least a week."

"Well, at least you have eggs. Onions. Omelette. Sound good to you?"

"Well, since you offered."

"As you wish." He placed his right hand over his heart.

Mesmerized by his dazzling dark hazel eyes and bow, she could see how they were begging for her to trust him again. These were the eyes that used to sparkle with mischief when she taught him how to make Rice Krispie treats or when she talked about love. But they were the same ones that had lied to her, a lie that could still pierce her soul and sink her heart into despair.

"You okay?" He refilled her cup of coffee.

"Still sleepy."

Turning away, he started breakfast. As she watched him, she wondered why her heart and mind felt like a thousand puzzle pieces scattered on a table. She had the picture in her hand to put it together, but she lacked the resolve and energy to start figuring out how all the pieces fit to form the picture.

"Your toast. Just butter, right?" Setting the food in front of her, he left to check on his omelette. She made the sign of the cross, prayed, and ate her toast.

As she sat there waiting for him to join her, she thought she saw him pray, but her sensible side didn't want to ask him. Instead, she chewed her meal and stayed silent.

"Is your food okay?" he inquired.

Emma was chewing, but she didn't realize that she was staring at him again, "Yes, thank you. This stuff was sitting in my fridge? You've come along way from melting butter in a pot."

"I'm surprised you remember."

Decreasing her chewing speed and swallowing, she said, "You didn't have to do this. Did I have orange juice in my fridge?"

"No, you had a couple of oranges and lemon. It's nothing. It's the least I can do. I was out of line yesterday. I woke you up. You found my phone."

Placing his fork down and sucking in his breath, he opened his mouth.

"I don't want to talk about our past anymore," Emma blurted out.

"Em—"

"Last night, other than our usual arguments, it was nice to hang out. It was nice not to have a night doing Martin's things or discussing work. I enjoyed seeing you through Beth's eyes."

He opened his mouth, but no sound came out. Instead, he grabbed a napkin and wiped his mouth. "Okay, but if you won't tell your staff about us, you should tell Martin." His voice and manner were soft and serious. He focused on her reaction in a way that took her back to the past, to an intense admiration that stirred in her heart the utter belief to listen to his advice.

"How do you know I didn't tell him?"

"He invited me to hang out. He loves you. If I were him, I would kick my ass for hurting you."

She bit her lip to stifle her agreement.

"He's protective of you. I assume as he prepares for his future, he wants to make sure there are no skeletons in your closet. If he becomes a candidate, you'll be on that stage with him."

"He likes to hint about a future, but there's nothing—"

"I wonder what it's like when he's being direct. I'm surprised he's not here."

"Why?"

"Emma? There were times he forgot we were in the room."

"You're imagining things."

"When did you become so dense?"

Emma shook her head. "He's not open with our relationship."

"Come with me." Grabbing her hand, he led her to the Poang chair.

"What are you doing?"

"Proving I'm right." He sat and had her sit on his lap. "You were sitting together. Martin's hand was firmly around your waist. Holding you this close. You draped your arm around his shoulder. Every time he wasn't speaking, his mouth grazed your neck, and his hand stroked your leg."

"This is ridiculous."

Swallowing her moan, she tried to keep the back of her neck straight then fall back to give him more access to the nape of her neck. But her body wasn't listening to her.

"We assumed you were glad to see us leave," he whispered into her ear, causing her lips to turn to him.

"Beth is nice."

"She is, but I haven't met anyone nicer than you."

Closing her eyes, she savoured his praise.

"I never thought you would be with a guy like that."

"Handsome, smart, and well-physique," she responded with her trademark wicked sarcasm.

His lips hovered over hers as he confessed, "He brings out something in you that makes you different. In a good way." His breath was already invading her mouth.

She responded in a husky voice. "I guess."

"Maybe he can get you back on the stage where you belong."

"Excuse me?" Leaping off his lap, she stood away from him.

"Emma, what I meant to say was that I —"

"Why, so you can humiliate me again? I don't want to be on that stage for you, him, or anybody."

"Forgive me for wanting you to be you again. I thought you would want to share the best of you with him."

"Or, kissing me might do the trick?" As soon as she blurted it out, she shut her mouth.

"Do you *want* me to kiss you?"

Shocked by his question, she was trying to figure out *what* she wanted. Everything about this conversation was too confusing to figure out early in the morning.

"You are the last person I want to kiss."

"Right, but if I were to kiss you, I would be a good reason for you to break up with Martin. Better than telling him you don't love him enough to marry him."

She squeezed her eyes shut to fight every tear that wanted to fall. When she opened them, Christopher was standing in front of her, shell-shocked.

With a clenched jaw and a hand ready to slap him, she declared, "You haven't changed. You're still a presumptuous and arrogant know-it-all. You don't know me."

"That's not—"

Her place filled with the sound of Martin's ringtone. She glared at him with the venom of a snake and answered her phone.

CHAPTER 17

Emma worked furiously in her office. After the incident this morning, working was a good form of therapy. Unfortunately, every five minutes, she had to deal with Christopher, who didn't agree with how she changed their original plans.

"Emma, we can't do this," Christopher yelled.

"You only despise it because it's not your idea."

"It's contrived."

"Am I missing a personal touch? Who cares if we raise the funds needed for the Centre?"

"Find a solution. You have an hour." Christopher stormed out of her office.

She took her pen and threw it at him.

"Is that round 1000? Every time I'm here, the two of you are always yelling at each other. You realize you have no colour in your cheeks, right?" Amalie observed as she entered Emma's office.

"What are you doing here?"

"Richard called in reinforcements. He mentioned that you might need a referee."

"Go tell your new best friend I'm right."

"Richard wasn't exaggerating. Are you okay?" Amalie hovered over Emma's desk.

"Don't worry. We understand what our roles are in this relationship and what we want. Why are you really here?"

"Your sister sent me to check on you. Plus, I had to drop off something to Christopher. Oh, when you get back to your place, I unpacked another box. I couldn't help myself."

"Fine."

Amalie tilted her head and tried to get Emma's attention. "Are you positive you're okay? Are you upset with me?"

"Should I be?"

"Well, when I proposed that you share your experience, I didn't mean to cause such a fuss. And, I'm sorry that I've been working with Christopher in secret. I want to tell you what we're doing, but I love a good surprise. Thought we were on the outs."

Emma tossed her hair back and sat up in her chair. "This has nothing to do with you. Were you at my apartment on Monday?"

"Yes, I told you. I was dropping material for the gala and—"

"You became distracted and consumed my food?"

"The chicken pasta was divine. I found these books inside a while ago, and I wanted to ask you and—"

Emma was smiling, fully engaged in the conversation.

Tilting her head to the left and shutting her right eye, she glared at Emma. "Sneaky rabbit. You didn't answer my question."

"What question?"

She leaned towards Emma and stammered on her words. "Is this about Christopher? I mean…did you work with him…like before? And now… you can't… or something. Is this him?"

Amalie pushed a picture across to Emma. It was of her and Christopher sitting on a picnic table leading a group. She was teaching, and he was staring at her with a goofy grin. Coughing away the twitch of nostalgia, she fought the memory materializing quickly in her mind. She loved telling those kids stories about a trees history or why swimming at night was dangerous. As she tapped her fingers on the edge of the picture, everything she loved was in that photo, but, like the picture, it was outdated and irrelevant in the present. But she waited too long for Amalie to believe any explanation for why Christopher and she were together when the truth was in full colour.

Emma placed the picture on her desk. "Where did you find this?"

"It fell out when I was putting one of your books away." She showed off her pearly white teeth as if she was an innocent cat who ate a mouse.

"How long have you known?"

"The first day he came, I thought I recognized him. See, I've unpacked your boxes and searched through your books and albums, and he's in there. As soon as I met him, I assumed you dated him and wanted to keep a secret, so I kept my mouth shut. Aren't you proud of me? I love to share news about people."

"You mean gossip?" In a subdued voice, she pushed the picture away from her. "We worked together. We never dated. Anything else?"

"So, nothing happened between you two?"

Emma crossed her arms across her chest. "Nothing happened."

"But, he seems very good at anticipating your every move and how you like things."

Emma waved her away and turned back to her computer. "I have work to do. If you only have personal questions, I won't answer them."

"Right. The real reason I'm here."

"Is to discuss business? The Campaign for the Centre?"

"Whatever! I'm here to discuss the retreat. The one you promised to attend six months ago with me. I'm here to do the pre-conversation."

"When is it?"

"This weekend."

Emma pursed her lips together. "Are you sure?"

"Yes, but if you prefer, we can meet later," Amalie suggested.

"No! You're here now."

Amalie's eye narrowed as she pouted her lips, "You forgot."

"Sit."

Amalie grinned and leaned back in her chair. Silenced filled the room. "Dylan and I had a lovely evening."

"Dylan?"

"The guy I'm seeing."

"Three months, right?"

"Yes. He came to my place. We talked about our previous relationships. He was sincere, but then I remembered how Colin fooled me with his sincerity. So, I remained reserved and didn't follow my feelings. But, the wine and his sheer honesty inspired my hormones."

"You drank wine?"

"I didn't drink."

"He didn't—"

"No. He wanted to leave. I escorted him to the door, where I kissed him goodnight. He leaned his forehead to mine so we could take a moment and really consider what we wanted to do, but my hands were seeking a means to undress him. As he placed me on the bed, I wanted him. But when his bare skin touched mine, I broke into a cold sweat."

"Amalie, he didn't—"

"No. He heard me whimper and drew back. He recognized that I was shivering. I couldn't move. He sat me up and waited for me. Grabbing my throw blanket, he covered me with it. Fear laced his eyes, but he remained calm and patient. He held me in his arms until I fell asleep. When I woke up, he was reading a book. He grinned and kissed me on the forehead without a desire for an explanation."

"Sounds like a nice guy."

"I trust him. But as we grow closer, I believe his tenderness is concealing something darker in him."

"You haven't told him about your past?"

"No, because he might treat me differently. But, he senses something is wrong."

"Amalie, fear will always be there. Your past always binds you to moments that paralyze you into that anxious young girl, but if you don't trust yourself, then you'll be alone."

"Thanks for sugarcoating my problem. It's my fault." Amalie covered her face in anguish.

"No, it's Colin's fault for abusing you. The only thing you have to decide is if you want him to wreck your future."

"Dylan is so sweet, but I wonder if I can trust him that much."

"Amalie, we bring emotional baggage every time we start a relationship. When I started dating Martin, I was nervous. I had a defensive wall around my heart, but over time, his patience and determination chipped those fears away. I found a way to trust him. You can't let your past dictate your future or even taint the hope for something greater. Tell Dylan the truth. How can you trust him if you can't trust him with your past?"

"Do you trust Martin? Have you shared your past with him?"

Amalie stared at Emma with the eyes of a puppy wanting to be wrapped up in her owner's arms. Emma sensed that

Amalie needed a word of encouragement or a story from her life to inspire her to tell Dylan the truth.

God, don't make me do this!

"Well, I —" As Emma cleared her throat, Richard charged into her office with Christopher hot on his heels.

"Sorry, Emma, but tight…as... Christopher wants to talk to you."

"Emma, you're being childish for approving these…sorry. Should I come back?" Christopher blurted and then bit down on his tongue.

Emma's eyes were glued on Amalie.

"No, I'm having a moment. You need to talk," Amalie responded as Richard followed her out.

"Do you need something?" Her eyes were stern and serious when she acknowledged his presence.

"Is she okay?"

Emma nodded and kept still like an elite poker player at the final stakes table. "Yeah, just playing mentor. Would you like me to share how mentoring requires you to listen to a crying mentee?"

Smirking and shaking his head, Christopher tossed Emma's advertising storyboard and banner layout for another fundraising project for cancer research. "That explains this—"

"It's fine." She was pretending to evaluate the material.

"This isn't what we discussed nor agreed upon."

"Well, I thought your plans were stupid when I arrived."

"Can you be a professional? Pout, cry, and ignore me. But don't let your emotions influence your judgement."

"My emotions only misguided me once, and they'll never influence me again."

"I'm sorry for this morning; it came out wrong. We're at work. Let's work together. These projects are important. I'm here to help the Centre. I'm here because it helped me—" He stopped mid-sentence.

She observed how his professional demure faded. "Helped you what?"

His exhale was deliberate as he sat down across from her. Leaning forward with his hand clasped together, he apologized. "My recent behaviour hasn't been professional. That's on me. But as a colleague, respect that I'm here to help you transition into your new role, to be successful."

"How? By commenting on my work or relationships?"

Resting his chin on the folds of his hands, he replied, "Work. This morning, I don't know why I said what I said."

"Really? There had to be a reason you assume Martin can tell me what to do and why I don't want to marry him."

Closing his eyes as if he was praying for a way to answer her calmed Emma down. The silence that followed seemed to relax both of them. It was as if they needed this time to stop and consider what they wanted to protect the other person's feelings.

Opening his eyes, he met her gaze. "You've been here every night. If you're not trying to avoid him, why are you here late?"

"Maybe I want to work with you so you won't ruin my work. You've lied to me more than once. " Emma stood and hovered over him.

He rose to his feet and spoke in a measured and wounded tone. "And there it is. I assumed…I thought we at least could've had a professional relationship. I get it."

"Get what?"

"You can't trust me. Doesn't matter what I do or

say, you'll never believe me. Fine. But I refuse to let our history and your ego ruin this opportunity."

"This has nothing to do with trust nor my ego."

"Hate me for the rest of your life. But I'm pulling rank. We aren't partners. You and your team will report to me. Final decisions are mine. Is that clear?"

"Depends. Are your feelings affecting *your* judgement?"

As he stood, he glared at her but remained silent. Balling his hands into a fist, he stomped out of her office.

***

Peeking through her office door, Amalie asked, "Is the coast clear?"

"Yeah. Come on in," Emma responded as she turned from her view and invited Amalie to sit on the couch with her.

"Did you argue with Christopher again?"

"We view things differently. But don't worry about it. He made it perfectly clear who was in charge."

"See, we need a retreat."

"I can't go. Martin needs me here. I have work—"

Amalie pulled a mirror out for Emma. "Have you seen yourself? Work is getting to you. Time away will give you the perspective to understand Christopher's point."

Emma pushed the mirror away. The last thing she wanted to see was her tired face and pale skin, then listen to Amalie defend Christopher. Her patience was not an iron gate.

"I'm not taking his side. Please, if not for you, for me. I need your help," Amalie pleaded.

Breathing through clenched teeth, Emma rapidly tapped her fingers on the table. She was trying anything to control the anger boiling inside. "You don't need me anymore,"

Emma insisted.

"I need my mentor."

"Martin will kill me. I barely have time for him. Besides, a retreat is a solitary exercise."

"You always need a friend."

"You don't need me."

"I need someone to challenge me so I can decide. You need this time, Emma."

"Take time for what?" Martin smirked as he opened Emma's office door.

"Our retreat this weekend," Amalie replied in a childlike voice.

Emma rose from the couch and started reading the ideas on the board.

"We have a fundraiser this weekend," Martin hissed through gritted teeth.

"I need her to come. I'm trying to find the courage to commit to a relationship and need someone there to help me, you understand?"

"It doesn't explain why Emma has to attend."

"Are you blind? First, she needs to go to help me. Second, she needs to get away from her work and recharge. Christopher is driving her nuts. You're driving Emma nuts. Don't you want her to focus on what's important? Clear her head so she can figure out her future."

"Thinking, again?" Martin glared at Emma. "Wasn't that why you went to Austria?"

"Martin, please let her go. I need my mentor," she pleaded with him like a child begs for ice cream.

Straightening her back, Emma ordered Amalie to leave her office. "Martin and I need to talk."

"Sure. Pick you up tomorrow night?"

"It starts tomorrow?" Martin shook his head in disbelief.

Amalie shrieked with joy. "Oh, yeah. It's a three-day affair."

"So much for my afternoon surprise. I guess you beat me to it," Martin announced as soon as Amalie left the room.

"I couldn't back out."

"Yes, you could. That girl takes advantage of you."

"Amalie needs help. I want to give her a chance to find happiness with one honest man. I've found it," she claimed in the hopes of soothing his ego.

"Emma?"

"What?"

"It's a weekend."

"Yes."

"We had plans."

"I understand. But she's right. I need time away. Helping her will allow me to clear my head. She doesn't trust herself to be with Dylan. Please, understand why I'm going." She wrapped her arms around him.

"Emma, I need you at my side."

"I'm sorry, but ever since Christopher's team arrived, it's been frustrating trying to get any work done." She buried her head into his shoulder.

"No more late nights with Christopher."

"Pardon me?" She didn't like how Martin's tone sounded like he was accusing her of betraying him.

"When you get back. For one week, at least, you'll work a regular thirty-five-hour workweek. You'll join me and my clients or staff for drinks, whatever it is, I get your evenings."

"But... that's... not..."

"It's obvious that Amalie needs you now. You need a break. I don't want to be a jerk, but we've been dating long enough for me to demand time with you. What's a week?"

"I've been—"

"Distant. This project has taken my evenings. Sonja's crazy wedding plans have robbed my weekends with you. We need to discuss our future. Aren't *we* worth it?"

"You're very important to me." She kissed him on the lips. "This campaign is more than I thought, and when you mix family, friends—"

"A history with an ex," Martin chided.

"He is not my ex."

"Whatever."

"Martin?"

"Enjoy."

A chill raced up her spine as Martin kissed her forehead and turned his back on her.

"Okay, you win," she shouted.

"You'll stay?"

"I'll go on this retreat, and when I come back, my evenings belong to you."

CHAPTER 18

Amalie drove two hours straight to arrive at the Galilee Centre before nightfall. Emma sat in awe at how Amalie described how the sun shimmered on the lake, and the sky glowed with a warm orange ribbon-like quality across the sky. It made her yearn to stand at the lake's edge and clear her mind of the doubt and her heart from an influx of anger and frustration. She doubted that the time away would help, but Amalie's eagerness and worry helped her to forget the problems she left behind. But, in their rush, Amalie needed a nap as soon as they arrived, and it left Emma alone to explore.

At first, she didn't want to go alone, but something inside her heart urged her to go on this journey. Wandering on a trail, her brisk pace helped to quiet her mind and to forget Martin's slumped shoulders. Experience taught her that when she didn't make Martin the most important person in her life, he became like an only child who realized he had to share his parents' attention with a new sibling. She could only imagine how many more text messages and calls she would receive while on retreat.

Damn it! He was right! AHA!!!

Her scream vibrated through the leaves. Emma closed her eyes, desperate to ignore Christopher's voice in her head. When she opened them, they adjusted to what was in front of her. A sunset that permeated the sky with warmth shining across the water. It was true. Standing at the lake's edge, she stood on the brink of finding her answers. The problem was she had too many questions to ask. She took another breath to relax, but the silence didn't offer her peace. Instead, her thoughts confirmed that Christopher was right; she was using her job to avoid being with Martin.

But, work wasn't a sanctuary for her anymore. With Christopher's arrival, work had become a competition, which made her question whether she belonged there. She wished she could blame Christopher's presence for the sudden discomfort, but these mixed emotions and ideas were not recent. They grew stronger every time Christopher was near. Watching him work with passion made her doubt her own commitment to the job.

Every heated discussion chipped away at the wall encasing her heart, but with enough power to sting her soul. The pain always stung as it did when she overheard him telling his friends how he tricked her. A voice that reminded her how her pristine and perfect life was a lie.

She had to run again. The lake had given her no answers. Feeling her legs burn, she rested against a tree to survey her surroundings. It was a moment that gave her some peace that she could clearly see ahead of her. Her run had put her on a path towards a small chapel. A chapel that glowed under the setting sun and wanted to rest there.

As she came to the threshold, the chapel doors were ajar. Swatting the flies away, she entered the sacred space. The smell of pine and old wood from the pews invaded her senses as if they were welcoming her home. The sun's ray burst chrisms of light from the stained glass windows, which gave colour to the barren and worn tile. As if the Holy Spirit beckoned her to follow, the light on the church tiles led her to the cascade of colour surrounding the altar. It was as if she was entering heaven and finding comfort in the smells and sights of the intimate sacred space. Her skin tingled with fear, and her blood percolated with anger, but as she stood in front of the altar, all of it seemed less menacing to her soul. Her eyes followed the brightest trail of light, which led her to the familiar red candle burning beside the tabernacle, which the icons of Mary, Joseph, and Jesus guarded. Kneeling in a pew, she let her body and soul rest. When she was at peace, she cried.

"Are you okay?" a soothing voice asked her as he gave her a tissue.

"I always cry in churches."

"Then you're ready for the retreat. I'm Father Anthony."

"Nice to meet you."

Fr. Anthony was everything you'd expect a Franciscan priest to look like. With a clean-shaven haircut and a beard the length of wisdom, joy radiated through him. He was dressed in the brown habit with a simple corded rope, known as cincture, with three knots around the waist. The three knots reminded the friar of the three cornerstones of the order: poverty, chastity, and obedience. His eyes were sincere as if they had studied the laws of love written in our hearts and had found a way to live it with a fearlessness and grace that can only come from knowing God in an intimate way.

She pulled herself up and sat quietly in the pew, waiting for him to say something or leave. But he sat there contemplating the crucifixion before him. The calm and peacefulness surrounding him unnerved her.

Why is he sitting here? There are other places to sit.

Even though leaving was obvious, her heart convinced her it would be rude. She sat quietly beside him and kept her eyes forward. Before her, was the crucified Christ, an icon to remind mankind what God's love is for humanity. A reminder that suffering and death are not the end of one's story, but only a part of it. Contemplating the magnitude of

God's love, she could not stop herself from crying. She faced the priest.

"Father? If someone had everything at her fingertips, love and stability, why isn't it enough for her? How can a person who hurt you still affect you in ways that they can verbalize everything you're too afraid to say aloud? And when they say it, it hurts because what he is saying isn't far from the truth."

Father Anthony gave her another tissue.

"Sorry, you must have other things to do. I should leave you alone."

"Perhaps your heart hasn't caught up to the expectations in your mind," he sighed as Emma stared at him like a deer that yearns for running streams.

"Silence is an interesting thing. It reveals what's important, and the Lord waits until your ready to listen. Embrace the silence. You have these questions but haven't given yourself the space to listen for the response. Ask yourself this question, as you've sought the answers within yourself, have you discovered it? You tried every solution and reasoned it out to some decision, but you still feel the power of doubt and fear influencing your choices. Consider trying something different. You see that over there?" Father Anthony pointed to the tabernacle. "Seek God. And wait."

"No quick answer or scripture quotation to make me feel better?"

"If it only worked that way. Usually, you have moments of clarity and fall back into old habits until you have another epiphany when you can let go of the sin that God has already forgiven. I never thought I was smart enough to be a priest because of the mistakes and decisions I made, but here I am, offering you advice when I'm not supposed to meet the retreat participants for another hour."

"Coincidence."

"Faithful eyes would see that we're meeting now so you can understand how the doubts you're having are real, and I'm here to say you're not crazy, but to take the time to sort them out."

"Maybe I need to confess something."

Nodding, he shifted his gaze to her, with an expression of hope that only sinners could see. In one quick motion, they both made the sign of the cross, and she asked for him to bless her as it had been years since her last confession. After confessing her sins and after the absolution was given, they continued to talk with a sense of trust and hope between them.

"Nothing comes instantly. For your penance, write what you're feeling. Review it and see what God is trying to tell you. What you seek will not be instant, so don't try to rush into anything. Prudence is a gift, not a burden. Remember that, and I'm sure you will find the peace and joy you seek."

Feeling her cheekbones rise and her lips curve upwards, she nodded with less fear about the future ahead. He left her to pray on her own. Moved by his words, she rose and knelt in front of the tabernacle where Christ was present and waited for God to respond.

As Emma prayed, silence surrounded her. But fear and doubt did not come. Instead, a joy filled her heart and urged her to find a paper and pen to write down the tidal waves of emotions gushing forth. Finding a pen and a notebook near her, she found a place for the humming to cease in her head. She enjoyed how she could note every perception and emotion without editing the feelings it produced. Her writing cracked her defence system and permitted her soul the freedom to vent. As she wiggled her hand, she read her words and discovered her problems were less daunting. But the answer still eluded her.

"Emma?" She smelled his aftershave and cringed.

God, you're kidding, right?

Turning slowly, she glanced up to see his familiar perfect rustic hair and figure hovering over her. He was dressed down in jeans and a hoody sweater. His appearance resembled the boy she had trusted with her hopes and wisdom years ago.

"What are you doing here?"

"I…uhm…retreat…Beth." He placed his hands in his pockets.

"There you are." Amalie ran towards them. "You beat everyone here and— Christopher?"

Emma hated how Amalie was studying them. She could see the corners of Amalie's mouth turning up, and her eyes dancing with glee. "Are you here for the retreat too?"

Christopher nodded but didn't say anything.

Amalie waved her hand. "Well, great minds think alike. You needed a retreat too. It's nice seeing you in casual clothes and rendered speechless. You weren't talking business? This is the House of God. For my sake and those here, a truce, please," she instructed them as if they were her children.

"Of course, it's a retreat." Christopher placed his right hand above his heart, bowed, and found a place to sit away from them.

Tearing her eyes from him, she refocused on the cross.

"You okay?" Amalie tugged on Emma's arm.

"Yeah, I took the long way to get here. I'm a little winded. But I'm here for you."

With joyful anticipation, Amalie squeezed Emma's hand and watched the other participants join them in the chapel.

***

Dressed in their brown religious habits, Father Anthony and Sister Clara welcomed the retreat participants. They had a glow about them that Emma could not understand. Yet before her were two people dedicated to service and ready to help others find their way out of turmoil, confusion, and regret. Admittedly, these were three things she yearned to sort out in her life.

"Welcome. My name is Father Anthony, and this is Sister Clara."

"We're your facilitators. You came to discern important decisions for your life, or your loved one thought you needed a break from work to destress. No matter the reason, you're here," Sister Clara continued.

Emma groaned. It was audible to her neighbours. She coughed and waved an apology to them.

"Are you okay?" Amalie murmured in her ear.

"Sorry. Nervous, I guess."

"State your name," Amalie instructed.

"What?"

"It's your turn to share something. Say your name and give them one reason why you're here," Amalie instructed through pursed lips.

She scanned the room, realizing that everyone was staring at her. Finding her voice, she stated her name and explained how she needed a break from work to assess her future and to support Amalie as she discerned the next step in her life. After the longest minute ever recorded, Father Anthony and Sister Clara moved on to the next person.

For Emma, this was torture. Not since her acting classes did she have to gather in a circle and share her feelings. These types of circles always produced emotions that actors in training always wanted to explore in depth to understand the psyches of their characters. For actors, it was never enough. The good ones always delved deeper into the hearts of the characters to see what was better to play on stage. It was this strange practice, where an actor lives someone else's life without risking their heart.

"Take this moment to appeal for guidance. Be open to searching and accept what you find. Embrace your fears. Christ stands with you." Fr. Anthony's lilting voice returned Emma to the present moment.

"Courage," Sister Clara suggested as she moved around the room in a very quiet and calming manner.

For some reason, meeting Fr. Anthony helped her to buy into the retreat experience and listen to the voice that gave her the courage to discover the answers. Hearing the voice of everyone asking for help finally relaxed Emma's heart. No life was perfect. Everyone needs helps. You have to ask and open your eyes, ears, and heart to receive it. By the time Father Anthony rang the bell to end the conversation between each other, Emma was ready for silent prayer. But as the seconds passed with everyone embracing the silence, Emma came acutely aware that she didn't want to be alone with her thoughts.

CHAPTER 19

Silence was easy during the night because one is asleep. But as soon as the sun rises, people want to talk to someone. Emma was like that. Being alone with her thoughts was not an option. Listening to others would've helped this morning, but the silent exercise was continuing through breakfast. Her only comfort was eating. Eating would give her something to focus on, as opposed to feeding her hungry spirit with self-reflection.

Waiting in the breakfast line, she was mesmerized by the display of food. A buffet of scrambled eggs and pancakes with an array of fruit trays made sure everyone ate healthily. But the sweet smell of freshly fried bacon always won against a fruit platter. Bacon was that guilty pleasure that was very hard to deny. It never failed, people will pile it on their plate as if it was their last day on earth. Emma was one of those people. With the glee of a child on Christmas morning, she piled the bacon on her plate. The task kept the thoughts and feeling jet-setting through her mind and heart at bay.

Lost in her love for bacon, Emma returned to reality with the touch of Christopher's fingertips against her skin. She didn't even have to verify her suspicions when there was only one person who sent a jolt of energy through her blood. Slowly, she glanced up with the hope that she was wrong. Christopher's eyes gazed back at her, but she couldn't tell what was running through his mind as his demeanour was blank and unemotional. Yet his loose-fitting attire and five o'clock shadow concerned her. It suggested that he did not have a good night's sleep last night, either. This made her happy because it felt like they were equal. The only drawback was the heat rising in her cheeks as his rugged and unkempt appearance was as attractive as the man in the well-tailored suits.

He bowed his head and released the spoon, but he continued to study her. She didn't need his eyes probing her thoughts. Grinning, he stepped away without placing food on his plate. She scooped another pound of bacon onto her plate and walked away immediately to join Amalie at the table.

As more people joined Amalie and Emma at their table, their clanging forks and cups further rattled her senses. The rustling trees and the buzzing sound of insects didn't relax her spirit. They only added to the growing discomfort of remembering her past and neglecting her responsibility to Amalie. She had not been the support team Amalie needed on this retreat.

Emma sipped her coffee and chewed her bacon. She smiled at Amalie and glanced over at Christopher. Burning with envy, she hated how he appeared relaxed and at ease, now with a plate of food in front of him. Seeing her didn't unnerve his calm and confident nature. Emma convinced herself that he was acting cool to lull her into a false sense of security. Stuffing her mouth with more bacon, she chewed her irritation away.

Aha!

Emma stabbed the eggs with her fork. Amalie glanced over at her with concern. She groaned and chewed her food, shooing Amalie's concern away. As much as she tried to enjoy her breakfast, even the taste of bacon could not erase the bitterness in her mouth from watching Christopher eat and being unaffected by her presence.

After morning prayer, Fr. Anthony instructed the participants to reflect on the assigned scripture passages in relation to their experiences. As Emma read each passage, her frustration subsided. The words calmed her spirit until she noticed her hands were shaking. She drew in several breaths, wanting to talk to share the thousand thoughts in her head or solve someone's problems. But they were still in silent prayer. Answering the reflection questions became her only outlet to communicate and examine her heart.

During the last session, were you disturbed by anything? Why?

As she answered the question with a resounding yes, Emma laughed out loud. She had to confront the truth. Christopher bothered her. His presence reminded her of who she was before he betrayed her. Her other relationships never yielded the same emotional scars.

How many more months till you break up with Martin?

She wrote the question in her journal and stopped writing. She read the question over and over again, pondering if the question was from her own mind or a thought planted by Christopher. She closed her journal dramatically. Hearing her voice answer the question terrified her.

***

"So, how did we do?" Sister Clara surveyed Emma's group.

Amalie, Emma, and Christopher were sitting in the same group. The group had been divided into two, with Fr.

Anthony leading the other one. Emma hated the idea of sitting in a circle. In theory, sitting in circles is supposed to make every person feel equal and safe because you see everybody. Cringing and fidgeting, Emma sat in front of Christopher and didn't feel either of those things.

"Our groups are becoming smaller. We want to give you an opportunity to share."

Sister Clara's voice was sweet and assertive. It reflected her personality to the tee. Wearing her brown habit like a superhero, Emma could tell that she was determined to lead her group with an iron fist, but also giving the participants enough support to share their feelings. She was younger than Amalie, but the wisdom of God was in her. It compelled you to speak even if it might hurt to hear at the time.

"Well, I want to apologize for my emotional outburst. I'm restless. Dylan is an answer to a prayer that I can't believe is being answered," Amalie confessed in her squeaky voice.

"Then what's your problem? It sounds like you're telling yourself these things to save yourself from getting hurt," Christopher commented as he straightened in his chair.

Holding her hands together, Emma faced Christopher. His tone was serious and emotionless, a tone that reminded her of the boy she met who thought he had all the answers.

"What do you mean?" Amalie grilled Christopher for more information.

"Your mind," holding his finger to his temple, "is telling you these things to keep you from listening to your heart. You said it yourself. The real question you need to ask yourself is, would he be worth it? All the potential trouble? Disappointment? Someone once advised me that sometimes your thoughts will betray you, but you need to take a leap of faith and trust that they won't break your heart. In your case, believe that Dylan will not intentionally hurt you. It's what Sister has been saying, faith means trusting the unknown when you have reasoned it to death."

"Yes, but life experience teaches you that if you don't listen to reason, you're bound to be fooled," Emma retorted.

"Reason doesn't inspire you to love," Christopher shot back.

"Reason makes us choose love and how to love. But sometimes, what you define as love blinds you from the truth." Emma hollered back Christopher.

Leaning forward, Christopher professed in a thick and husky voice, "And fear keeps you from real love. When fear consumes you, you forget what it means to live with love. Hope makes you believe that it's possible to become better regardless of how you started. What you've done before doesn't have to define you for the rest of your life. God created us to love each other the way He loves us, even when we screw up."

"Too bad life shows how people use those emotions to make you feel worthless," Emma responded as she sat forward on her chair.

"But if it's real, it leads to forgiveness, right?"

Feeling the weight of his words, Emma understood the truth in his statement. But it hurt to accept it. To accept it would mean she would have to do it. To do it meant maybe finally finding the peace she yearned for in her soul. Her eyes clouded over with tears.

"Emma, are you all right?" Sister Clara passed her a tissue.

"Sorry, I can't help wondering… um… Martin…"

"Your boyfriend, right?" Sister Clara encouraged Emma to speak and trust this was a safe place to be honest.

"Well, like Amalie, I'm at a crossroad. Martin's ideal, considerate, and kind. But I'm scared he'll change if we…I… get married."

"Did he propose?" Amalie asked with excitement.

"No, but it's in the air. I'm afraid that it will change my life. Is he doing these nice things to get married? Am I blind in seeing who he is?" She murmured as if she was talking to herself.

"Christopher has a point," Sister Clara added as she handed Emma another tissue. "You need faith to embrace the possibility of being loved. Forgiving the person who hurt you is difficult. But harder than that is to forgive yourself when you make a mistake for being naive or foolish to believe it when the truth was yelling in front of you. In my experience, it's easy blaming the person who hurt you. Easy target. In some cases, it's even justifiable, but you shouldn't let it keep you from moving on. In the end, it's you who keeps you from moving forward. Ask for the grace to find how your worries are valid, but realize that your past and those decisions can't stop you from living your life. Your experiences are guideposts on the journey, not the destination."

As on cue, the bells chimed for the participants to enter into silent prayer again. Emma rolled her eyes.

CHAPTER 20

Once the bells chimed, Emma made a beeline for the great outdoors. It felt as if Christopher's words articulated her heart's desire, and Sister Clara provided the wisdom for her to understand them. But the truth didn't set her free. Instead, his testimony increased the gnawing doubt and melancholy that was consuming her.

As Emma watched others stroll down different paths, she stood on the terrace, praying that this feeling would go away as easily as taking a hike. Inhaling fresh air only reminded her how cold it was outside. She leaned on the banister, trying to warm her cold hands, but nothing helped. She slammed her hands down, wanting her heart yearnings to be heard.

Scared to confront Christopher or Amalie, she headed towards the lake. The trek towards the lake wasn't on a carefully groomed trail. Instead, the path was brittle and bumpy. The tree branches blurred her sight from seeing beyond the horizon as her feet climbed through the dirt and muck. She aggressively pushed the branches and leaves from hitting and scratching her. But it wasn't nature that was irritating her; it was her own stupidity for taking the unkept path.

After a few more twig scratches and countless other bug bites, she found the clearing. The wind was causing the water to crush the land with a fierce current to warn you that a storm was coming. Yet, the sound of water hitting rocks provided her some rest from her thoughts. It was a subtle comfort, even though the treacherous forest paths tried to stop her. As the sun came out from under the cloud, the shining light on the water opened her eyes to see the trees' greenness and the sky's blueness. It allowed her to hear the birds' tweets, harmonizing with the rustling sounds of leaves. She reached into her pocket and found a pen and paper. With a renewed sense of hope, she sat down and started to write the jumble of thoughts and memories.

***

I didn't want to go. Charlotte and Sonja wanted to bond with the other counsellors. When we arrived, Christopher announced that the three angels appeared. Charlotte was polite as she craved Winston's attention. I rolled my eyes at how they flirted. As usual, Lionel and Michelle joined Sonja. She accepted the beer they offered and, like a well-trained seal, drank it. I stood around the campfire by myself.

"Well, here you go, your highness."

I know I should hate how he gave me a nickname, but it was an appropriate one. As he offered me a beer, I shuffled a few steps backwards, wishing to show my refusal. But, he never understood social cues.

"Beer makes you honest," he suggested.

"You don't need a beer to be honest."

"That easy?"

"That easy."

"You're lucky. I've never been good at being honest."

"I'm not surprised."

"Really? How would you describe me?" He leaned forward.

Without missing a beat, I retorted, "You are a self-centred, self-gratifying, attention-seeking fool who can't see that he's a good guy."

He blinked and swallowed his beer. I hadn't meant to sound rude, but he always found a way to annoy me, that having witty comebacks became the only way to simmer my feelings of unease around him.

"Give me a chance for rebuttal after I've finished this one."

Then downing half of his beer, he asserted, "Unlike you, who is heartless and unfeeling, I need five beers in me to be in your league of honesty."

***

The words in her journal paper were smudged from her waterfall of tears. What she saw was how Christopher was being friendly, and she greeted his offer with sarcasm and trepidation. But it didn't matter. He professed anything to win her trust. Every interaction was a lie. The truth of his intentions towards her still made her actions innocent in comparison, but as she reviewed her entry, she wondered if she had wounded him with her words and actions as well.

"Emma, are you okay?"

Christopher's hand gently touched her shoulder. The physical contact made her feel safe to reach out and squeeze his hand, a gesture where she didn't have to say anything to invite him to sit beside her. Sitting beside each other in silence, she leaned on his shoulder and cried. Feeling the warmth of his arms around her shoulder, she rested in his arms.

All Emma heard was the lapping water on the shore, which had calmed in the last hour, and her soft whimpers. A bird's cry echoed in the air, and it broke the trance between them. Realizing where she was and whom she was with, she jerked away. He didn't say anything. Unable to make eye contact with him, she rose and ran down the clear trail to the retreat house.

CHAPTER 21

After dinner, Emma was in a comatose state as people shared experiences in the group. Emma focused on the Woman at the Well painting in front of her. It was a story about a woman who comes to fill her water jug at an unusual hour with whom Jesus engages in a conversation. As Jesus questions her, her sassy and standoffish demeanour begins to fade as he shows her life for what it is and what it could be. Emma had heard the story a thousand times, but as she pondered on the woman, her eyes were telling her how she yearned for the hope and life Christ was offering her but was too scared to trust what her heart already accepted as the truth. Emma understood that the fear of being loved for who she was and forgiven for all she had done. It was a forgiveness not from ritual, but from admitting one's fault to your beloved and finding true peace and reconciliation. One that frees you to forgive and love. Shaking her head, she didn't want to dwell on her thoughts, so she focused on the group's discussion instead.

"Does anyone have anything else to share?" Sister Clara clapped her hands together to elicit a response from anyone in her group.

Amalie cleared his voice. "Love hurts. I mean, a man who declared he loved me hurt me. I was in love and thought it was enough to change him. But, he was an ass who got high on punching me. He was in love with himself. My body and heart paid the price. He took my ability to trust my judgement, and it became a roadblock to love someone. How can I move on when I haven't even forgiven myself for being stupid?" She tried to control her emotions, but it was hopeless.

Sister Clara placed a comforting arm around her. It was a kind gesture that seemed to soften her sobs. As Emma watched, she wondered why she rejected the same comforting gesture from Christopher.

"Let's get ready for our evening prayer hike. You'll walk in pairs to talk to someone. I encourage you who fear this intimacy to recognize the freedom in talking to someone who won't judge you but will listen. If you open yourself up to the experience, it will lead you to places you never knew existed," Father Anthony encouraged as the groups merged to find their assigned partners.

It led Emma to pray. She begged God to be left alone. She didn't want to explore the explosion of feelings and memories running rampant in herself. With an absolute request, she begged God not to go on an evening stroll with Christopher. Every conversation with Christopher made her remember the naive and vulnerable girl who believed she had someone to trust and love. She was the girl who fell too easily for admiration from a person who wanted her for his own personal gain.

Sitting in the foyer, Emma watched each pair leave the retreat house with flashlights in hand, relieved that she was waiting in the foyer for her partner Santiago Cruz. As she waited, couples stepped with trepidation and fear. Giggling, she understood the absurdness of being with a stranger and bearing one's soul to them. It was an unrealistic request. But as she massaged her hands and tapped her foot, she watched each couple embrace the opportunity to chat with a stranger. It gave her hope that Santiago Cruz may be someone to share her fears and experiences with because he didn't have a past with her and would never see her again after they parted ways the next day.

Clearing his throat, Christopher whispered, "Our partners didn't show up."

She closed her eyes, praying that his statement wasn't true. She pleaded for God's mercy. Leering at him, she hissed, "I suppose you planned this?"

Exhaling with an audible *pfft* sound, he stood up to leave.

Sister Clara approached Emma. "Aha, there you are. Santiago wanted to be with his wife. If you don't mind," Sister Clara stopped Christopher at the door.

She clapped her hands to wake Emma from her trance. When she didn't move, she nudged Christopher to help get Emma unto her feet. The sister beamed with hope for both of them.

"Sister, maybe I should go on this hike by myself. She's too tired for an evening stroll."

"I'm sorry. Are you okay?" Sister Clara asked with a tone of tenderness.

"It's warm."

She smiled, fully aware that Sister Clara's eyes were ablaze with determination. They were eyes that urged Emma to have faith and trust in God. It confirmed Emma's theory that those who take their vows and serve the Lord are given the charism to never take no for an answer.

"An evening stroll will clear your head. The air is a very pleasant temperature." Sister Clara sat beside Emma to shove her forward.

"Right." Emma finally stood up, unable to say no to Sister Clara's warm and persuasive nature.

She shoved past Christopher, feeling her temperature rise as he trailed behind her.

"Your path!" Sister Clara yelled as she came running out

of the retreat house to catch them.

"Our what?" Emma clenched her hands together.

"Each pair have marked paths to follow."

"So as not to lose anyone, I suppose?" She tried to control her sarcasm.

"I have faith in people. Harm will not come to you."

Grunting, Emma trudged ahead as Christopher took the map from Sister Clara.

Strolling along the quiet lake, Emma kept her distance ahead of Christopher. She was grateful for the space. His heavy steps behind her told her he had questions.

You cried on his shoulder, and in the next second, you ran away from him. He must be scared to say or do anything. Aha!

She wasn't ready to talk to him, especially when she had felt something change between them this afternoon. Leaning on him, she was with the man she had worked with and the boy who broke her heart. And she felt safe, to be honest with herself and him. She acknowledged who she was then and now, and she was no longer afraid to let him back into her life.

"I wish I never kissed you," Christopher called to her.

Her body remained still as if she was sinking into the ground. Feeling her breath stop in midair, she focused on her shoes. She felt like her heart and mind betrayed her again. She couldn't face him.

"Emma? Did you hear me?"

"Yes."

He stood in front of her, tipping her chin upwards. She closed her eyes and inhaled his intoxicating scent, an aroma that had become familiar and refreshing over the months. She was not sure whether to embrace or slap him. On the exhale, she followed the urge to slap him.

Wincing and rubbing his cheek, he murmured, “That's fifteen years in the making.”

“I didn’t slap you because I’m angry about what happened between us. I slapped you because you have determined this is about our past.”

“It is.”

“Unbelievable!”

“Emma, you haven’t forgiven yourself for trusting me. For letting what I did to you affect your life. I see it in your relationship with your coworkers and Martin.”

Exasperated and with flailing arms, Emma exclaimed, “That’s brilliant! I’m not furious at you; I’m angry at myself? For your information, I’ve had great relationships with men I trusted, men who loved me and didn’t hurt me.”

“Then why aren’t you married? Why aren’t you happy with one of them?”

“What? I’m happy, even if I’m not married,” she shouted as she poked him in the chest.

“You were miserable at the airport.”

Poking him harder, she spat out, “It was a long delay from Austria.”

Christopher reached out to touch her hand, but she yanked it away. “In the park, you were crying.”

“I was held at gunpoint.”

“*Twelfth Nigh*t made you cry. You were never afraid to share anything when you were with—” Christopher clenched his hands together.

“That girl didn’t realize how someone could be so cruel and heartless. It, as you used to say, was a life built on the hopeless dreams of a silly girl. You showed me everything I believed in wasn’t real.”

“I never called you silly. But this, right now, is crazy.”

"It's crazy because you think one kiss changed everything."

"It was more than a kiss. Em, I ruined your life."

She paced back and forth, trying to figure out what she wanted to say. As she glanced at him, all she could say was, "Wow! Nice suit and good manners, but still the deaf and blind bastard who doesn't listen or understand."

"You used to enjoy life. You believed in someone like–"

"Listen carefully. What happened between us didn't change me!" She stabbed him in the chest again with her finger but did not make eye contact with him.

"Then, look at me."

"Excuse me?"

"I'm not the boy who assumes he has all the answers and hides from his feelings. I'm the one person you could never lie to. So, look me in the eye and tell me the truth. What are you feeling?"

She stood on her tiptoes to challenge him. He didn't flinch as she glared at him. She was so close to him, that she could make out every blood vessel and speck of colour in his retina. The exact words were on the tip of her tongue to vanquish the small thorn of doubt and regret from her life. But as she inspected his eyes for deceit or sincerity, time couldn't conceal her soul nor the desire to be honest with him. Yet, like a five-hundred-pound weight around her neck, her painful memories outweighed the need to tell him the truth. "My life is better without you."

He searched every contour of her eyes. Closing his eyes and nodding at the pace of a turtle, he moved away from her. "Then, be happy."

Crossing her arms and shaking her head, she hated how indifferent he sounded. She searched for any word to convince him of her happiness, but the spirit of truth could only be muted for so long.

"I can't. Everything I've ever loved has broken my heart." The words fell from her lips. He placed his hands on her shoulders. It took every ounce of her willpower not to fall into his arms.

"Then let me help you to find the confidence to trust yourself again so you can love and have the life you've always wanted for yourself."

"You don't know what I need."

Holding his breath and shaking his head, he finally said, "Em, it's obvious even if Martin is an ass... astute person. You want to love him and the life he's building for you. You need to trust yourself so you can love him."

"It's early in our relationship."

"Emma, I know you." Something in his voice made her heart weep because it was true.

"Why are you doing this?" She lifted her chin to stare at him and noted how his eyes were dark with an anguish to say something that he was too afraid to tell her. It was as if his soul was like hers; conflicted in choosing between their desires or losing each other again.

Taking a small step backwards, he lowered his head and pushed the dirt with his foot. "You have always professed, if you love yourself, it comes out in what you do. Because once you love yourself, you can share it with someone else. Love never ceases to give, Em."

"Did I say that to you?"

"Yes, but you've shown me what it means to have someone love you, and I owe it to you to make sure you have ... because I —"

His shaky hands reached for her trembling hands. He kissed and blew warm air on her cold hands. Drawing her closer to him, he moved his lips from her hands to her forehead. His lips felt warm against her skin. Resting her hands on his chest, she revelled in his scent and felt dizzy as the hard thumping of his heartbeat scorched her fingertips. Christopher breathed in deeply, "I... owe everything to you. If you never humiliated me, I wouldn't be here. You taught me how to have faith in God and in myself. You've given me my career. My passion... and…I—"

"Beth," Emma whispered, pushing away from him. A sweeping sadness engulfed her heart. Her lips set in a grim line, knowing that his love for Beth gave him the confidence and compassion to say these things to her. "The only reason you want to help me is because you owe me something for pretending to like me? You're grateful that I humiliated you because it helped you find—"

"Love. You deserve to be loved."

"I love Martin."

"Fine." He paused. "If he makes you happy—"

"You don't believe me?"

"What do you believe?"

She stepped away from him, "I should be with him."

"Okay, then let me help you trust yourself to love—"

"I LOVE MARTIN!" she screamed.

"Em, I don't doubt you love him. What I'm trying to say is, you helped me trust myself to love—"

"Beth."

"What? This isn't coming out right."

"Unbelievable! I fell for your lies again! You're trying to make amends so you can have a clear conscience—"

"Em, that's not even close."

"So you can have a clean start with Beth. I get it. And

here I thought—" She raised her head and stared at him, unsure how she wanted to complete that sentence.

"What?"

She puffed up her chest and straightened her back.

"Em, talk to me."

Biting her lip and raising her hands to stop him from coming close to her, she found the words to break the bond between them, "Consider yourself forgiven. You owe me nothing. Don't worry. Martin makes me happy. He loves me. To prove it, I'll tell him how I used to love writing and singing. It'll rehash how I wasn't good enough. I was a dreamer who wasted my time. Then, I'll tell him what happened between us to prove that I trust him. But you'll need to leave town because he'll kill you. But then you can explain how you wished… it never happened."

"You're misinterpreting everything I'm saying."

Throwing her hands up, she hollered, "Why don't you call me a flake? Taken in by your charms. I'm not that naïve young girl you fooled once before!"

"Em, I never said you were naïve. If I made you believe that… I'm sorry. But, I need you to listen, please."

Backing further away from him, she covered her face, trying to wipe away any trace of sadness. "Listen? To what? How I've made all the wrong decisions in my life, from my work to my relationships. I'm inadequate and broken."

"Em, I've never doubted your ability nor your talent." He studied her as if he learned the full picture of God's plan for him. "How badly did I hurt you? I thought I was the only one who cared about us? At the time, I never considered you had the feelings I had… but I'm here now. Please, let's talk about this." His voice was soft and tender.

She wasn't sure what to believe, feel or say as she

searched his face for clues. There was a despairing darkness to them, but a lightness she had not seen since his arrival. But they were also begging for her to listen to him as they did when he pleaded on that stage for her compassion. Turning away from him, she couldn't find the courage to believe what she saw in his eyes. Her instincts had been wrong too many times.

"No, I get it. Thank you for helping me acknowledge how I've been incapable of having what I want. Maybe this is what I need. I haven't felt this great since the day I found out the only reason something happened between us was because I was in love with the idea of love. I was an easy target for you, wasn't I? Easy to tease. Full of ideals about love, but incapable of loving. Your lie helped me to grow up to see the world in black and white. Thank you for saving me from my false ideals."

"Em, I'm not here because you need me to save you. I'm not doing this from obligation. I'm doing this because I–"

Christopher stopped and stared at her.

"What?" she pried, unsure if she was interpreting his thoughts and feelings correctly.

He kicked some dirt around. "Martin loves you. I've seen you together. I want to help you see how everything you want is here already. He'll love you and do everything in his power to never hurt you. He'll be the one you share your life with, infuriate you with his idiosyncrasies, and sit beside you as you admire the stars. Ever since the day you exposed me and said goodbye, that's all I've ever wanted for you. I'm sorry for making you feel like nothing, and maybe that's why I want someone who'll make you feel better than I did or do. I want you to be deeply in love so you can grow old together and build a home despite the bickering. I'm saying this as a friend because we were and are friends. You deserve to love someone and have a life you love. As your friend, I could never lie to you."

She exhaled as if she had been holding it in for fifteen years, feeling her past and his words consume her heart. With the weight of truth and her past decisions on her shoulders, she whispered, "Except you did. Our friendship started as a lie, and everything we shared after that I can't trust if it's real." She placed her hands up with less energy, but enough to stop him from coming to her. "I'm fine."

As she slowly moved past him, she couldn't make eye contact with him. She felt his fingers graze her hand as he tried to intertwine them together, but she yanked her hand away from him.

"It hurts being around you. It always hurts. But, you're right, I wished you never… kissed me. My life would be better… without you in it," she uttered as she turned her head to the stars, wishing that her soul wasn't being torn in two.

She ran back to the retreat house to escape the pain from consuming her heart. It was different from the feelings she had experienced when she stood on those campgrounds outside his window as a teenager, where she heard him laughing at her with his friends. Now, it was as if she ripped her own heart and stomped on it with her foot.

CHAPTER 22

She returned to her room and screamed into her pillow. The audacity, she thought, as he stood with confidence, saying how he regretted kissing her, then judging her life decisions. All this time working with him, and he dared to analyze her relationships and job through the lens of that summer as if it led her away from her dreams.

She flipped onto her back and examined the plain and bare ceiling above her, coming to the conclusion that he had hurt her again. Frustrated, she got out of bed and decided she needed to prove him wrong. She loved her life and the one that Martin was offering her. So, she planned to call Martin and tell him that she was ready to commit to him. But as she held the phone in her hands, she started to hyperventilate.

Martin wanted a future with wedding bells, her at his side for every photo op, and a family to complete the idealistic life. But as an hour passed, she still hadn't mustered the courage to call him. She held the phone in her hand and paced back and forth in her room. When she grew tired of pacing, she sat at the small desk and read her journal, skimming it for clues.

She read her answers but didn't find anything to calm her mind. Flipping through, she came to the centre and found a prayer.

On the left was a sketch drawing of a Celtic heart, labeled as the trinity. On the right was a prayer written by Joseph Whelan, S.J. It was titled *Fall in Love:*

Nothing is more practical than finding God,
than falling in Love
in a quite absolute, final way.
What you are in love with, what seizes your imagination,
will affect everything.
It will decide what will get you out of bed in the morning,
what you do with your evenings,
how you spend your weekends, what you read, whom you know, what breaks your heart,
and what amazes you with joy and gratitude.
Fall in Love, stay in love, and it will decide everything.

Wiping her tears, she focused her attention ahead and contemplated the picture of the Sacred Heart of Jesus. He was pointing to his burning and pierced heart, reminding her that God's love burns for humanity. The love one must aspire to will include suffering and sacrifice because it leads to the fullness of love. She had known this since her childhood, but experiencing the heartache and loss solidified the teaching in her heart. Her past and present stood squarely in front of her, and she didn't know what to do because the remorse and resentment of that experience no longer existed. Closing her eyes, she picked up the pen and wrote those jumbled sentiments on paper. As she wrote at a rabbit's pace and reread the words, she wept with a joyful sorrow.

***

It was a late, chilly summer night at camp Ibig Pagalingign. As per usual, I dressed poorly for the evening watch with Christopher. We were patrolling the lake perimeter for campers in search of a romantic skinny dipping adventure. Since this was a gruelling shift, Christopher brought blankets and sleeping bags for us to sit and stay warm during the night. It was a romantic gesture that only stirred the anger inside of me. I didn't want to engage in our usual banter of wits. Speaking to him was like Russian roulette. But, he kept staring at me in a way that was making it difficult for me to concentrate and stay angry at him.

Lucky for him, the temperature dropped. I don't know why I always forgot to bring my sweater nor why he always remembered to bring one for me. But, I would not give him the satisfaction tonight. Feeling the cold breeze gnaw at my skin, he smiled with a hint of mischief in his eyes. He offered me his sweater before the words passed my lips. I should've accepted, but in my usual stubborn way, I said no.

Grinning, he placed his sweater around my shoulders anyway. He always smiled when he could do something for me, knowing I was fearlessly independent and never asked for help, especially from him. I felt immediately warm. But the acceptance cost me as it gave him an opening to ask why I was refusing to speak to him. I was surprised he noticed. He chuckled, saying he had known since breakfast. He claimed that he either mentioned something to offend me or, more likely, I was jealous that he had spent time with Michelle.

I was not amused, so I reminded him that he promised Lily, Calvin, and Tonia to take them fishing yesterday. Immediately his smug grin disappeared. He knew where he was at that time. He was making out with Michelle or Amber. In one stroke, his arrogant armor was destroyed because I reminded him of his responsibility and how his selfishness had disappointed three special needs campers who worshipped him. Guilt was written all over his face, but he tried to argue his way out of it. I didn't back off because he needed to see how his actions had consequences.

When our fight was reaching the peak of bitterness and anger, I accused him of choosing his libido over his responsibility. This made him angry. He stood up and told me that he could never live up to my Princess' expectations for him. I rose to my feet, yelling that I was angry because he made a promise and didn't come through. But I had gotten used to seeing him choose his wants before others.

I took my index finger and poked him hard in the chest. He tried to reason his way out of the situation, but I wouldn't let him charm his way out of this problem. There was no doubt my disappointment in him was displayed. Something came over him because he kissed me. I guess to stop me from poking and judging him. It worked. I forgot my name when he kissed me.

After a few minutes, he pulled away and apologized quickly for doing it. I didn't want him to apologize. Yes, I was disappointed, but it did not change how I felt nor how I wanted him to kiss me again. He was hesitant and stepped away, so I grabbed and kissed him. We were both in jeopardy of doing something we did not want to admit we wanted from the other person. He pulled away, running his hands down my arm. He was hesitant to kiss me again.

Instead, he grazed my forehead with his lips and gazed into my eyes. I was shivering, but it was not from the chill in the air. I offered his sweater back to him as his goosebumps were like pebbles under my fingers. We both smiled and kissed each other again. This time, I enjoyed the sensation of being kissed by someone who was intent on making me happy. I pulled him down and on top of me. With each tender kiss and touch, I wanted him. I heard him groan as my body arched into him. We were both immersed in each other that we almost didn't hear kids yelling for help from the lake. Stunned at the sound, I did not want to respond. He smiled and helped me to my feet, and we ran to help them.

The next morning, I rushed to Christopher's cabin so we could talk about what happened. I had stayed at the hospital with Maria to make sure her evening swim partner Ben was safe. I should've stayed at the hospital than search for Christopher.

When I arrived at his cottage, I heard voices and laughter from his cabin. Christopher was telling Michelle, Donald, and Wilson a story about me. They jeered like hyenas, ready to eat their prey. It was the moment when I realized how foolish I was to believe that Christopher felt the same way I did for him.

The shrieks of laughter still fill my heart with embarrassment. The way he recounted everything that had happened between us was far from the love stories in a Jane Austen novel. It had an air of mockery where something private between two people was their form of entertainment. I can still hear the exact words he used to describe that moment to his friends.

"When she kissed me, I had her. Her eyes bore into mine with a desire I had never experienced. I had never seen anyone as beautiful and passionate in my life. I felt how much… she needed me… and, in that moment, I won my five hundred dollars."

You could hear my heart breaking as every feeling I had about him transformed into pure rage. Those who have experienced a broken heart, no words could express the emptiness it causes. How every ounce of colour fades from your skin, and all you hear is the beating of your heart trying to slow down as the pace only inspires you to fly from the pain. Everything I believed in love was wrong! Being there for someone and understanding them didn't lead to love. Following your heart didn't lead you to love. But all those things I thought were the definition of love led me to him. I had kissed him because I thought I loved him and believed he felt the same way.

His lips were tender in that moment, but they now felt like ice to my lips, freezing everything in my heart that believed in us, in him, and in love. Every word that followed erased every tender moment we shared about our family and friends. The longer I stood there, every affection I had dropped to the ground and was buried in the soil of my sorrow. It was all lies. Confronting him in private was too kind.

Within minutes, I devised a way to humiliate him at the evening talent show. Who knew I had the skill to deceive and hurt someone? I fed on the fact that he loved being in front of an audience, and it would feel good to embarrass him in a roomful of people.

I avoided being alone with him, even though he tried to talk to me. I told him that we could spend some time together after the show. He understood and quickly outlined what he had planned for us. I guess he wanted to try again and fully win the five-hundred dollars.

He seemed proud and supportive before I took the stage. He squeezed my hand and kissed me on the cheek for good luck. I jerked away from him slowly, trying not to puke, but he made sure to make eye contact with me. Our eyes locked together, and I remember seeing an expression I had never seen. I didn't recognize it, but it made him squeeze my hand tighter as if he was trying to hold on to our friendship. His eyes begged me to give him one minute before taking the stage, but it was too late. I was announced.

As I sang Kelly Clarkson's 'Cry,' I felt the need to show him mercy rather than give in to my anger. Maybe I didn't want to be wrong about us. But as I peered into the crowd, I saw his friends snickering at me. Sounds that mocked my ideals and feelings. His voice taunting me. I glanced over at him, and his shoulders were hunched over. It was the first time his arrogance and confidence evaporated from his manner. I could see he was sorry for getting caught, but something in his posture told me he realized the gravity of his decision had annihilated our friendship. The realization that he had chosen to use me as one of his toys rather than cherishing me as a friend. But, I didn't care what he felt. I only wanted him to feel the humiliation and anger that consumed me.

I called him to the stage for my encore piece. Everyone yelled for him to join me. He couldn't resist. He appeared confident, but his eyes were wide with sheer terror. He knew that I knew the truth. I exposed the truth in front of everyone and ignored every instinct that told me how revenge would not stop the pain in my heart. It felt too good to make him feel as worthless as he made me feel.

***

By her own hand, she examined her past in a new light. She had kissed him back, and when she found out the truth, she chose to humiliate him. Her reaction was justified, but it was cruel. And what did it gain her? A piece of her soul that could not trust herself and a fragment of her humanity that could never forgive those who offended her.

Lifting her head from her words, she contemplated the icon of the crucified Lord. The sun had started to rise, and the rays were casting its light on His face and arms. The arms that stretched out to those who betrayed him was *the* example of love personified. A love she believed in but never understood.

There she realized what her life had been from that moment. It was a life where she had tried to avoid the pain and loss of being hurt again. And it was in those choices where she was left with only a bucket-full of unresolved feelings, a mountain of self-doubt, and a shattered vision of love.

CHAPTER 23

"You okay? You have bags under your eyes." Amalie sat beside Emma before Mass the next morning in the chapel.

She nodded with little energy to pretend she was all right. Emma barely slept last night as she analyzed her writing and evaluated her relationship with Christopher and everything after that moment. When he told her that he wished he didn't kiss her, it sparked something inside of her that she didn't understand. She tried to write it down, but all she had were memories that hurt in a different way.

"Sorry. I had a late night." Emma massaged the back of her neck and tried to sit-up.

"How was your evening stroll?"

"Sad." The word slipped out of Emma's mouth.

"Sad? I'm sorry."

Emma reassured her. "Don't worry. I realized I needed to remember things."

"You have good impulses. You've always been on the money about me. For example, you suggested that I had to decide if I could trust myself, and once I did, I could have a future. If I don't risk, no reward, right?" Amalie wiped away the tears.

Emma passed her a tissue. She was used to having tissue on hand for her friend. When Amalie had a breakthrough, she sobbed for hours then found the peace needed to make a decision. Emma recognized the calmness in Amalie's relaxed shoulders; Amalie had made a decision about her future as she cried tears of joy.

"What are you going to risk, Amalie?"

"I'm going to tell Dylan. Everything. I mean, if he rejects me, then he doesn't love me, but if he understands, then maybe something is there. Christopher was right. You were right."

"Christopher was right?"

"That I had to balance my heart and mind. You see, I'm at a crossroad where I have to make a choice."

"Right, a choice. Dylan will be thrilled," she murmured with little enthusiasm.

"Are you okay?"

"Yes, sorry. You were right. I needed a retreat to discern my choices and understand where I'm going."

"With Martin?"

Grinning with a lack of confidence, she nodded. "Right. He needs an answer."

"Are you going to marry him?"

"I'm not sure," she answered as she shrugged her shoulders.

"Do you love him?"

"I need some air."

After last night, as she wrote out everything, words and feelings were spilling out of her. Thoughts and emotions that had long been buried had resurfaced, and she didn't have a plan of how to deal with them.

Sister Clara was at the back of the chapel, greeting people at the door.

"Sister Clara, have you seen Christopher?"

"Dear, he left last night."

Staring at her as if she spoke a foreign language, "Oh."

"If you ask me, your conversation helped him discover his answer."

"His answer?"

"I shouldn't say, but he was trying to figure out if he loved someone enough to marry her. After your walk, he left the centre to tell her."

Emma's stomach churned. The thought of him marrying Beth never dawned on her as a possibility. When they were together at her place, they were friendly, but not in the way where they had a secret language between them. He had spent many hours with her at the office, and she never realized that he would have time to commit to someone. But Beth seemed ready and willing to adjust to his lifestyle. Sighing, she acknowledged that the boy who thought love was fleeting had found someone to love till death. At least she was right about something. Beth was a woman who taught him to love and helped him mature into the man who could commit to someone regardless of his past sins. She was happy for him but didn't like the hole it left in her heart.

"Did you need something from him, dear?" Sister Clara asked.

"No, it can wait. I'll talk to him at work."

Feeling her cheeks burn with embarrassment, Emma buried this surge of emotions and decided to focus on the future ahead. Amalie was right; she was at a crossroads. She had to make a decision.

***

As she opened the door to her condo, her half-empty boxes greeted her. It felt barren and unfinished. Surveying her space, she had to make this place her home, a home to raise a family. Unpacking some boxes, she found items to warm up her space, like the framed photos from her trips to Paris and London. But she left her books and journals in those boxes. There was no room for them on her shelves. When she finished, she congratulated herself for attempting to spruce up the place, but it did little to erase the loneliness in the air. Succumbing to the fatigue and self-pity, she rested outside because she didn't like how she decorated her condo. Everything she pulled out made the space feel like a museum.

"Emma?" Martin called out.

She was still sitting on the terrace, resting under the moonlight and stars. Coming out to join her, he kissed her on the forehead. His lips thawed her cold skin and brought her back to reality.

"I brought food. You hungry?"

"Starving."

He escorted her back inside.

"What are you doing here?" She sat and watched him intently set the table.

"I needed to see you."

Martin brought a plate of Chinese food for her and placed the flower arrangements on the table. He pecked her on the lips and encouraged her to eat. There was a tender bitterness as his lips touched hers, which sent a shiver of fear to her heart. She picked at her food and eventually chewed and swallowed it. The food had no taste.

When dinner was over, he guided her to the couch, and he sat across from her atop of the coffee table. Silently, they held each other's hands. She didn't remember the last time they ignored the raw physical attraction between them and had a quiet meal together. It unnerved her to sit silently with him.

"Do you know how much I love you?" he whispered, lifting her chin to gaze at him.

"I do."

"Then, what are we doing?"

With as much passion she could muster, Emma kissed him. She craved to bury the loneliness in her soul and to find the strength to say yes to the life he offered.

"Emma, this works between us. Trust me. But, we need to be—"

Emma pulled herself onto his lap and straddled him. She moved her body up and down to arouse the bulge that was already activated to take her. Being physical worked, but she could see that he wanted something more from her. As she tugged at his shirt and unbuckled his belt, she needed him to give in to her desire.

"Emma... we need to talk."

"Move in with me. I'm all in. It's not conventional, but you need some type of commitment from me and I from you, so—"

"Wait, you're okay with that arrangement? Are you sure?"

She had a thousand reasons why this was a bad idea. It went against everything she had been taught and believed, but it made the man who loved her happy. It wasn't the path she wanted to take, but it was the way to be with someone who wanted her, and was a type of commitment she could offer. Why this way? She didn't have an answer. All she knew at the moment was how it helped her forget the one who left to marry someone else.

CHAPTER 24

From her office window, Emma watched the sun rise above the skyscrapers. She soaked in the sun's warmth on her skin as it intensified her anticipation to see Christopher. Her plan was to apologize for what transpired between them, congratulate him on his pending wedding, and to thank him for encouraging her to finally make a commitment to Martin. It was her hope to rebuild their professional relationship as they were both settling down with their significant others. The thought did nothing to alleviate the anticipation of seeing him.

"Good morning!" Richard greeted Emma in his irritating Monday morning manner.

"You're early."

"Bonus points, please. Kidding. Needed to work on our other campaigns. You realize, we can't always focus on the Centre," he responded with equal sarcasm.

"Have you learned anything?"

"Learned?" He raised his right eyebrow.

"From working on the St. Michael's Centre campaign? Do you approach your work differently working with Christopher's team?"

He placed her coffee in front of her as he studied her face. "Why?"

Emma leaned toward him. "I was reviewing your table ideas. Inspiring, to use pictures from the Centre as the centrepieces. It's a brilliant way to show what happens at the Centre."

"I'm an amazing assistant."

"Maybe not for too long. This is quality work. Have

you considered becoming an event planner?"

"As much as I love taking credit for everything, this was Christopher's idea. I told people to be natural as Amalie took their picture. He provided the design and layout. He wanted to capture the generous spirit and compassion you encounter when you're there."

"These unposed shots capture the real joyful moments," she exclaimed as a memory came floating to her mind.

Richard giggled, "Funny, he mentioned it last week. I never noticed until he pointed it out. 'Tight-ass' was right."

"Hurts to say, doesn't it?"

"Must be. You've never praised him."

She threw a pencil at him as he left her office. His astute observation concerning her relationship with Christopher was a sobering revelation to her. But, she pushed it aside and focused on her work. After a few minutes, peering down at the world calmed her nerves as there was no sign of Christopher or his team. Martin's text ringtone brought her back to the present.

Sorry, I wanted to have breakfast with you, but I needed a change of clothes. I had a wonderful time talking about our future. Having the papers drawn up. See you tonight. Leon has concerns and requires us to discuss the pros and cons of moving in together. Love Martin.

She gasped for air. Despite her decision, the doubts and fear in her head didn't disappear. They intensified. But, she convinced herself that this was the right decision for them. He was present and loved her. What more could she want?

"Good morning, Emma."

Emma turned towards the voice. She was disappointed to see Kyle in her office.

"What can I do for you? Is your boss here?" She faked her usual assertive voice.

"No, that's why I'm here. Christopher is in London," he answered in a flat tone.

"I see," she uttered, struggling to stifle the disappointment in her voice.

"Mr. X called Christopher back."

"And he always goes?"

"Yes."

"Well, it's good, Mr. X trusts me. I'm surprised Christopher agreed. We never agree. Isn't he worried I'll change everything?"

"No, he trusts you. We see how you disagree with each other, but you find a way to compromise. We're intense, but Christopher wanted us to work hard for you. He mentioned we could learn a lot from you. The love you have for your sister's Centre and Amalie is inspiring."

"Thank you." She half-grinned as she tried to control the wobble in her voice.

"He taught us that when you set the bar high and push yourself to reach those goals even if you don't reach it—

"… you're left with something amazing," Emma blurted out.

"Yeah. So, you've been drinking from the Riley Kool-Aid tank too. The work speaks for itself." Richard pointed to the plans for the campaign around her office.

For the first time, Emma noticed the work surrounding her. From her office's chaos, now was a well-organized room of plans and pictures flowing together.

"We're here for support. So cheer up. We'll miss seeing how you never let him get his way. When we do these things, everyone agrees with him. But, you never conceded. It was fun. This has been the most entertaining project we've worked on."

Emma tried to stifle her laugh and couldn't help but agree with the sentiment.

"When will Christopher be back?" She examined the plans and pictures in her office.

"He won't."

Her hand stopped on a Post-it Note that he had moved the last time they were in her office together. "I see. So, he's gone, gone? Will he be back for the gala?"

"Mr. X always has Christopher working. When he calls, it means he has a new project for him. It's unlikely that he'll come back."

"Never tires from running Mr. X's affairs?"

"He works as if he is trying to prove something. Mr. X tells him to relax and stay in one spot. Get married. Have a family. But, as you can see, it's impossible to tame his determination."

"Right."

"Before I forget, this is for you. Christopher said it was important and would explain everything I told you in detail." Kyle handed her a sealed envelope.

After he left her office, she sat with the envelope in her hand, letting the news settle into her heart.

"We heard the wonderful news!" Richard burst into her office.

"What good news?" Emma stuffed the envelope into her purse.

"We're free from the watchful eyes of 'Tight Ass.'"

"Right. Um …set up a meeting for this afternoon. Call

Amalie and my sister. Let's meet to review and ensure everybody understands their role and the new setup."

Rising to her feet, she ordered, "Let's stay on top of this. Um…I need to step out for a while."

"Relax. We got this."

***

The post-rush-hour commuter silence was settling in between the towering buildings where Emma decided to sit and process the information. Christopher was gone. It was everything she wanted. But the news did not elate her heart in the way she thought it would.

She played with the envelope in her hands. It was too much for her to hope the contents expressed her heart's desire. But what scared her more was that this was a goodbye letter, a document that would sever any connection to him forever. Holding her breath, she unsealed the envelope and unfolded the letter. Unable to control her hands from trembling, she prayed to God that the contents did not match the worst-case scenario in her mind.

Dear Emma,

In this day and age, I should've emailed you or sent you a long text message, but I've learned from those Austen books that you made me read that the best way to express yourself, one must use pen and paper.

For the last few months, I've enjoyed working with you again. You bring out the worst and best in me. But, I can't get past our history. After last night, I don't believe I can ever get past the fact that I hurt you and can do nothing to remedy the pain I caused.

While working with you on our projects, I prayed time

would mend the wounds between us. It's too much to ask of you to forget and forgive what I've done. But until yesterday, I didn't realize how much my decision cost both of us. It cost me the one person who saw beyond my arrogance and accepted me, even implied it was okay to be me. You were my first true friend, the friend who taught me how to love. I will always treasure the time we had together and everything you taught me.

When I saw you at the airport, I didn't realize how much I missed you. Your timing was heaven sent. You walked back into my life when I needed you. Every argument and conversation we had since has forced me to reevaluate my life and realize what's important to me. Trust me, in my position, few people challenge me, but, as per usual, you never relented on your beliefs nor silenced your opinions. It helped me see problems and solutions in new ways.

I wanted to tell you why this Centre holds a special place in my heart. It's the place where I went after you told everyone about that bet. I met Mr. Xavier Holmes at St. Michael's Centre. He became my mentor and helped me through university and my career. I never imagined how this place was my opportunity to make amends with you.

I'm sorry for using our working relationship as a means to tell you how to live your life. I don't blame you for not trusting me nor my opinion, especially concerning your relationship with Martin. When I held you in my arms, I thought I was being helpful. But, our past seems to always get in the way. We can't even trust each other as colleagues.

Understand, I'm not saying this from duty or obligation or to make amends for past sins. It's out of respect for our past and current relationship. I hope I can convey everything I was trying to say to you last night without sounding like a blundering fool. You still make me nervous.

Back then, you were right about me. I was using my parents' divorce as an excuse to live my life without responsibilities, choosing to be in relationships where I felt good regardless of the other person's feelings. Thank you for showing me how selfish I was and living my life with no purpose. But, I was someone who could have lasting and loving relationships. When I met you, I was too young and foolish to believe and trust what you saw in me. I wished I told you the truth sooner and had faith you would understand and forgive me. But, I was always afraid of losing you and your friendship.

Our friendship, as it always has been, has been a source of inspiration. You taught me how to love and what it means to make a commitment, regardless of my past. You showed me that in friendship, you can find something you never knew you needed in life. Because of you, I learned how to be a friend.

As your friend, I treasure the time we worked together at the camp and now. I remember when we sat staring beyond the horizon across the lake or the view from your office where we didn't have to say anything to each other. I always wondered how we could do that. I have always wondered how you could sit under a tree or at your desk with chaos surrounding you and remain at peace or remain hopeful when life has been cruel and unfair to you. But in the last fifteen years, I've learned that your joy comes from your faith in God, in yourself, and others. I'm sorry for how my actions caused you not to believe in that anymore.

Before you react, consider the amount of time we've worked together. We've worked long hours, and in that time, all I have seen is sadness in your eyes. I couldn't figure out where that sadness came from when you have a great career, family, and a devoted boyfriend. Don't shake your head in complete disagreement. I noticed it every time you were with your staff, encouraging them, or when you're texting Martin. Em, consider what I'm saying before crumpling my letter. There is something in your eyes that tells me how you yearn to love your work and your life. I experienced it when I found you writing on Friday in the chapel and when you slapped me. I felt it when I held your frigid and shivering hands in mine. You've worked so hard giving to others, yet so distant from everyone. You allow people to help you, but you remain cautious and seldom attach yourself to someone emotionally. This is true at work and in your personal life.

It's obvious that Martin loves you. It's obvious everyone loves you. Don't be afraid. Trust yourself to love again in the way I've experienced how devoted and passionate you are towards others. You always showed me that prayers helped you organize your thoughts, and your pen kept a record. If you wondered why I wanted you to write again, I wanted to see your joy for life. Your writing is the way you remind yourself of who you are. Once you do that, I'm sure you'll embrace the love and support around you.

Sadly, it's obvious that I keep impeding your happiness and embracing the future ahead of you. I hope my absence will give you the opportunity to experience your life and the joy and love that surrounds you. I understand how I made it difficult for you to trust someone, even to love someone. Again, listen! It was in your voice last night. I didn't grasp the gravity of the pain I caused you because I didn't fathom how much you valued my opinion and our friendship.

Yes, Em, our friendship was real. Every conversation. Every story I shared with you was true. When I kissed you, it wasn't because I made the bet or wanted to fulfil a hormonal youthful urge; it was because I loved you at that moment. When you looked at me, as if everything everyone told you about me was true, I thought I lost you, and you would never know what you meant to me. Never doubt my feelings for you. But it was a kiss that changed us in the worst way. I lost my friend that day, and it's because of that experience that made you stopped trusting yourself and in love.

You once told me that love without ceasing can only lead you to what you seek. All I want for you is to allow someone to love you. If it's Martin, I'll rejoice and be at peace knowing you're happy and in love. But never sell yourself short. Everyone who loves you only wants the best for you. I understand it's true because I've found love and risked everything for it. Love helped me see who I was and to sacrifice everything for it.

Don't believe me? Take one more trip to the past and discern our relationship with all the facts. It'll help. If you could let your heart trust me on this one request, you'll understand how our friendship was real and special. Then, you will see you were never wrong about me or what you believed. You have always inspired and helped me to find true joy and love.

God Bless.

Love, always

Christopher

Her tears had smudged and stained the letter. His words expressed her soul's desires and appeased her spirit. The emotions exploding within her was too much for her heart to contain.

"Em?"

Closing her eyes, she folded the letter in her hands and sat up straight. Martin's voice brought her back to reality.

"You okay?"

"What are you doing here?" She made room for him on the bench and saw Leon behind him.

"I left in a hurry this morning and thought we needed to talk about moving in together, thought we could have a coffee. Plus, Leon wanted to ask you some questions."

"I hear you're committed to team Martin. We have plans for you!"

"Easy, Leon. My girl is out of sorts. Are you okay? What were you reading?"

She held the letter tight in her hands. "Nothing. Just wondering."

"Good thoughts. Me?"

Smiling as if she was parading in a beauty contest, she replied, "Who else?"

"That's the spirit! Since I have you both here, let's review some ideas for the campaign, " Leon interrupted them as he showed them the plans he had for their immediate future on his iPad.

CHAPTER 25

Sitting on the patio of Sunnyside Pavillion, Emma admired the pink and orange horizon off Lake Ontario. The sun was setting as the patrons started to fill the patio tables on the beach, but she didn't notice the sun's rays gleaming in the sky nor the chatter around her. Her slumped-over shoulders showed little joy or contentment.

"Em, you okay?" Sonja snapped her fingers in Emma's face to wake her up.

She smiled as if she was listening. "It's been one of those weeks."

"Another rough one?" Charlotte patted Emma's hands with a reassuring touch of support.

"Martin's political stuff."

As she promised, she worked a thirty-five work schedule and an additional forty on Martin's campaign. Leon had squeezed every ounce of her charm and intelligence to impress the political stakeholders. She was a sound bite dream to the media and a pleasant surprise to donors. Her presence softened Martin's aggressive nature and made him likeable at parties. Being on Martin's arm always drew the paparazzi. But, as much as she craved to relish in the spotlight, her soul wondered why her heart was still restless.

Emma sipped her drink again.

"Martin, then?" Charlotte asked.

"We spend every night together," Emma mumbled without glancing at them.

Sonja choked on her drink.

"We've decided our relationship needed to move to the next level."

"He proposed?" Charlotte drew her chair closer to the table.

"No. He's moved in with me."

Sonja and Charlotte sprayed their drinks on Emma.

"I'm surprised!" Charlotte shrieked as she regained her composure.

"Why?" she queried as she sought the source of their disbelief.

"You're the romantic. You're the girl who preferred everything in the traditional order, ring, marriage, house, then kids," Sonja explained as she glared at Charlotte for support.

"Yes, true, Sonja. But since she began dating Martin, she started to bend some of those rules about dating because she recognized that Martin was going to be the one, so she tried things that maybe only married people do, I guess. And this is the next step. What did your parents say? " Charlotte crinkled her nose.

Emma frowned as she recalled not telling them.

"Way to set up Martin. Are you enjoying every night with him?" Charlotte probed with wide eyes.

"Charlotte?" Emma gasped at her question.

"Humour me. I have children and a mortgage."

"But marriage is the best thing that ever happened to you, right? It's wonderful to share your life with one person for the rest of your life?" Sonja asked.

"It is. I love everything in my life. I have someone who takes care of me and nurtures my growth as a human being. But he drives me nuts. For example, it was cute to hear him sing along with radio jingles as my boyfriend, but now it sounds like fingernails on a chalkboard."

"Sonja, marriage is wonderful, and what Charlotte is saying is that it takes a lot of work." Emma glared at

Charlotte, but she didn't seem to get the message.

"Marriage isn't always roses. When you argue, you notice your differences. Then, you have kids, and his idiosyncrasies irritate you. Yet, being married has its perks. When I crawl into bed, I snuggle beside a man who loves me for me. There is a shared language between us that only married people understand."

"I don't think I can get married," Sonja cried.

"What's wrong?" Emma reached for Sonja's hand.

Running her hand through her dark brown hair, Sonja confessed, "The wedding plans are stressing us out. Guest lists. We keep adding names because our parents want to invite the whole village to our wedding. Yesterday, we were arguing about what gifts to buy our friends and family. A week ago, we were arguing how we're too accommodating to our future in-laws. I want to skip this wedding stuff and be his wife."

Charlotte and Emma brought their chairs beside her. They tried to calm her as she burst into hysterical sobs. Nothing was working.

"I spent the weekend with Christopher," Emma blurted out.

She felt her friends' eyes turn and judge her. As soon as she said it, she realized it didn't sound right. "But, not in that way," she added as Sonja and Charlotte's stunned reaction radiated a moral concern.

"What are you talking about?" Charlotte gawked.

"We were on retreat together."

"Is that what you call it?" The corners of Sonja's mouth twitched upwards.

"Nothing happened. He was on the same retreat, and now he's in London."

"But the campaign. Typical. Irresponsible as ever. I mean, someone brought him in to help, and in true Christopher fashion, he leaves you to finish the job," Sonja yelled with indignation.

"No, he told his boss I could handle it. He's not as calculated as we've made him." The words slipped from Emma's mouth as she fidgeted in her chair. She conceded, "I mean, he's mature and sensitive. He realizes what he's done, and it was nice to work with him as he is now. Yes, still arrogant, but reasonable and calm." Her friends didn't seem to be buying her explanation. "And, he believes in God and hopes and loves. He is everything we always thought he could be."

"What did you discuss?" Charlotte's eyes were wide with curiosity.

"Life. Our pasts. He helped me to realize how perfect Martin is for me."

"Christopher suggested you move in with Martin?" Sonja's voice screeched with skepticism.

"No, he apologized…um…I…" She paused as the epiphany rose slowly to her mind like bread rising in the oven, "…trust him."

Studying Charlotte's starry eyes, Emma did not want to provide any more information for Charlotte to have a fairytale ending to her story with Christopher. Before Charlotte could ask more questions, Emma turned to Sonja. "Sebastian loves you, and you love him. This chaos around you is your fear of the unknown. But when it's right and you trust and love each other, this appeasing and living up to ideals doesn't matter. Let Charlotte and I handle this stuff so that you and Sebastian can focus on each other and your future. The wedding is a day. Marriage is a lifetime of joy and sorrow."

"It's a miracle! Emma, the romantic, is back!" Charlotte squealed.

"What?" Emma swallowed the lump in her throat.

"It's been a while since you focused on love's feeling rather than the mechanics."

"Thank you. I guess."

"The past is memories. The future is unknown. But the present is where you change your life." Charlotte imitated Emma's speech and mannerisms to deliver her point.

"Did I say that?" Emma pointed at herself.

"It's nice to hear the idealist once in a while as opposed to the realist preparing for the worst-case-scenario," Charlotte stated with less dreaminess in her tone. "Why are you only moving in with Martin?"

"It's a commitment. At least... and who says it won't end in marriage, right? Okay, distraction complete. Let's focus on Sonja. Sonja, I promise to help organize a glorious wedding without sacrificing the marriage. I'm here to help, and so is Charlotte." Emma took out her phone and started making lists and plans.

CHAPTER 26

For the next few weeks, Martin was busy moving his things into Emma's place or strategizing with Leon. She hung on his arm, hinting that a wedding was on the horizon. She greeted his potential donors with the hospitality of a queen who discussed the king's plans for the future. She leaned on his shoulder in public, whispering ideas for his campaign that they would work on when they got home. To her, anything was better than dealing with the voice inside her head.

As Martin ordered food, Emma sat in the bedroom. It wasn't her room anymore. His pressed suits occupied half the closet, and his hair products found space on top of her dresser drawer. His second phone was on the night table. In the blink of an eye, the man of her dreams had moved in.

But, are you happy?

She tried to find the voice's owner to that comment in her head, but she only saw Martin's dumbbells.

"You okay in there?" Martin knocked on the door before entering.

"You don't have to knock. This is your room too." She held her hand out to him.

"Are you okay?" Martin sat beside her and cradled her hand in his own.

Her back straightened, and her throat tightened, "It's been a good week. My team works well with Christopher's team despite his absence, which helps, and Sonja's wedding is coming together. The campaign—"

"I want you to consider a break."

She squinted her eyes. "A break?"

"It's obvious you enjoy your work, but you're not in love with it."

"I have the skills needed to carry out those goals. Remember, it's what you love about me."

"Yes, but I can't help wondering if Christopher was right. I mean, he described you as being brilliant at your job, but he mentioned you loved writing. I want you to consider that if you choose to take a break and write or do something less taxing on your time, I'll support you. Having you on my speech writing team, my marketing team, or you at my side is something that sounds ideal. If I'm nominated and elected, our lives will change. You see that, right?"

Half-smiling as pain whirled in her stomach, she muttered, "Yes."

"I love having you when I want. We're both on the same page regarding our future, then?" He kissed her, and his grip tightened around her waist. She felt knives poke and prick her body.

"What did you order?" she tore her lips from him.

"Chinese. I ordered your favourites." He pushed her underneath him.

"What are my favourites?"

"General Tsao Chicken, Beef Broccoli, Pork Fried Rice."

"Sounds delicious." She didn't want to correct him. "Um…my…parents are coming."

"Yes." He unbuttoned her shirt. "You invited them."

"I didn't invite them," Emma reminded him.

"Yes, you wanted to tell them. Remember?"

"Right." His hands yanked her pants over her legs.

"Martin! We need to stop."

"I understand your parents are coming. The food is on the way. But I can't help myself."

"You can't be serious!"

"That doesn't mean we can't relieve the tension in your shoulder," he murmured as he kissed her shoulder. "... or your neck."

"We need to clean." She was trying to avoid vomiting on him.

"Forget what you have to do and focus on me," he whispered in her ear.

His jealous tone recharged her will to listen to her body. She pushed him off and stormed out of the room. Channeling her confusion and anger, she searched for any task to complete.

"You've got to be kidding," Martin yelled as he watched her set the table.

She remained silent as she meticulously laid out the plates and utensils.

"Did I say or do something?" He stood with arms crossed, hovering over her.

"My parents are coming. We don't have time. I didn't invite them. You did."

"I'm sorry, but I was trying to have time with my girl before her parents arrived. People in love understand what it means to be together."

"Why did you invite them?"

"I'm not their favourite person."

"So, you should be on your best behaviour, and having sex before they arrive isn't the way to do that."

"Sorry, but I've moved in, and we're more like roommates without the benefits."

"So, time with your girlfriend isn't what you want?" she hissed.

"I guess the only time you have for me is when you're not at work, or no one else needs you!"

"What was happening between us was about you."

"Sorry, I'm tired of working so hard for you to want me. Do you even love me?"

As the question hit her heart with precise and deadly precision, the plate slipped from her hand onto the floor. The crash sent her to her knees. She tried to clean the scattered, broken pieces. But as she picked them up, her uncontrollable tears fell to the floor. "I'm sorry," Emma whispered.

Martin placed his hands on top of hers to stop them from shaking. She dropped the broken pieces to the ground and fell into his arms.

"Hey, it's okay. I shouldn't have lashed out."

"I broke your plate."

"Then we'll buy a new one."

"Why are we arguing?" She pushed herself away from him.

"I've no idea. An hour ago we were close, and a minute or two we were —"

"We're sitting in a mess."

Releasing a pent up breath, he concluded, "We're still adjusting to our proximity. We can't hide from each other, and maybe the pressure is putting undue stress on our relationship. Your parents coming over adds another layer."

"They like you."

Martin scoffed. "Keep telling yourself that."

"They do. And my opinion is the only one that counts. I'm committed to you."

"Relax. We had a fight. I'm stressed. You're

stressed. I'm busy. Your work and friends are a priority."

"We've been spending time together, right?"

"Yes." His voice was tight.

She watched as he pushed away the broken pieces away from her and cleaned her hands. His silence drove another knife into her heart. "Martin?"

"We need to clean this place. I want your parents to love me." With slumped shoulders and a shrug, he helped her to her feet. Scared that she had caused another rift between them, she found his lips to reassure him of her commitment to him.

He tucked the strands of her hair behind her ear. "Hey, don't cry. It's only a plate." "This is going to work…I…do love you. I'll be better," she swore and kissed him with every intention to convince him.

With those few words, he nodded and kissed her forehead. His lips were cold against her skin. Shaking off the reaction, she pecked him on the lips and pulled away to finish setting the table. Martin went to replace the broken plate, then he swept the shattered pieces away.

CHAPTER 27

Emma needed a distraction from the tension inside her condo. Distracting herself with the sight of the glorious green trees below and the lit skyline made her wish she was anywhere but with her parents and Martin.

"Your father and I admire Martin's ambition and his intentions towards you. But, your living arrangement isn't right for you," Beatrice stated as she joined Emma on her terrace.

Emma let out a frustrated sigh, "You hate him."

"Hate is a strong word. We want something more for you."

She mumbled, "You always do."

Beatrice stood in front of Emma and reached for her hand. She caressed it with a mother's touch. "You used to. Are you feeling okay?"

"I needed air. It's tense in there."

"Understandable, you live with your boyfriend."

"You're disappointed?" Emma avoided her mother's concerned expression and stalked away. "He loves me. He wanted a commitment."

"No doubt. Brave man to ask you if he could move in. It's been a year."

"Moving in is something I wanted. It was easier…and I…"

"Do you want to marry him?"

"Mother!" She hoped her outburst, as it always did, told Beatrice to change the subject.

"You're a grown woman who can make her own choices. Yet, I do have the right to tell you that you seem unhappy.

This is surprising since Annabelle told me that the gala and campaign are on track to being a success."

Gagging at her mother, she asked, "She called you?"

"Who else? You haven't called me since Christopher left."

Emma plastered on her pleasant-daughter mask to convince her mother that her prying nature was not needed. But, Emma understood how her mother used her parental power to rattle her confidence and unearth the truth.

"I've been —"

"Busy." Beatrice's voice was firm. Emma hated how her mom always seemed one step ahead of her. "But it seems you're not too busy to unpack your things."

"I needed to fit Martin's stuff."

"Good, those boxes have been there since you moved in."

"BUSY!"

Without blinking an eye or raising her voice, Emma felt Beatrice probing her soul. It was a mom's superpower that they gained access to as soon as the child starts to grow in the womb. This was a power given in abundance to Filipino moms who could stare and say one word at their child until who then would tell them the truth. It was a tone that forces a child to face their mother and listen with an open heart and mind. There was not another option when this unbreakable connection forced one to tell or confront the truth.

"Are you happy, dear?"

After sitting down, Emma sighed and searched the stars for her answers. She didn't want to hear her mom's advice.

"Um…sure."

"Your sister mentioned you might sing at the fundraiser. It's been a long time since I heard you—"

"I'm not doing it." She bit her lower lip to temper the boiling fury percolating in her heart.

"Okay. How is work?"

"After this month, I can relax."

"Is that why you're so tired? "

Her mother took a quick picture of Emma with her phone and showed it to her. She had to concede. The dark circles around her eyes were heavier, and her face didn't glow like a woman in love. Handing the phone back to her mother, she grunted, "My sister has been keeping you well-informed."

"I'm concerned for your well being. She mentioned you've started working longer hours again. Is Martin okay with this arrangement?"

"He understands it's only temporary."

Beatrice reached for Emma's hand again. Emma sucked in her breath. Her mother always could articulate the truth hidden in her heart. Like a good mother, she would pry and dig until she got her to admit it aloud, but never force her opinion on her. Emma could feel the question her mother was going to ask her.

"Did Christopher leave because of you?"

"No."

"Did he leave because of the bet?"

"What bet?" Emma cringed and darted her gaze away from her mother.

Does my mom read minds now?

"You never told me what happened during that summer at the camp. It was him, wasn't it? Christopher made a bet to sleep with you, betrayed your trust, and humiliated you. Ever since he arrived, it was obvious he was the other party involved."

She sat, stunned at her mom's intel and wisdom. Beatrice had succinctly placed her past and present before her, without judgement but with clarity.

"You were never the same. After that summer, you were more mature and serious. My little girl was growing up, but the lessons you learned came at a cost." Beatrice hugged her tightly and let her cry.

As she whimpered, Emma explained, "What he did, he apologized. He wished he told me and never made the bet. See, I had overheard him tell his friends that he could get me to sleep with him. As we became friends, he realized he had made a mistake. He was afraid to admit his feelings. But anytime you express your feelings, it is risky because the other person you love may not reciprocate those feelings."

She brushed Emma's hair and lightly kissed her head like a mother saying goodnight to their child after they had fallen asleep. "It is difficult because we recognize how being vulnerable to someone else will lead to disappointment, especially when you fall in love. And you wished you didn't let your temper lead you to humiliate him and destroy what you believed was a special friendship. Then in the way you reacted, to realize you are not as pristine and compassionate. You acknowledge you're an imperfect human, prone to hurt others at times. Our passions and emotions drive us to wonderful things but burn us, and we seek vengeance."

"How did you know that's how I reacted?"

"Sonja and Charlotte told me when you came back. Plus, you are my daughter. This calm and demure nature only comes from seeing my life over the years and learning from those experiences when I didn't live up to my own expectations. I am not very good at forgiving myself. Your patient father has the forgiving heart. He always forgives. I do too, but it takes a while for me to forgive myself. Sound familiar?"

For the first time, she saw herself reflected in her mom's words. But she didn't judge herself. It was a relief to have someone who understood her torment and offered compassion to accept her weaknesses and to see how she could learn from them.

After a few moments of silence passed, Beatrice brushed Emma's hair aside. Tilting her head and gazing at her daughter's posture with a neutral smile, she reminded Emma, "You are unique because you believe in the impossible. You see someone's greatness before weakness. Believing everyone deserves love. But in reality, in your youth, when your ideals on love were trampled on, you stopped believing in *you*. In your usual one-hundred-and-eighty-way, you stopped trusting your instincts on love. Since then, you end your relationships before it becomes serious, risking your heart for what you love is something you couldn't do anymore in your relationships and in your work. But I can see that the man who changed my daughter has changed her again. Did he leave to give you space?"

"No. His boss reassigned him. I didn't have a chance to say goodbye and finally close that part of my life."

"Well, then live your life free from your past."

In her mother's embrace, she felt safe to be herself and cry. Emma felt scared but ready to settle into her future.

CHAPTER 28

After talking to her mother, Emma tried to have fun being Martin's plus one when time permitted. It was easy being the dutiful girlfriend, so much so when they arrived home from the political parties and community events, they were exhausted. On top of that, Sonja's wedding plans were occupying an enormous amount of her time, that her maid of honour role was becoming a full-time job. No matter how hard she worked, though, the fundraisers and wedding plans piled up in her office, which only increased the amount of time she spent away from Martin.

Tonight was no different. Being in her condo with her workers was a glorious room of chaos and organization. The office space at night wasn't producing the results she wanted, so they moved to her place. It was a space that energized her team, but it was one where she had no desire to work. Martin's campaign material was scattered throughout the condo to only remind her of the future ahead with him. It should have inspired her, but it only reminded her that she needed to be at Martin's donor dinner.

"Yes, I'll be there," she repeated to Martin.

"We agreed to eat together."

"Yes… but... but... Annabelle needs me to finish. Plus, wait, check and finish the decorations. I promise. I won't be longer than an hour. I swear."

"Emma!" She hated his whiney voice, especially when it was exponentially loud.

"I promise. I'll be there." She hung up the phone. Annabelle, Amalie, and her staff stared at her. They each gave her their best impression of a supportive smile. The gesture of kindness did not help temper her mood.

"I got called in for an emergency?" Annabelle shook her head at Emma.

"Trouble in paradise?" Amalie inquired.

"I've been late a lot this week, but I've made most of those meetings. With Sonja's wedding coming up and all of this fund-raising stuff, I haven't found the time to be with him. Let me review those plans."

"If he needs you, go," Amalie suggested.

"I made a promise to Annabelle." She pointed to her sister.

"Right," Annabelle tooted her two cents.

It was useless for Emma to spar with both of them when one encouraged her to go, and the other one stressed that she stayed.

"Do you have glasses?" Annabelle was opening the kitchen cupboards.

"Just cups. Cupboard above the coffee maker."

"Seriously, Em."

"I drink coffee. Martin drinks coffee. There are some wine glasses in there, or you can check if Martin has water glasses in a box over there."

"We have glasses at the office," Amalie mumbled.

Annabelle scoffed. "Yes, but it's half an hour away from where Emma is meeting Martin. Em, don't forget to take time for yourself. If he cares, he'll give you space. You did his fundraiser last night. It's time to do *your* thing," Annabelle instructed Emma in her sisterly, responsible manner.

"Let's finish our work," Emma agreed and reviewed her plans.

An hour later, she was sitting in her Poang chair when

she noticed the organized chaos. Her team was working well with Christopher's team, but her heart and mind did not swell with pride. There was no sense of peace and anticipation for the gala. She hated to admit it, but as their plans started to materialize, she wished Christopher was here to see and celebrate with her.

"You okay?" Annabelle waved a hand in front of Emma's face.

"Yeah. Sorry. Watching all of this come together is moving." Her voice wobbled.

"Get out of here. I can see everyone out," Annabelle suggested.

Emma dismissed the suggestion. "Go home. You have kids. Martin is a big boy who doesn't need me with him all the time."

The long hours had taken a toll on her patience. Sternly staring at her sister, she wanted to make it clear that she had her life under control.

"Why isn't your name in the program?" Amalie passed a mock-up of the program to Emma.

"We agreed a long time ago that I was not part of the presentation."

"I thought—"

"What?" Emma glared at her in a way to not even dare to broach the topic with her again.

"Nothing. I thought you would sing after —"

"After what?"

"The retreat. You moved in with Martin, so I thought you might be feeling up for it. I mean, if you were willing to break your rule about living arrangements, then singing would be nothing, right?"

Amalie's recent moody and sassy comments were beginning to irritate her. Her patience and temper had limits before she became unpleasant.

"You and my sister will be fine."

"You should do it. Your voice is important for the night and—"

"AMALIE! I created a nice opportunity for you to share your story. You don't need me because you're a confident young woman. No one wants to hear me. We're here to raise money for the Centre. We're there to hear how it benefits people seeking help, like you."

"Christopher said —"

"What did he say?" Emma leered at Amalie.

"By the time we got here, that you would agree to do it. I thought —"

"Whatever you and Christopher were hoping is not going to happen. He's not even here, so drop it. Amalie, I know you envision my singing will be this great moment and will inspire people, but I don't indulge myself in fantasies and what-ifs."

"Okay, so don't write a song. How about singing, 'No Day But ToDay.' Picture this, I give my testimony, and then you sing. It'll be great with the display. Please, it'll make my work make more sense."

Emma never heard Amalie plead her case with such passion and desperation. But it did not move Emma to say yes.

"Are you referring to the project I haven't seen?" Emma questioned Amalie as if she was cross-examining her in a court.

"Uhmmm, trust me, you should sing a song."

"I don't see how it's relevant to a project I haven't seen. Let me see the showcase."

"You promised Christopher that I had creative control

over it, and…you didn't want to be involved and…you trusted me enough to make sure it was okay." Amalie's voice wavered in intensity but never lost the tone of determination. "Do you remember the first time we met? I was sitting in front of Annabelle's office, and you were humming. Your voice calmed me down. Your story, especially in song, will perfectly tie into my story. It will bring everything full circle. It shows how I started as this scared young woman who needed a kick start, which you gave, and in turn, I helped you find your voice. See, this Centre is where we met and found a way to love again."

"She's right," Kyle quipped in as he packed his things.

"I'm not asking for opinions," Emma growled.

"It makes sense. It's a great way to show how the Centre doesn't assist those seeking help, but changes the person who is helping. I mean, you haven't sung in public for years, and now, because of your relationship with Amalie through the Centre, you found the courage to be heard again." Kyle continued with an opinion that had no intention of forcing her to do something. It was an honest observation.

She tapped her finger on the table, irritated at the onslaught of demands. The pressure almost persuaded her to do it, but her heart couldn't say yes.

"I'm in charge, and we'll follow the approved program. Amalie, you have your assignment, so finish it. I've given you free rein to create and design the venue without input from me. I will keep my promise to you and Christopher. Finish whatever project you are so determined to keep private. But do not test my patience."

She mustered all the assertiveness left in her blood to remain strong in her convictions. Scowling at everyone, she could see how scared they were to cross her. She had won the battle, but it did not provide her the comfort or confidence she still yearned for the upcoming event, if she was being honest with herself and her future plans.

CHAPTER 29

It was just after sunrise when Sonja arrived at Emma's condo. Martin was not happy waking up early on a Saturday morning. But time to a bride two weeks from her wedding is always in short supply. Fortunately for Sonja, Emma arrived in time with take-out coffee and breakfast. When she did, she noticed that Martin's eyes were displeased.

Through gritted teeth, Emma grunted to Sonja, "I told you we were meeting downstairs." Then smiling at Martin, she said, "Let me help Sonja with two things. Then I am yours. I promise."

Martin waved goodbye and slammed the door to the bedroom.

"Not a morning person? Sorry, Em. I forgot we were meeting downstairs. But we're here now. He won't mind, will he?" Sonja bowed her head in contrition.

Emma placed the coffee down on the kitchen counter, trying to ignore the irritation she had towards Martin's response. Emma had no choice. She was either going to disappoint her boyfriend or friend. She chose Sonja. Her plans were a good distraction rather than dealing with Martin's morning moodiness. Sonja had an endless wedding to-do list, which was easier to accomplish than dealing with him. Every time he strutted in and out of their bedroom, he made it a point to make his presence known as if he was a dump truck unloading manure onto a children's park.

"Thank you. I mean, you're helping your sister and me. I mean, Mr. Perfect is perfect."

Emma acknowledged the comment with a nod, even

though his recent behaviour was less-than impeccable. Recently, she noticed the change in his demands when she worked overtime, and his eye twitched every time she read a text from Sonja or Amalie.

"Did I say something?" Sonja inquired after taking a sip of her coffee.

"No, it's early, and I worked late, and my sister sent over those programs for me to review and personalize. Plus, Amalie keeps pestering me to sing."

"You're going to sing?"

Emma groaned to Sonja's enthusiastic response. "No, Amalie is like Christopher. She believes if I sing, people will give more."

"Well, I want you to sing at my wedding."

"No. I'm not doing it for charity. I'm not doing it for your wedding."

"You're right; it's too much to demand. Ignore me. I'm two litres full of coffee and a crazy bride who wants too much." Sonja cleared her throat and reviewed her to-do list with Emma. Hearing Sonja list her activities made Emma's heart beat faster. She could hear her thumping heartbeat, urging her not to peek at Sonja's sad-looking expression.

"Ask," Emma grumbled.

"Ask you what?"

"Sonja?"

Staring at her as if the idea came to her, she asked, "Do you remember the song you sang in *Guys and Dolls*, 'I've Never Been in Love Before'? Can you sing it? I mean, me and Sebastian want to dance to it."

"Really? Sebastian? The one who loves techno dance music?"

"You're right. I heard it countless times when we were in

high school. Repeatedly. But it's okay, forget I mentioned it, even though you promised to sing it when I found the right guy. But what's a promise?" She pretended to text something into her phone.

"Consider it my wedding present. Don't tell Amalie, or she'll have me put on a production number or something for the gala."

"Thank you. You're the best. Have you been sleeping?" She hugged her tightly.

"Adjusting to my new life."

"Makes you wonder, right?"

"What?" Emma squinted her eyes above the rim of her coffee cup.

"If you grow tired of living in limbo with Martin, I'll be helping plan *your* wedding."

She finished her coffee and forcing a smile as she responded, "Right… that makes sense."

"Well, that's settled. Rest, I don't want bags under your eyes."

Two hours later, Emma went back to bed. Martin was showering as she tried to fall asleep. Sleep didn't come to her. Inhaling, she sat up in her bed, realizing how much stuff had piled up in her room. She glanced at her nightstand and found the bible nestled in between her work. Thumbing through the pages, she came upon St. Paul's letter to the Corinthians.

…If I speak in the tongues of mortals and of angels, but do not have love, I am a noisy gong or a clanging cymbal. And if I have prophetic powers, and understand all mysteries and all knowledge, and if I have all faith, to remove mountains, but do not have love, I am nothing. If I give away all my possessions, and if I hand over my body so that I may boast, but do not have love, I gain nothing.

Shaking her head, she closed the bible and pondered St. Paul's words. Age and experience had made her wiser in understanding love. But the passage didn't fill her with the warmth of confidence that her life was a reflection of St. Paul's definition of love. Instead, it was a cold reminder to reevaluate her intentions, desires, and decisions for the future. Why had she thought living with Martin was right for her, and why did she yes to singing at Sonja's wedding?

"Em," Martin stood above her with a phone in hand.

"Sorry, did you need something?"

"It's Amalie. She's on the phone."

She took the phone from him as a chill rushed through her fingertips.

"Good morning," Amalie belted cheerfully.

"Hey. What can I do for you?"

"I'm checking to see if you got my email."

"Your email?" She reached for her tablet and searched her inbox.

"I sent my speech to you. I need you to review it before the gala."

"Sorry. Work, the wedding, and everything in between kept me busy."

"You sound busy, so I'll…um…well…talk to you later?"

Pulling the phone away from her, she counted to ten. Emma could not ignore Amalie's tone of contrition. "Are you okay?"

"Yeah, I didn't want to bother you, and I thought that maybe you were upset and didn't want to talk to me."

"How are you?"

Martin slammed shut his sock drawer. She had forgotten he was still in the room getting ready for a lunch date with her. She noted the tension in his shoulders as he left the room. But, something compelled her to talk and make peace with Amalie.

It was an hour later when Emma entered the living room. As she approached Martin, he continued to watch baseball. He pointed to the unpacked picnic lunch on the kitchen table.

"If sorry are your next words, save it," he blurted with a curt and cold tone.

"I've ruined the day again, haven't I?"

"You love helping people; I get it." He switched off the television and got up from the Poang chair.

"Keeping up with your life is a full-time job. Give me space to do my thing. Then it's you and me. I'm yours after Sonja's wedding and the gala. I promise." Her confident-sounding voice was her attempt to convince herself that everything was going to get better between them, even though something in her heart didn't believe what she was saying.

"Emma, are you happy?" He tilted her head up.

Emma nestled herself against his chest, hoping her despair and fear would disappear into his skin. "Please, let me show you how much you mean to me. No more meetings or calls. Just you and me."

As she kissed him, she felt the tension dissolve between them. He smirked and sauntered over to the picnic basket and repacked the contents for a quiet afternoon together in the park.

CHAPTER 30

"You told me that Martin was the love of my life," Emma shouted at Christopher.

"I didn't say that." Christopher shook his head.

"He's a great guy."

"I'm confident he is."

"You told me he would make me happy."

"He will, especially in this arrangement."

"Don't say it like that!"

"How am I saying it?"

"I've settled. I should've suggested we get married."

"Safer this way, though, right? No commitment. Easier to walk away. But I'm sure he'll propose soon, and you'll say yes."

"I will."

"Makes sense. Martin's a professional and well-groomed man. He's serious and attentive. He's close to your ideal man."

She swallowed a lump in her throat. "Close?"

"Do you remember the lessons you learned from Guys and Dolls? The heart craves what it chooses. But, you can't fall in love with an ideal. It's not real."

Emma sighed. "What defines a real relationship?"

"Chemistry."

"Chemistry?"

"When you discover agape love, you don't trust you found it, so you test it."

"That's chemistry?"

His eyes glowed with insight and a certain twinkle of fearlessness and confidence that was reserved for her. "No, chemistry is the moment you encounter peace in their presence. It's easy to be yourself. They can see through the facade, and despite how you try to fight those feelings, you explore them. You feel safe enough to risk your heart beyond your prejudices. You can fall in love, even though that person has the potential to break your heart more than once."

"'Guys and Dolls' has a wealth of lessons." There was sarcasm in her voice.

"Maybe you're seeing how you're in love with the man in front of you."

A comforting silence embraced her. She was enticed to ask him another question, but Christopher spoke first. "You should answer the door. It's Martin."

***

She was sitting in her bathtub engulfed in bubbles. The scent of pine and lilac was from the soap and not from trees or wildflowers. Sadness filled her heart to realize that she and Christopher weren't beside a lake, under the stars and quarrelling. It was a dream.

"Emma, you okay?" Martin knocked on the door again.

"Fell asleep."

"You sure?"

"I have a million things to do before Sonja's wedding."

"Shouldn't you be at Sonja's place?"

"Why?"

"Today is Sonja's wedding."

She jumped out of the tub and quickly dried herself off.

CHAPTER 31

After causing Sonja a panic attack before the wedding, the rest of the day went smoothly. Emma was the attentive maid of honour, fixing the bride's dress for every picture at St. Claire's and in the annex garden. As a well-trained monkey, she pursed her lips together and tolerated the whims of the photographer. She was grateful for the diversion. The wedding kept her thoughts from dwelling on her dream and the feelings it rekindled in her heart.

Weddings always flooded Emma's mind with romantic ideals and sentiments, which, now, were sinking her spirit into melancholy. But it wasn't because she didn't believe Sonja and Sebastian had made the wrong decision. She wished them the best. In fact, she didn't have any malice or disdain for the whole "till death do us part." What she disliked was the spectacle of overwrought dresses and extravagant flowers, which tarnished the simplicity of the ritual itself. In her soul, she understood how committing to love another person in sickness and health was a leap of faith within every human being beating heart. But she was unsure if she could love someone forever.

As she stood in the reception line, she ignored the nagging voice that begged her to examine her feelings. It was a voice that grew louder as Sonja's wedding approached and was at a fever pitch now. Being at the wedding, witnessing them exchange their vows, reignited memories and a harsh emptiness that only champagne could cure at this moment. Her fourth champagne almost worked to numb her thoughts and feelings to enjoy the celebration of love around her.

"Sonja let you mingle? You are stunning," Martin commented as he brought her another glass of champagne.

"I'm surprised that you're having a good time."

"I get to admire you from a distance, and I'm even able to talk to you at the same time in person, makes this a special day," he announced for those around him to hear.

Through pursed lips, she pretended to be happy with Martin, a man who was pleasant from afar, but in her presence was a sarcastic and mean drunk. "How much did you drink?" she interrogated through gritted teeth.

"Do you suppose six or seven being too much to drink? I lost count."

Sonja approached them and squealed, "Aha, there you are. I'm stealing my maid of honour."

"I'm sure she'll be happy with you. Until the warden releases you." His words were slurred as he mockingly bowed at Sonja.

"He likes a good open bar," Emma explained to her.

"I've never met a lawyer who didn't."

"I'll be fine. One more distraction to go until another one arises," he commented rudely, toasting their glasses and sauntering off to find another drink.

"Are you guys okay?" Sonja raised her eyebrows with concern.

"Yes, he's pacing himself with the drinks. If you avoid pulling me aside, he'll stop drinking and speaking loudly."

"Well, he's loud and obnoxious, considering he wanted a favour from me."

"A favour?"

"Forget it. This is my time. You're mine."

Mustering fake enthusiasm, she allowed Sonja to pull her into more pictures. The spectacle and the demands of wedding guests were peeling away at her patient facade. She was trying to be the perfect maid of honour and Martin's girlfriend, but being surrounded by love and joy was sucking the energy from her to be the poster child for maid of honour and girlfriend of the year.

When the next wedding game started, she excused herself from it. The groomsmen-centred game was the opening she needed to slip away from her duties.

As she sat by herself outside, she felt the pain in her feet and back. But the time didn't offer her the rest she desired. She was exhausted from living up to the expectations of her life. Being outside with alcohol-induced numbness was exactly what she needed. But physical exhaustion and alcohol could not protect her mind from the truth nor her heart from regret.

"Emma?"

She placed her champagne glass on the stone bench. She was hearing voices as if she was Catherine from *Wuthering Heights*. As she turned to leave the terrace, she recognized a familiar frame ascend the steps. When he reached the plateau in his well-tailored suit, she thought she was dreaming again

"Sorry, I didn't expect... well, I noticed you from a distance and you were sitting there, and I couldn't... I wanted to say hi. What are you doing here?" He stammered in a high-pitched voice.

She wanted to believe that he was happy to see her again. "Sonja's wedding,"

"Right. You're stunning." He cleared this throat. "Sorry, are you okay?"

"I'm taking a break from the festivities."

Nodding a couple of times until his eyes connected with hers, he lamented, "I'm sorry."

"For what?" Her voice was airy and quiet.

"I wanted to apologize for not saying goodbye to you in person, but Mr. X had an emergency. It was in my letter, which I hope made sense. I needed you to understand what I was trying to say and accept that I want the best for you."

"Right, Mr. X called, and you had to go. Kyle informed me. Our teams are working well together."

"I'm sure they enjoy hearing one voice bark out the orders."

She grinned and coughed. Her stomach wasn't making it easy for her to appear calm and collected. "Thank you for trusting me. It'll be a wonderful campaign with a spectacular gala to kick it off. The other projects are going well."

"I expect nothing less. Kyle mentioned Amalie is still working on the top-secret one for the evening. Thank you for allowing her to do it on her own."

"I promised you."

"I'm glad you didn't undo everything I set in motion."

"I considered it. But we spent so many hours arguing, so it wasn't right."

He replied, beaming with pride, "Thank you. Are you okay?"

His tone shifted into a deep whisper. It was a tone he used when he suspected that she was trying to hide something from him. Emma felt uneasy that she recognized it, and he had noticed her discomfort.

"The emergency with Mr. X keeps you busy. You haven't returned to check in on me."

He scratched his nose, but she could see his grin. "Mr. X. thought some time in London might be good for me. Besides, you didn't need my help."

"Why are you here?"

He cleared his throat. “Personal business. My team doesn’t know that I’m here. It’s better if you don’t tell them. Makes them nervous. I’ll be moving them so —”

“You didn’t send them flowers.”

“Urban myth.”

“You sent *me* flowers.”

“It was a gift. It was a stupid idea. I thought you would understand the sender’s intent.” He shook his head as he examined the ground.

“It was a gift?” She realized she had misinterpreted the message.

“Yes, I was trying to communicate something with them as you taught me how flowers send a message.”

He stood in front of her with his hands in his pocket. Studying his stance, she remembered how he had done the same thing when they hiked through a field of wildflowers. It was the first time they were alone, and she had picked flowers and stuck them in his face. At the time, it was an innocent gesture, but one where she got so close to him that the heat steaming from her face shocked her. To conceal it, she started to explain what flowers meant when you sent them to someone. Remembering with clarity, she murmured, “In friendship, I’m filled with joy. It’s heavenly to be with you. Yellow roses and Easter White Lilies.”

“You do have a way with words.”

She examined the ground, trying to stop the wave of emotions racing through her veins. “Um…are you in London, permanently?”

“Well, that depends.”

“Depends?”

“If you need me. Are you okay without me?”

She smirked as those familiar eyes still mesmerized her. Her past, present, and future were converging, and it was urging her to stop pretending. On the verge of hyperventilating, she couldn't lie to him. At that moment, she sobbed and fell into his arms. He held her up, but she was too afraid to let him go. Guiding her to the stone bench, he placed his jacket on her.

His touch was warm against her skin, causing her body to lean on him and rest her head on his shoulder. With every minute, his touch warmed her body as his affection for her well being made her forget the obstacles between them. It was safe in his arms, even though she shivered under his touch.

"Where's your sweater? You're shivering. Overdoing it, again?" He rubbed his hands up and down her arms.

"I don't even remember eating. I'm hideous."

"Look at me. Breathe with me. Do you hear me?"

She nodded. His affectionate voice calmed her soul.

Studying her worn face, he stated with confidence, "Hours of sleep for the previous week would be about four hours each night."

She grinned with an affectionate affirmative.

"I'm guessing you were working on multiple things at work and helping Martin. Add in Sonja's wedding and your devotion to help execute her plan, doing everything again? Are you trying to avoid something or someone?"

Her muscles tightened to reveal how his innocent joke, as it had done before, articulated what her heart protected from others seeing and hearing.

"Uhm…living with…. Martin has been harder than I thought."

"You moved in together?" His voice lost that sense of hope and confidence.

"Don't look at me like that."

"No, it sounds great. It's a commitment, sort of. Should I get him?" he asked in a hurried voice.

"He's drunk. Things have been weird. But, we're good. I guess moving in together was too soon."

"You could say that again," he mumbled.

She analyzed his expression, wanting to discern if his stern face and edgy tone indicated that he disagreed with her decision or if he was jealous. "Why are you here?"

"I'm attending an engagement party in the other hall. I needed fresh air."

"Too much happiness in there for you?" She was teasing him.

"No, it makes me wonder if I'm as happy with my life."

"I understand that feeling."

"Yes, you would," he uttered as he rubbed the back of neck.

"So, you came outside?" she inquired.

"You always claimed that fresh air always gives someone clarity to discern if you're paranoid or if your gut is trying to tell you something. Guess we both needed air?"

"I believe the last time we were together, we got clarity." With a hesitant hand, she tilted his head to meet her eyes.

"One can hope."

"Thank you." She leaned in closer to him.

"Don't worry. It's just a jacket."

"I'm not referring to your jacket. You always find a way to keep me warm. Thank you for your letter. I'm sorry."

"For what?"

"I've treated you unfairly."

He covered the hand still lingering on his face with his own. "You have every right not to trust me for the way I treated you and our friendship. I really care about you… then and… now…and… I miss arguing with you."

The lightness in his voice mellowed her anxiety. It was an anxiety not due to the wedding, Martin, or her dreams, but being near him. But, with his presence, her feelings and thoughts didn't feel overwhelming.

"When we were together, we said things —" She cleared her throat.

"Which needed to be said —"

"We were young and foolish back then, making ill-advised choices and letting our feelings outweigh reason when understanding and compassion were better options. We aren't those people anymore. I hope we're not those people. You are what I always knew you were, and now, well, because of you, I appreciate what I have in front of me."

Resembling a child listening to a story on the cusp of the end of the story, he whispered, "And what do you have in front of you?"

"A man who loves me. A man who wants to build a life with me. Who tries, at least. It's not a perfect arrangement… but…Martin is willing to follow my lead on this one. You were right. He loves me."

Christopher moved closer and ran his hands down her arms. Releasing a reticent and steady breath, he withdrew his hands from her and moved away.

"Good. I should record this moment. Her Royal Highness, Emma, declared I was right. I should get Martin."

The corners of her mouth twitched to meet his smile. Reaching for her, he brushed her tears away and drew her closer to him. She placed her hands on top of his so he wouldn't let her go again.

"Martin is drunk. Hates it when I'm not at his side."

"Understandable, he loves you." He paused. "You know how I felt about you… back then… so I understand what he may be feeling."

"I just don't …if—" Her voice trailed off as her head shook.

Gazing deep into her eyes as if he was searching for light in a dark tunnel, he reminded her, "You know you can trust me, right?"

She closed her eyes as she let the question sink into her heart. It felt like a million tiny pins piercing her skin.

"Em, open your eyes. Let me help you say what you need to say."

She opened them and probed his eyes for the truth. What she found frightened her, but it also gave her hope. It was true; she could trust herself to be with him without pretence or a past standing in their way.

"There she is," his breath was warm over her lips.

She felt a jolt of joy hum between them. Feeling his breath against her lips, she wanted to lean in so she would know how he felt about her now, and he would understand how she felt about him.

"You can't even imagine how much I've missed you," he murmured.

"I can," she responded, feeling his lips graze hers with the same warmth as she remembered. As their lips brushed ever so lightly, the electricity that vibrated between them could light the whole world.

"Emma, are you here?"

Martin's voice rang through the air. Shock bolted her from her position. As she stood up, she fell into Christopher's arms.

"Whoa, relax, Martin, we're over here."

"Christopher? Emma? What did you do to her?"

"I needed air," she explained quickly

"She fainted."

"I can see that. May I?" Martin pushed Christopher away from her. He took Christopher's coat off Emma and replaced it with his own. As he did it, an engagement invitation fell out of Christopher's coat pocket. He read it before handing it back to him.

"Shouldn't you be at your engagement party?" Martin shoved Christopher's jacket on to him.

Sirens of stupidity rang in Emma's ears as she glanced at Christopher. The sound of naiveness fuelled her soul with doubt again. She leaned on Martin's arm to help her balance. "We should return to the wedding. Sonja needs me."

"Are you sure?" Christopher stood between them and the path back into the hall.

"Send my best wishes to Beth," she snorted, offering her hand to shake Christopher's hand.

"Emma, it's not what you think—"

"There you guys are," Charlotte screamed out of breath as she reached them. Noticing that Christopher was there, she studied Emma's pale face and tried to make light of the situation. "Christopher, you're still rugged and handsome. What are you doing here, being someone's knight in shining armour?"

"Celebrating his engagement to Beth," Emma pushed Christopher aside.

Martin let go of Emma's hand to block Christopher from touching her. "Charlotte, help Emma back inside."

When she was a safe distance away, Emma turned around and saw Martin and Christopher talking. By Martin's puffed-up chest, she knew Martin was telling him how he would take care of her.

CHAPTER 32

The dance floor was filled with people enjoying the good wine and company. But the lights and sound of a wedding feast were making her feel nauseated and confused.

"Where have you been?" Sonja inquired as Emma lumped herself down beside her.

"Sorry, needed air."

"You look flushed. Are you okay?"

Emma crossed her arms across her chest and replied, "Christopher is here."

"Where?"

"At his engagement party!"

"Here?"

"Yes." She reached for a bottle of wine on the table and gulped it down.

"You're singing. Remember? Wedding present. Trust me; you want to be alert for this." Sonja took the wine bottle from her.

"I need to lie down."

Sonja did not give her that option as she grabbed Emma's hand and dragged her towards the emcee, who was standing in the middle of the dance floor.

All of a sudden, the spotlight blinded her as the emcee's voice blared through the hall. "And now, for a special treat. May I introduce the dearest and most beautiful maid of honour, Ms. Emma Alamayo."

Sonja nudged Emma forward. Her body was shaking and shivering as she waved her hand at the guests.

"Emma, how are you? Have you enjoyed the food and drinks tonight?" The emcee shoved the microphone in front of her.

Laughter filled the room, and Emma was taken back to the day when the laughter of others broke her heart. She stared blankly at the emcee and the guests around the room. They were a blur, only being highlighted by phone lights and camera flashes.

"What do you want to tell our happy couple? I heard you prepared a special song."

Feeling her cheeks burn, she tried to remember what she was supposed to sing and say to the happy couple. She nodded her head instead.

"I guess Emma has really enjoyed the drinks tonight."

Another roar of laughter filled the room. Chunks of water deposits were starting to well in her eyes. With no desire to relive that experience, she straightened her back and took the microphone.

"Sonja and Sebastian, I'm so glad you found each other. You were lucky to find someone who loves you, who will protect you and never use you. Continue to be honest with each other because you make us believe that love is real. Enjoy this song as my gift and hope for your future."

The music track played, but she didn't recognize the tune. Sweat beads trickled down her back. She was in front of an audience unprepared. This night was one endless nightmare.

"Emma?"

How did Martin get here?

Martin stood in front of her as Charlotte forced her to sit in a chair she had brought out for her. Her parents stood behind Martin, inching forward to hear the question and her response. She saw Ravi and Leon with a camera crew in tow to her left. Closer than her parents.

"There's a reason you didn't recognize the song. According to Sonja and Charlotte, you like grand gestures of affection. With the help of your family and friends, I present a song you wrote in your youth. It is a song expressing my desire."

As her family and friends began to sing with Martin, he knelt in front of her. Cheers swelled with the music as if this was the ending to some rom-com movie. But she couldn't hear the lyrics nor see what was ahead of her. She needed air to clear her head from the fog of disappointment minutes ago to the anticipation in front of her.

"Emma, I can't see my life without you. In front of your parents and friends, will you marry me?"

She gawked at Martin. Lights from cameras and phones were blinding her. Her parents were somewhere near. She tried to see their reaction, but Leon's associates, who made sure to capture the romantic moment, blocked her view. Emma closed her eyes and immediately recalled all the ways Christopher broke her heart and how Martin had never hurt her. In front of her was a man in love with her who offered her companionship and security. A man who loved the woman she was now, not the broken one that Christopher conned and had found a way to break her heart again.

She contemplated the life Martin was offering her. It was a life where he would adore her, a future that fulfilled her ideals of security and love. It was safe to love him. She accepted what she was getting in him. It was at her fingertips. Swallowing the lump in her throat, she ignored her soul's relentless cry to be patient. Feeling her parents, friends, and Martin's anticipation, she felt them urging her to say yes. She had no choice. Leaning in, she kissed him and gave him the answer he wanted.

CHAPTER 33

"What time is it?" Beatrice kissed her daughter's head and joined her at the Alamayo kitchen table.

It had been two weeks since her engagement and one month till the gala fundraiser. In theory, both should be filling Emma with a cascade of emotions ranging from joy and fear. Instead, she felt indifferent to the range of thoughts in her head without any emotional connection to them or desire to sort them out.

"Three in the morning, I guess." Emma sipped her tea and placed a cookie in her mouth. Beatrice sat beside her and took a cookie from her plate.

"Why are you here?" Beatrice waved her hand across Emma's stoic face.

"I couldn't go home tonight."

"Martin knows you're here?"

"I suppose. I texted him, " she answered as she shrugged her shoulders.

"Let me guess, Annabelle is driving you nuts?"

"The closer we get, she becomes more nervous, but it's usual." Her voice sounded lifeless.

"Did you tell Lillian, Emma?"

"I will. As soon as we launch the campaign, I can focus on it."

"Your wedding?" she probed with a nurturing twinkle in her eye. As she poured herself a cup of tea and refreshed Emma's cup, she waited for Emma to speak again. "Rough couple of weeks? Makes sense. You're engaged. It would make me depressed."

Mother, sarcasm at this hour?

"Mom, I didn't want to go home and strategize with

Martin and his team. They want to get started on wedding plans, and it's stressing me out."

Emma sighed as her mother sipped her tea. She admired her mother's confidence to remain silent and calm as she evaded answering her questions. Finding the mental strength to conceal her feelings was unnerving. "Martin's fine. He's super excited to marry me and wants to make a splash. He wants to set a date, and it's one of those things where we make plans to make plans, and then he gets called out for work or a meeting with some donors, and when I don't see him, I feel like I'm not there for him."

"Sounds reasonable. You went from moving in to engaged within a couple of months. As well, you're about to embark on launching your first fundraising campaign, in a new job that has the potential to help your sister. You have a right to be stressed."

Annoyance bubbled in Emma's throat. Her mother was digging with a teaspoon to hear the truth and had struck gold every time.

"Your sister called. She's concerned."

"So, she sent in her enforcer?"

"The name you and your sisters call me. Enforcer? I prefer interrogator. Or an over-concerned mother. Your sister thought you might need someone to talk to since you had an argument today. Is that why you're here, or do you really want to talk about your engagement? You're not glowing."

"Glowing, Mother? That's not even a thing." Emma paused for a moment. She shut her eyes tightly and regretted the tone she used with her. She buried her head into her hands.

"Do you love Martin?"

"Of course," she blurted out.

"Are you in love with Christopher?"

She glared at her mother in shock. "Excuse me?"

"Dear, you've forgiven him, yes?"

Emma got up and placed her mug in the sink. She rested her hands on the counter, holding her head down in defeat. In a few minutes, her mother had succinctly vocalized the question she had been too afraid to ask and answer herself.

"We've made peace… but... he's engaged."

"My dear, do you *love* him?"

Emma whimpered as she turned away from her mother and started to clean the kitchen countertops.

"Have you forgiven yourself for not telling him?"

"Telling who, what?" Emma tossed the cloth down.

"Ever since he started working with you, you've been different. Focused. Determined. You've been working long hours. It's easy to see when you come for dinner."

"I've always worked long hours."

"Yes, but since he returned, how many extra hours have you worked? Were you proving something to yourself or him? Exploring your feelings for him?"

"Doesn't matter. I'm marrying Martin, and Christopher is marrying Beth." Emma returned to sit with her mother. Opening a bag of chips, she hoped that eating a chip would either convince her mother everything was okay or she would find the answer she was seeking in the bag. When the answer didn't appear, she put a handful of chips in her mouth and offered some to her mom. Beatrice accepted and began to eat them but didn't say anything. As if she was reading Beatrice's mind, she got up again, holding the chip bag tightly in her hand while making her way to the porch door.

There she observed the bright stars in the sky in contrast

to the shadow of darkness, which concealed the fenceless, beautiful backyard.

"Maybe I had a crush or something in my youth, and when he came back, he reminded me about who I was. The best parts, but then again, I was foolish to believe him."

"Are you conflicted because you're letting your past impede your happiness with Martin? Or, are you using Martin as an excuse to hide from your feelings for Christopher?"

Emma gasped as she dropped the bag of chips. "I don't know." She paused as she reached down for the bag but relented as sitting on the floor became a more enticing option for her. Leaning her back against the door, she let the silence embrace her weary soul. Her mother's wisdom penetrated her thick skull of reason and stubborn heart to listen and sort out the confusion.

"Martin is a good man," Beatrice confessed as she joined Emma on the floor.

"He thinks you hate him."

"We don't hate him. But, it doesn't matter what your father and I like. We can always grow to love him if you do." Her mother put her arm around her and invited her to lean on her. "You don't resemble a woman in love."

"Mother, you're speaking nonsense. I love Martin."

"Are you trying to convince yourself that you're in love when you love someone else?"

"I don't love Christopher. He broke my heart." She groaned from a place that had never healed from the experience and had been wounded again. "He has a way to make me reevaluate my life and discern if I'm making the right decision. When he's around, he makes me see another side of the world, and it opens up these new possibilities that I have no idea what to do. "

"Yes, you do. Dear, Christopher didn't take your confidence or your ability to do that. You stopped listening to your heart on your own. Yes, the experience was painful. You allowed the moment to define you and influence your decisions. He reminded you to see you have choices and the ability to make them using your intelligence, experience, and heart."

"And if it hurts?"

"How does it hurt?"

"That I might have made the wrong decision and can't change it."

"Give yourself time. You need to listen to what your head and heart are saying. They're saying the same thing."

"He told me that all he wants is my happiness, and I want that for him too. That stupid moment changed what that means to me, but I want it for him and myself. He's found it, which means I can find it too."

"Does Martin make you happy in the way you want it for Christopher and others?"

Biting her lips, she leaned on her mother and held her close. "I'm not sure."

"Whatever you decide, we'll support you."

Emma picked up the bag of chips and started to eat with her mom. It was nice to be loved and supported. As they munched on the snack, Emma was less fearful about what she needed to do but still couldn't find the courage to do it.

CHAPTER 34

After a long week at work, Emma had left early to shop and prepare a simple dinner for her and Martin.

When she entered her condo, she gasped when she saw Martin. "What are you doing here?" She dropped her multiple grocery bags onto the floor.

"I live here, remember? Skipped work today?"

She noted his annoyance as she watched him place his tuxedo jacket on.

"I wanted to make you dinner to apologize for last night."

"You forgot," he stated.

Studying his formal attire, she couldn't register where they were going tonight.

"We're attending my pre-nomination party."

The blood drained from her face as she gulped for air. "I forgot. I'm so —"

"Sorry." He brushed past her.

"I *am* sorry." She held onto his arm, desperately trying to hold on to him. His eyes were black and hollow when they leered at her.

"Whatever." He wrestled his arm away from her.

"I mean it."

"Okay. But, check your phone. You'll see that I've been trying to reach you to ask what dress you would be wearing tonight."

"I'm here now. I'll get ready."

"Whatever, it doesn't matter."

"I promise, it won't take me longer than —"

"I should go before I say something." He headed towards the door.

"If you say nothing, you're saying more than you think."

He turned around and grunted in disbelief. Her tears were fresh and flooding from her eyes.

"We're engaged, Emma, and I thought being engaged would be this amazing thing between us. When we moved in together, we grew apart, and right now, this…isn't working. I thought we were finally making a real commitment to each other, but I guess I'm the only one invested in our future."

"Martin, I love you."

"Emma, being together shouldn't be this difficult. We're supposed to be making the world sick by how much we love each other. We should find reasons to be together. You find reasons to work." His voice was poignant as if he was giving his closing statement in a case he was sure to win.

"I've made it to your functions."

"Late."

"Dinners."

"Late."

"That's not true." Her voice sounded like a screeching car.

"I can't do this right now," he spat at her.

"Martin! Let's talk, please. I've been distant; it's just that—"

"How convenient —" he hollered but stopped midway as his phone rang. "My ride is here. I'll tell Leon you're sick."

"Martin! Don't leave, please."

"It's your turn to wait for me." He slammed the door behind him.

She shut her eyes, trying to erase the venomous disdain

piercing her heart. When she opened them, she was alone with Martin's things and her unpacked boxes surrounding her. What Martin had organized was now scattered everywhere as if he was moving out. His words were burning in her ears. The walls felt like they were closing in on her, and she had to leave.

But the truth of Martin's words followed her. He was right. She was using work to avoid being with him. It had been easier to be the charming fiancée in public rather than one in their private quarters. His proposal was so romantic that saying yes was the only option. She would be a fool to say no to a man giving her a life like everybody else had in her social feed and family. It was a choice that satisfied her ideals, but as soon as she had said yes to Martin's proposal, the doubt and despair within her intensified.

She wiped the teardrops from her face. When she adjusted her eyes to the light, she was standing in a church during Mass. Unaware of how she arrived, she stood paralyzed at the back, watching the priest lift the host for consecration. It caused her to weep as the truth crystallized in her mind.

She blinked and found herself soaked and sitting in the back pew of the church. Those who attended Mass were passing her with concerned looks, then whispering to their neighbour, unsure if they should help her. Fear crept into her mind telling her that they were labelling her as a broken and weak woman.

"Emma?"

"Christopher?" She blinked and saw her dearest friend dressed in a hoodie and jeans. He wasn't the businessman anymore. He was a friend from the past who she trusted in the present.

"What are you doing here?" He stopped and studied her expressionless face.

"I was roaming around, I guess I came in here because it's raining, and now I'm here. What are *you* doing here?"

"Mass. May I join you?"

She moved over and let him sit beside her. A priest came by to see if everything was okay. Nodding at him, the priest expressed friendliness, telling her that everything was going to be okay. No more words needed to pass between the priest to understand her state and how she had someone to help her.

"I'll lock the door behind me, Father Joseph. She'll be fine."

They sat in silence. She felt his arms drape his sweater across her shoulders and his hand holding hers in his. He traced circles on her hand, waiting for her to say something. His touch reminded her of that day in the park when he made her feel safe after Curtis barged into Annabelle's office. A moment, like now, where she didn't feel alone.

"It's peaceful here." Her voice was a whimper as she settled into the pew after sitting in silence for a while.

"Always is. People say you can talk to God anywhere, but when I go to Mass, I can hear Him."

"Do you know this for a fact?"

"I do. I learned it from you."

A lump lodged itself in her throat as she examined her hand in his. It was small and fragile in comparison, but it felt like it belonged with his hand.

"We were having a peaceful night watch. We were gazing at the stars, and you quoted Bronte, '*We know that God is everywhere but, certainly, we feel His presence most when His works are on the grandest scale spread before us; and it is in the unclouded night-sky, where His worlds wheel their silent course, that we read clearest His infinitude, His omnipotence, His omnipresence.'"*

Her eyes widened in wonder and awe. The memory of them reading *Jane Eyre* together led her heart to rest in that joy. It was a time when she lowered her defences and opened her heart to him through literature.

He continued, "Do you remember the time you showed me a picture of the famous Notre Dame stained glass windows? You described it as this place that makes you raise your head to the heavens, to the light, even when you stand in the darkness. It takes you to another place. You said that's what you experience when you're at Mass. You told me that you always find something when you go to Mass, especially when you're in despair. I didn't believe you, but when I walked through Notre Dame and attended Mass, I realized you were right."

"That I was a foolish girl to believe these places were a treasure trove of answers or ways of finding—"

"Joy…and hindsight into your sorrow." In a tranquil voice, he turned to her. "It is the fool who sees the soul... that *'fortunately, has an interpreter - often an unconscious but still a faithful interpreter - in the eye.'"*

"Bronte again? Who *are* you?" As she touched his face, she perused the unshaven hairs as if she was trying to convince herself that the soft hairs and warmth under her fingertips were real.

He cooed. "What do you mean?"

"You speak with confidence and faith, quoting one of my favourite writers with an understanding that you understand what she's saying."

He gazed at the Crucified Christ. "You inspired me. You always have."

"How?"

"You were never afraid. You believed in God and lived

your life accordingly. You taught me how to believe and trust in God, and from there, especially after you exposed me, I learned to believe in Him and myself. You taught me that despite the pain we inflict on each other intentionally and unintentionally, we weren't born to carry the weight of our sins by ourselves. Anger is not part of our DNA."

Holding her breath for a moment as the revelation crystallized in her heart and mind, she finally spoke. "Because God's love and forgiveness is our code. I was naïve to the world's reality."

"You lacked personal experience, Em. Sometimes you suffered from someone else's ill-advised decision, like when I thought happiness was winning a bet, never acknowledging how one friendship would show me the difference between happiness and joy."

A tidal wave of tears fell.

"Hey, no need for those. Are you okay?" He tilted her head to search her eyes.

"Martin and I had a fight," she blurted out.

"That's a relief," he murmured.

She gawked at him.

"Sorry, it's exhausting watching how attentive he is to you. His goodness couldn't be real."

"There's the cynicism." She smirked.

"It's not cynicism. I'm being honest. I've seen you two together. You're matched in both intelligence and nature. But you're human. Remember, I watched how he texted and called you every day to remind you that you were late. His patience with you is something extraordinary."

"Is that cynicism or sarcasm?"

"A touch. It's comforting to learn that Martin isn't

perfect. Your relationship isn't perfect. It doesn't have to be."

She cleared her throat as she focused on the image of the Crucified Christ again.

His arms were stretched out, but at second glance, His countenance was calm as it was lifted to the heavens. There was a sense that He was suffering, but something in his outstretched arms called out to you to trust in God's love for humanity even at the moment of his death. This act of love could defeat any darkness, a love that could forgive and lead one to reconcile with the one who betrayed and offended.

"Whether you want to admit it or not, your past resurfaces when it needs to or not. Fear and disappointment are chains that keep you from seeing what you have, and love helps you to let it go."

"Did I say that?" she questioned as the words didn't sound like her.

"No. I learned that truth on my own." He nudged her shoulder with his own.

She studied his features. His eyes twinkled with understanding, and his voice soothed her restless heart. The friend she had trusted was sitting beside her. But time and life lessons had withered his face with wrinkles of wisdom. He was the same boy she enjoyed spending time with and had grown into the man she had always believed he would become. He was a man she had learned to trust.

"Wise, but still so arrogant," she teased and rested her head on his shoulder.

"From you, it's high praise."

"You've always put too much value in my opinion. I'm a shadow of that confident person."

"Never fear shadows. There's a light shining somewhere nearby."

Feeling the warmth and sincerity in his voice, she heard him. He was using her words to understand herself. Contemplating his eyes full of tender patience, she smiled, and he returned it with an expression that acknowledged the pain between them didn't bind them anymore to anger nor fear. They had reached the point of forgiveness and reconciliation, where she didn't have to pretend to be strong and confident for him.

"Hey, don't cry. I'm saying thank you."

"I'm sorry. Martin and I..."

"Did he hurt you?" He checked her arms.

"No, not physically. We needed to talk, and he walked out on me. But who can blame him? I've been a terrible fiancée. Person."

"You're engaged?" he asked through gritted teeth.

"Yes, he proposed at Sonja's wedding reception."

He let go of her hand and glared at the diamond shining from her left hand, "Congratulations."

"Thank you. Is being engaged this difficult?"

"Each couple is different. But, I've seen couples live in a bubble of bliss."

"Is Beth in this bubble?"

"I guess."

Moving away from him, she grasped to find the right words. "I'm sorry; I shouldn't be telling you. Everything will be fine as soon as work slows down, and I can concentrate on Martin's campaign. I'm fine."

"And your wedding?"

Smirking as she realized that her wedding was the next project to complete. "Right."

He placed her hands into his own. "Does he love you?"

"Martin?"

"Yes."

"He loves me."

"Do you trust him?"

As she leaned forward, "Sure."

"Do you love him?"

She lowered her head, trying to figure out what her heart and mind wanted to say. "He's everything I ever wanted, but I —can't live without —"

Before she could finish, her ringtone rattled the church walls. She wanted to finish her sentence, but he reached for her purse and retrieved her phone. Pausing for a moment, he handed her phone to her.

"Hello."

Her heart stopped as Dylan's cold and calm voice told her that Amalie was dead.

CHAPTER 35

"Martin! This is Christopher. Emma needs you. We're at your place. She just found out Amalie died."

Standing in her kitchen, he hated bringing her home. He had suggested driving her to her parents, but her eyes instructed him to bring her to the solitude of her condo. As he hung up her phone, he had to contact Martin. It was the right thing to do, despite his better judgement.

He gently led her from the church to his car. Her frail and limp body rested in his arms as fear boiled through his veins. He was helpless to do anything. On their way to her place, he let the silence fill the car. Christopher was grateful for the unexpected traffic jam from the church to her place because it helped her to rest and to find solace in the rear red lights and the quiet of the night. He thanked God for this gift. It provided her a break from dealing with the news that Amalie was dead. Carrying her limp body broke his heart for he didn't know how to take away the truth nor the pain that came with it.

As he sat in the Poang chair, he watched her sleep and pondered on what to say and do. First, he had to respect her relationship with Martin. There was a line of comfort and intimacy that he could not cross. Christopher accepted that truth. He was her friend and not a lover. There was no intimate knowledge regarding her contacts or insight into how to respond to comfort her. In her life, he was the man who broke her heart and was helpless to her in this moment.

Another hour passed, and he wanted to punch a wall. A man in love would come running to his suffering lover. But there was no response from her fiancé. It infuriated him to see how Martin rendered his friend speechless and left her to suffer alone. When she told him what happened, he had to conceal the fury towards the man who intentionally hurt her. And now, losing her friend without her fiancé present to comfort her was shattering his soul.

He was infuriated when another hour passed. He slammed his cup on the table and buried his head in his hands. She didn't deserve another man disappointing her. But when he gazed at her, his anger subsided. Feelings of revenge and fury could not alter the situation nor help the woman who changed his life and still held a special place in his heart. For her sake, he remained calm and attentive. He owed her that much.

But, as he beheld her beautiful and delicate features, as he had done since the day they met and reconnected, he loathed how he had shattered her spirit. The agony of that decision was always there, and it propelled him to do anything he could to make amends. Though he didn't want to believe that Emma was in love with Martin, her palpable conflict and agony in the church showed him that she was trying to let her past go to build a life with Martin. She was trying to reclaim her voice and happiness and share it with someone else. But her work, her past — and now a death — would rob her from experiencing it any time soon.

As Christopher paced the room, he moved towards her bookshelf, where the rock still laid upon the shelf. Unnoticed and untouched, the rock held her unnamed bound books. He shook his head and felt the sorrow of unfulfilled dreams, remembering Amalie's quest to rekindle Emma's artistic soul. She had told him how she placed her old journals on the shelves in the hope that one day Emma would find and read them. Then she would remember and see that she still had something far greater to offer the world.

***

"You're still here." Her soft whisper pierced his soul with indescribable sorrow.

"I didn't want to leave you alone."

"You carried me up here?"

"You fell asleep."

"I should call my parents."

"Now, you want to call your parents?" He pinched the bridge of his nose together.

"Better not, it's late."

"It's almost midnight."

"Thank you." Stretching and smiling at him, she pulled herself up to sit.

"It's nothing. Cup of tea then?" He handed her a cup and watched how the steam brought some life back into her eyes.

"You don't have to stay. I'll be fine."

"Amalie died today; you don't need to be brave for me."

Sighing with the sorrow of death, she contemplated her space, and how Amalie tried to help her organize, but created a mess instead. "Her life was on track. And now it's gone. What was the point? Set her up for death?"

"This isn't your fault."

"I set it up so someone could take it away."

"Emma?" Christopher took the cup from her hand and sat beside her. He framed her face in his hands. "Listen. This isn't your fault. You gave Amalie the courage to love. Courage to hope. Her life ended because an idiot got into his car and rammed into her."

***

She hugged him tightly as if he was the rock to cling to when the current was taking her downstream towards the falls. Her skin burned through his fingertips as her breath cooled his temperament. As he warmed her arms and back with his hands, her tears soaked through his shirt. He needed to reassure her that she would never be alone. Kissing her forehead with the lightest and most tender care, every ounce of his soul wanted to take her grief away. If she ordered him, he would follow her command.

"It's okay. I'm here," he whispered over her quivering lips.

"I know," she murmured before finding his lips.

It was a bittersweet kiss, which he responded in a way to soften the sorrow of losing her friend. Her pain scorched his skin between each tender peck. He rolled his hands up and down her arms drawing her closer to him. As the kiss intensified, it vanquished the present pain. Her hands quivered over his shirt buttons. He cupped her hands in his, feeling the rock gash his heart. He moved his lips to her forehead again, ignoring his need to console her and help her forget the truth.

"You should rest," he uttered, resting his forehead on hers.

"I'm sorry," Emma touched her lips in embarrassment.

Bowing and shaking his head, he whispered, "Shh! You're in shock."

She pulled herself up and tried to balance herself. But her legs collapsed under her weight.

"Whoa, let me help you. Where were you going?" He steadied her balance.

"I need to sleep in my own bed and pull the covers over my head, so I can wake up, and this will have all been a nightmare."

Unable to find the strength to hold herself up, he picked her up and carried her into the bedroom. She wrapped her arms around his neck. Without words, he placed her down on the bed and tucked her under the covers. It was a gentle offer, but one he could follow without breaking her promise to someone else.

"I'm sorry. I shouldn't have kissed you... I mean, I'm engaged… and you're—"

"Shh!!! Get some rest, Em. I understand."

"One more thing." She grabbed his hand.

"Sure," he murmured with a sweetness of love as he sat on the edge of her bed.

"I don't want to be alone tonight. Stay till I fall asleep."

"Of course," he replied, tucking the strands of her hair behind her ear. "I'll be here till you don't need me anymore."

She made room for him, and he embraced her in his arms. As he held her close, she cried herself to sleep. Once her breath found a calm and peaceful rhythm to take her to sleep, he released a groan that only people who have lost hope can utter. The truth was clear. He was standing in for Martin. His friendship wasn't enough to help her mourn her friend. He could only offer her so much which wouldn't cross the line of intimacy and trust that can only reside between one's lover and her beloved.

When he was confident that she had fallen into a deep sleep, he pulled himself from her embrace. He noted Martin's cologne on the dresser and shirt and ties in the closet, as well as framed pictures of them together; he didn't belong. Without him, she was happy and engaged to a man who could give her the world without the baggage that defined their relationship. Releasing a breath from the depth of his soul, he accepted that it was Martin who had a future with her. It was a future where he would comfort her in times of sorrow and then celebrate the joy and peace he had always hoped for her. His prayers for her had been answered. It was a bittersweet consolation.

The kiss exposed his heart. He had feelings for her that were more than he deserved to feel in this moment of grief. These feelings urged him to console her, but he didn't want to cause her any unnecessary guilt in betraying her vow to Martin. He couldn't take her innocence and beliefs again. Breaking her heart was not an option, so he couldn't allow himself to care for her in a way that was not fair to either of them. His presence would only confuse her in a time when she needed to mourn her friend and plan a joyous life with the man she loved. He had to let her go.

"Christopher, is she asleep?" Martin whispered as he strolled through the front door an hour later.

He closed her bound journal. "She's asleep. Take care of her." He handed him the journal.

Martin nodded, and Christopher closed the door behind him.

CHAPTER 36

When Emma woke up the next day, she was numb. But as she stirred her spirits into reality, Martin's warm body was pressed against her. Her heart sank as the support he offered wasn't as comforting as the one Christopher offered her. But, as the truth sunk in, having anyone near helped to ease the pain piercing her soul. Amalie was dead, and Emma was powerless to change the truth. For the days leading to the funeral, that feeling never left her.

"You okay?" Martin squeezed Emma's hand.

The day of the funeral arrived in the blink of an eye. Emma was standing with Martin at the gravesite. Watching the coffin of her friend lowered into the ground, she didn't know how they arrived at this point. An hour ago, she was at the church. She sat and watched Amalie wheeled in and then rolled out. Within two hours, Amalie was six feet underground, having dirt laid upon her as her family wept from the grave to the pub.

"Is it me, or is it loud?" Emma pushed her beer towards Martin.

"Irish funerals. Are you ready to go?"

Nodding with a heavy heart, she assessed the room. There was this deep sadness that hung over the celebration, but an odd sense of joy ran through every kind gesture amongst the gathered. She didn't want to be here. Her legs weighed a ton, and her mind was an empty, silent void.

"Please, can I have your attention?" Megan's voice rang through the pub.

It surprised Emma to see Amalie's grief-stricken mother

stand amongst her guests with a beer in her hand.

"We, the family, thank you for the support. Yes, the manner in which someone had taken Amalie's life is tragic, but she doesn't want us to cry. Since being returned to us, she reminded us how to enjoy each day. She came out of a relationship that destroyed her spirit. But with your help, she returned, determined to love again. Ms. Emma, you stood by our girl through every nightmarish storm and offered her the support and love that we couldn't provide her. To you, Emma, thank you for giving us back our daughter. You showed Amalie how to love again and trust herself. Please, do not dwell on how she died, but be inspired to live your life in joy and happiness, which, Emma, you helped her recover. She embraced the challenges ahead. Ms. Emma, you gave our daughter hope to live. She found love with Dylan and a safe place to reconcile with her family. Do not weep for my daughter, but let her spirit inspire you to be brave. To Amalie."

Megan raised her pint above her head. But a mother's pain overtook her strength and resolve. Her sobs echoed through the pub breaking everyone's heart. A mother's lament was unbearable for Emma.

"Please take me home," Emma whispered to Martin as she took his hand in the hopes the sorrow would not follow her out the door.

CHAPTER 37

Everyone provided Emma the space she needed to mourn. Martin didn't demand her presence at his planning meetings or fundraisers. Even though her team wanted to cancel the event, Mr. X encouraged them to make the gala an opportunity to celebrate Amalie's life. Emma agreed. She still went to work and tried to lead her team, but they always insisted they would take care of everything. They wanted to take care of her as well as she had taken care of them.

"Annabelle, I'm fine. Are you sure you don't need help with Amalie's showcase?" Emma sat on her office couch, hoping her sister would say yes, but as Annabelle packed the programs for the gala, her sister said no. "We're good. We have a plan and the map. People will understand if you can't write a speech."

She ignored Annabelle's comment. She had to share her story with people even if it exposed her regret and grief for not bending to Amalie's desires. Every time she started to write it, she had to acknowledge how she let her fear dictate the decision not to appease her friend's request when she had asked her to share her story.

"I can help," Emma pleaded.

"I got it. Don't worry. Go home."

"Megan is on her way with the memorial picture."

"Martin called and insisted that you come home. If you're not home within the hour, he'll be dragging you out of here himself."

"This is how I mourn, Annabelle; I need to work."

"I understand. When you mourn, you work. When you're avoiding people or writing something you're connected to, you do any other job rather than the task which needs to get done."

Emma tried to pack the box of programs. Annabelle grabbed the box from her hand. With a sister's love, she confessed, "I'm the same way. If I distract myself enough, then the problem or feeling I'm avoiding will go away. We are our mother's daughters."

"And don't forget, we're very stubborn to accept help," Emma retorted.

"Emma, let your team do this. Go home. Write your speech. Call Lillian. She wants to talk to you."

She appreciated how her sister was trying to help.

"Annabelle, are you sure I can't help you?" Emma pleaded with her sister.

"Yes. Get out of here. I can wait. The next couple of days will be busy."

Emma said, "I'm okay. Megan will be here any minute. Go. You have a husband and kids to get home to. Hug them for me."

Begrudgingly, Annabelle hugged her sister and took the items for the hall with her.

Emma sat and let the silence dull her thoughts. Turning towards the door, she wished that Christopher would be there, wanting to come in and talk to her. But it was empty. There was no one there to help get her thoughts in order or listen. Even writing hadn't been a source of peace. Writing only forced her to remember how she had taught Amalie to hope in the impossible and seize opportunities despite the obstacles, to follow the voice inside that urges you to be fearless, to believe that God was always there to support you, that it's okay to follow your heart and see how your words change the world.

But her words betrayed her. Every time she tried to write

her speech, she was a liar. Prior to Amalie's death, she believed everything was perfect in her life when underneath, she would trade her life to share her stories. Amalie's death was forcing her to acknowledge how she had given the best of herself to everyone, encouraging them to love and live when she herself was the stumbling block to her own happiness. Christopher had seen it and told her, and Amalie's death made her accept it.

"Emma?" Megan stood, waving her hand in front of Emma.

Startled, Emma coughed and half-smiled at Megan. "I'm sorry. Deep in thought. This event makes me miss her less. She was so excited to come as our guest speaker."

"She loved you and the Centre very much. It was her home. I cannot thank you enough." Megan's Irish lilt had lost its vibrance. You could hear the melancholy vibrate against the office walls.

"Megan, I didn't help her. The counsellors worked with her every day. They made sure she received the best care and enrolled her in the right programs. I'm the girl who gave the cash to keep the doors open."

"You were more than a donor to the Centre and her mentor. You were her friend. She always claimed you were the first voice she trusted."

"I did nothing."

"But give her this."

Megan gave Emma a gold, ornamented journal from her bag. "The doctors had given her a plain notebook to take notes, and you gave her this one. You told her, use the plain one to indicate how the day is going, and leave the other one to write your dreams."

"I gave her this?"

She examined the journal and realized it was similar to

the books she had written in all her life. Thumbing through the pages, she read Amalie's thoughts and hopes, coupled with her favourite quotations and drawings of how she viewed her life. It made Emma believe that Amalie was sitting right beside her and urging her, in her usual pesky and honest way, to acknowledge and accept her calling as a writer.

"She sat beside you when you were waiting for your sister. She grumbled and complained about keeping a journal. You told her how you used to keep one to remember. Two days after, your sister introduced you as her mentor."

"She thought I was crazy."

"Yes, but you cared about her dreams. It moved her to consider how there was still a life for her to live. You should keep her journal. Read it; it'll help write your speech. Your sister mentioned you hadn't written it." Megan sniffed and wiped her tears. A faint joyful murmur crossed her lips when she pulled another package from her bag, "This will make perfect sense to you."

"What is it?"

"Amalie's gift to you."

Emma opened the box. In the box was a book with her name on it and a painting by Amalie. She had painted an image of an angel aimlessly searching the sky for something, but with a face that believed there was something invisible and great to behold.

"Amalie showed me your work six months ago."

Emma's hands trembled as she perused her words in black and white with pictures and images by Amalie. As she examined the contents, joy swept her heart. Tears welled in her eyes as some of the pages were filled with the Centre's client portraits and a poem or quotation from her journals. Words she had written in her youth were now telling how the Centre helped people and were intertwined with Amalie's journey to sobriety. It gave voice to the visions of a friend she had helped out of her own despair and darkness. She admired Megan's strength and courage. Megan handed her a letter from Amalie.

Dear Emma, this is your book. You have been so reluctant to do it, so I did it for you. One day, I rummaged through your unpacked boxes and found these journals. I found your short stories and poems, which I read and compiled into a book. Since you were in no rush to unpack, I figured you wouldn't miss them. So, I stole them from your place. I was curious, but as I read them, your words inspired me to publish it. You will find your quirky sayings that I wrote after our meetings. Remember when you instructed me to write down anything you said that I liked. I did. It came in handy when I needed to remind myself who I was, am, and who I hope to be.

Anyway, as we celebrate the Centre and its achievements, this is a token of my appreciation for your encouragement and a way to help others. You helped me find my voice, and I wanted you to find yours. May it show you how to love the life God has given as you helped me be grateful for the life God blessed me with. Love Amalie.

"These are my poems? My stories?"

"She was very diligent in writing things you suggested to her. You inspired her to live. Considering the events, my company wants to publish it in honour of my daughter. If you don't mind?"

"That she stole my journals from my place?" Her sarcasm and wit rang in the air. It had been weeks since she heard herself.

"The first was an accident, but every time she was at your place, trying to help you unpack, she kept finding your journals. It helped her explain her journey to others."

"And stop unpacking?"

"She couldn't help but read them. When she gave me pieces to see if it was any good, I couldn't stop reading them. I'm not sure how she pieced it together in such a short period, but the flow is seamless."

"Could explain why my condo seemed like I was moving out. She was never good at staying focused on a task."

"You're not angry?"

"Furious, but thank you," Emma laughed with glee as the gloominess around her felt like it was lifted to allow joy back into her life.

"So, can we publish it? In honour of my daughter."

"To Amalie."

CHAPTER 38

It was three in the morning, and Emma was sitting alone in the kitchen. She was thumbing through the bound book of her words. Inhaling the scent of new pressed paper and unmarked pages, she was searching these clean pages for inspiration. But, it was difficult to write when the truth was screaming at her to accept it.

"You okay? A cup of tea? Coffee?" Martin kissed her forehead and pulled a chair to sit beside her.

"Sorry, did I wake you?"

"I set my alarm. I needed to review my campaign material."

"Do we argue a lot?" The question fell from her lips before the thought crossed her mind.

"I couldn't find my phone this morning, and I was in a bad mood," he lamented as he ran his hand through his hair.

"Martin, I'm not talking about this morning. Do you remember the argument we had the night Amalie died?"

"I remember, I was selfish and refused to listen to you. I was frustrated that you always find a way to help other people, and when I need you, you aren't there."

"I told you I would go."

"I remember."

"And you wouldn't listen." She turned to him.

"Yes, that's in the past."

"Do I help people? Amalie's mom stood and thanked me at the funeral. But for what? Listening to Amalie and making her believe in hope."

"Emma, you gave them their daughter back."

"I was doing my job."

"Helping Amalie wasn't your job. You help others because you want to save the world."

"Or, am I trying to prove something to myself?" She buried her head in her hands. "Martin, if you died tomorrow, would you be happy?"

"I guess. Are you happy?"

He nudged her to look at him. Taking her hands into his, she felt nothing.

She drew her hands from him and clutched them together. "Amalie wanted me to share what the Centre meant to me, how I met her, and how it helped her to find herself. She wanted me to explain what it meant to be her mentor at the gala, and I refused."

"You're allowed to say no. You were just promoted to a new position on a tentative contract, and you were dealing with our political career and moving in together. You don't need to feel guilty for not saying yes to her. Emma, give yourself a break."

"Those are reasons, but not the reason why I didn't want to do it. I was afraid. Our last conversation here was an argument about me sharing my story because it would explain how she found the courage to share her story with others. I didn't say yes because I was afraid to expose myself and open myself to the rejection and criticism of others." The tears trickled along the contours of her cheek.

"What's really bothering you?" He handed her a tissue.

"I encouraged her to embrace her fears. I'm a hypocrite."

"You're not making any sense."

She passed her laptop to him. It was a blank page. Then, she handed him her book.

"What's this?" He flipped through the pages. "When did you write this?"

"I didn't."

"Your name is on the cover. Do you want me to read it?"

She nodded and went to get more coffee. As he read the book, she watched him for his reaction, but his manner was as stoic as a professional chess player trying to avoid checkmate.

Closing the book, he sighed deeply and uttered, "Emma, I love you."

Shutting her eyes, she knew it was time to let Martin go. This relationship had been the answer to her loneliness, a path to having her dreams fulfilled. But it wasn't enough to fill the emptiness in her heart. Lifting her gaze, she sucked in her breath and encouraged him to continue, fully content in facing the truth, which meant letting him go.

"But I'm not in love with you," he conceded with a sad confidence.

Emma closed her eyes and reached for his hand and held it. In those pages was her soul. It showed her how Martin was everything Emma wanted in a husband. He was her ideal manifested in a man. It was easy for her to love his manner, but it never fooled her soul. Her soul knew what she sacrificed to be with him. She had been the dutiful and supportive girlfriend who beamed with pride on cue, but those decisions stifled her soul, a soul that yearned to be loved and to love. It was a future that didn't include him because, as they both came to the same conclusion, they had never been in love with each other.

"How long have you known?" she met his reassuring and somber gaze.

"When you wanted to move in with me. It was an obvious sign."

"I wish I was in love with you. You're handsome, successful, and intelligent. I thought the only reason I didn't commit to you was because someone hurt me. By letting him go and the pain, I was free to love you in the way you deserve. When I did, I wanted to commit to the perfect life that everyone kept saying we would have together."

"Except for Sonja, Charlotte, your sisters, and your parents."

She frowned. "They don't hate you."

"True. They tolerated me and accepted our act."

"I wish I could love you. We would be amazing."

Half-grinning and frowning, he said, "True, but would it be love? When did you write this?"

"A long time ago."

"You sure? Some of it is recent."

May these give you a glimpse into a broken spirit. Use it to rebuild your life when your dreams disappear. Your dreams may disappear, but in good faith, they take a different form. Your heart's desires always rise to the top.

"Where was that?"

"Near the end. It's marked July fifth of this year."

"She liked to quote me word for word. I'm reading this book, and half the time I don't even remember saying these things to her."

"I never realized how your words inspire others." He paused as his head lowered. "What should we do? We're engaged. People expect a wedding."

Slowly, Emma removed the ring from her finger and placed it in his hands. She held the ring between their fingers. As she firmly closed his fingers over the ring, she kissed him on the lips. Its blandness signalled it was the right decision, but its hints of saltiness reminded her how much they cared for each other.

"When two people are not in love, they shouldn't exchange sacred vows to each other." She kissed him lightly on the lips and released his hand from her grip, feeling the doubt and fear evaporate into the air.

CHAPTER 39

With the somber emotion in the air filling the Omni room in the King Edward Hotel, it comforted Emma to have Amalie's pictures and her poems surrounding her at the gala fundraiser. The elegance of black tablecloths highlighted by the gold napkins and yellow flowers gave the room an elegant grandeur sense of beauty. Laughing to herself, Emma had to concede that Christopher had been right to insist on the gold and yellow throughout the ballroom. It felt like rays of light in the darkness.

As she scanned the room, Emma could hear Amalie's voice ring in her ears, but the words she heard were her own. Tears of joy trickled down her face as her friend, who orchestrated all of this, was not physically present to gloat. She loved how Amalie had Emma's words engraved in gold lettering to give context to the black and white images in the room. As she did with the book, Amalie brought the Centre and her story to life through the portraits and her youthful and wise words engraved on each.

Each word she read or heard in the guests' mouths made her heart swell with joy and pain. Though the moment chimed with the sounds of her words and echoed her passion for writing and helped to express the journey of the Centre's clients, she wished her friend was standing beside her, basking in the praise of the guests.

But, though her syntax was ill-formed, observing the guests, they understood the struggle and triumph of the Centre's clients. Through her faith-filled eyes, the guests learned how they had the power to restore hope in someone else's life in their time or talent. As she circled the room, she believed that God was guiding her back to her soul. But it wasn't in the form of a burning bush; it was in her youthful wisdom to see that she needed to trust herself and in the relationships that God had abundantly blessed her with. She needed to love her work, so her intimate relationships with family and friends would not seem like a competition or an obligation but a place to find rest.

As Emma admired the images on the walls and the texts throughout the showcase, she saw her life. Her life was full of people supporting and loving her, but there was always this wave of loneliness that was part of it. There were moments of despair and joy. Her eyes squinted in peace as her words revealed the restlessness she experienced in her commitments at work and her relationships as if she forgot what it meant to have a joy-filled life. It had been easy to cope with life's peaks and valleys, but to dwell and learn from them had taken time. But, her heart and mind were ready to have that honest conversation to pave the way for her to choose and claim the life she had always wanted for herself.

"Emma, this place is stunning. Has Martin arrived?" Annabelle hugged Emma.

"He had an emergency," she replied as she covered her left hand.

"A blind person would notice your engagement ring is missing. I've noticed for a week. Don't worry. I'm a trained professional. Everyone was working so hard to pull this together and are now standing in awe, so they won't even notice. Mom and Dad haven't even mentioned it. Besides, you're having it resized, right?"

Relieved, Emma loved how Annabelle's experience and wisdom provided her with a reasonable cover story for the missing ring. Emma hugged her sister for her understanding and support and waiting for as long as she did to ask her.

"If anyone asks, I'll tell them that story."

"Thank you. He's not coming. We broke up." Emma explained. It was the first time she told anyone.

"I figured. I haven't heard his ringtone for a week. I'm a professional in observing behaviour, especially yours. Now, I'll really tell people that you're getting that ring resized, provided I get exclusive time to hear the full story. We'll call Lillian. She should know why you're the epitome of happiness as opposed to misery, considering you broke off your engagement."

She squeezed Annabelle's hand. "I'm happy because I'm loved. Amalie pieced together some of my work into a book that her mom wants to publish. When I read it, I realized I wasn't in love with Martin. When he read it, he came to the same conclusion. It wasn't right to get married and pretend." She paused and admired the room one more time. "Thank you for helping my team decorate the hall."

"I'm organized, but I am not artistic. Amalie was artistic, but she didn't plan this showcase, nor, I suspect, put that book together on her own. My guess is that she had help as we did when we followed the instructions for decorating this place."

"Instructions?" She noted how Annabelle resembled a child who had scammed her father into giving her another scoop of ice cream. "Annabelle?"

"Kyle gave me the instructions."

She was surprised. Kyle was practical and a wizard with numbers than colour schemes. "This is Kyle's work?"

"I said gave. Emma, you know who put this together."

She scanned the room again, realizing that her heart had already acknowledged the truth. Christopher had pieced the showcase together. As his name crossed her lips, the guests parted, and he entered the ballroom with Beth. She watched as he showed Beth the portraits and her words in print. If Christopher turned and glimpsed her, he would see how her manners expressed sheer contentment and gratitude for his efforts. As he guided Beth with an intimate knowledge of every composition, she focused on the guests' needs, not wanting to ruin the night for them. He was showing his work to his beloved, and she was the friend who gave him the words for him to share those stories.

***

Emma was admiring the stars on the terrace. The fresh air filled her lungs as she tried to prepare for her presentation. Watching how tender Christopher was to Beth did not help her prepare for the presentation ahead. She was pleased he was happy, but the sentiment wasn't shared by her whole heart. A piece of it was cold like her body, which was shivering as she drew her pashmina around her shoulders. But nothing could warm the iceberg in her heart.

"Getting fresh air?"

The corners of her mouth twisted up as Christopher's voice floated into her ears. Her heart, which was in a state of pain and sorrow, felt at ease and elated to have him nearby. Turning around, she gushed, "It's wonderful you're here."

"Of course. I needed to witness a miracle. You changed some of our plans."

"Well, I had no partner to veto the change. He claimed I had his complete faith and trust to do as I pleased."

"I didn't say that. Are you okay?" He frowned.

"I wish Amalie was here."

"Yes, she would have loved the glitz. Her funeral was beautiful."

"You were there?"

"I was in the back."

"Figures. She was your partner in crime."

"I've no idea what you're referring to." He beamed with pride, confirming her suspicions.

"Thank you."

"I was paying my respects. No need to thank me."

"Thank you for being a friend to me when she died and scheming with her to assemble the showcase. You were right —"

"It was nothing." He raised his hands in complete humility and sincerity. "Considering the circumstances, I'm glad our work is some consolation to you. It makes the risk worth it."

She bit her lower lip, unsure what words were going to spill out. "I'm sorry for kissing you. I was out of line, and I needed to feel —"

"…no pain. I don't need an explanation." He paused as he placed his hand on his heart. "You are stunning."

"Considering I'm a nervous wreck."

Responding to the brightness in her face, he approached her slowly. To Emma, it felt like it took him an eternity to reach her.

"You're at peace." He brushed a strand of hair behind her ear. She didn't flinch at his touch. His breath and touch thawed the chill on her skin. Its warmth broke her heart more than on the day he betrayed her. Words filled her mouth, but she didn't have the courage to express her feelings.

Clearing his throat, he explained, "I came to say goodbye."

"Goodbye? You already left. Are you making up for the last time you disappeared?"

He laughed and then pursed his lips together. "I'm leaving for London."

"Ontario?"

"England."

She shook her head and gawked. "Wow, you're moving?"

"I made my decision. Remember, the day at the airport, I had to decide."

"I wasn't listening."

She grinned as she remembered how he pointed out that she wasn't paying attention to him. He took a deep breath and stepped back. Reaching into the inside pocket of his jacket, he pulled out an envelope. "This is for you."

Her fingers trembled in anticipation as she opened the envelope. She prayed it wasn't a goodbye letter. A wave of peace swept over her as she held a cheque for the Centre in Amalie's name.

"Mr. X wants to honour Amalie by sponsoring a yearly scholarship at the Centre. I thought it would be fitting for me to give it to you in private as a way to say goodbye."

She hugged him without reason. He followed her lead and held her close to him. Her tears soaked the shoulder of his suit. It was as if two wounded souls were finally able to communicate in complete honesty and authenticity. The moment confirmed the heart-wrenching truth to her. She had forgiven him and had the courage to trust him more than she did years ago.

"You still haven't learned." He stepped back from her.

"What?"

"Next time, bring a jacket. Your shawl is too thin. You're shivering."

He offered his jacket to her. She shook her head, never breaking eye contact with him. "I'm not cold."

He stepped away from her. "Okay. One last thing, Mr. X has an offer. He wants to make you and your team permanent. He sent me to officially offer you the position to run his philanthropy foundation."

Emma counted the stars above, and when she reached eight, she replied, "Please, thank him for the offer, but no."

"What? This is a great opportunity for you. I'm sure you and Martin can make it work."

"It's not Martin. I'm publishing a book. I'm going to try writing again."

"What book?"

Rolling her eyes, she shoved him lightly. "Amalie pieced my words into a book like the display in the hall. It's obvious I'm a writer, and I owe it to myself to be one. If it helped Amalie to find her voice, then maybe my crazy wisdom can help someone else."

Stifling his grin, he conceded, "Mr. X. predicted this would happen. I showed him your work after Amalie pieced some of it together. I may have suggested some passages to include. How about recording one of your songs?"

"I'm singing an original tonight. Wrote the theme song you and Amalie wanted."

"I'm sure it'll be brilliant. Full of pathos and pain, right?"

"Yes, I included my personal heartache and loss."

"And I hope, love."

He lifted her hands and brought them to his lips. Stroking her fingers, he gazed into her eyes. But, as he was about to speak, he examined her hand and realized that the rock which had pierced his heart wasn't stabbing his skin.

"Em? Where's your ring?" he whispered as he held out her left hand.

She glanced at her hand and winced in grief. "I—" She yanked her hands away from him. "Gave it back."

"Why?" His voice seemed drenched in hope.

"I wasn't in love with Martin."

He released a heavy pent-up breath as if he feared to say or ask her anything. "Then you're not engaged?"

"We broke up."

As he inched closer to her, he probed with a sweet, hopeful sincerity in his voice. "Is that the only reason?"

"Reason?" She bit her bottom lip to stop her heart from saying too much.

"For not marrying him?"

She closed her eyes, and with a heavy heart, she nodded yes.

"I see."

"I have to get back inside."

She peeked over his shoulder, relieved to see Annabelle headed towards them.

Hugging him quickly and pecking him on the cheek, she mumbled, "I'll miss you. I hope you and Beth will be happy in London."

"Em, I —"

"I have to go." She moved in haste before her legs gave way to the sorrow seeping through her.

"Are you okay?" Annabelle interrogated Emma as she reached her.

"Yeah. I have a song to sing."

"You sure?"

"Tonight is emotional."

"Okay." Annabelle glanced behind Emma. "Is that Christopher?"

"Annabelle, the presentation." Emma moved past her sister.

She entered the hall and quickly pulled herself together. Watching Amalie's tribute video gave her the courage and strength to perform even though her heart was a mixture of emotions. She mouthed the words to 'No Day But Today' as it underscored Amalie's video. It was better than simmering in her emotional tidal wave.

"Ladies and Gentlemen, Ms. Emma Alamayo."

She took the microphone beside the piano. "Please forgive me. I miss my friend. When Mr. Xavier hired me to lead this campaign, I didn't see myself sitting in a room where my words and Amalie's pictures would radiate the love and compassion shared at the Centre nor how I would rediscover my love of writing again. See, Amalie discovered I used to write and convinced herself that it would be perfect for the campaign if I contributed my work. I hadn't written anything for more than fifteen years, and I was too afraid to do it. But, tonight, I have an original song to express what the Centre means to the clients, staff, and volunteers. I didn't want to do it because it reminded me of what I gave up. The day I permitted fear and criticism to dictate my life was the day I let fear and the avoidance of pain influence it. But, as you have wandered the halls, Amalie proved me wrong. I taught her not to let her past mistakes stand in the way of her dreams. God didn't create us to wallow, but to learn. That's what the Centre provided for the clients, the staff, and volunteers. Amalie, my team, and in partnership with Mr. Xavier and his colleague, Mr. Christopher Gomes Riley, want to make sure the work being done at St. Michael's Centre continues for many years."

Emma cleared her throat and scanned the audience for Christopher. But she didn't see him. Shaking off the disappointment, she spotted her parents, who were smiling with the pride and love that can only come from those who raised you. Her sister gave her a reassuring nod, holding her phone up so Lillian could listen. She was loved, and that's all she needed to continue with the presentation.

"Sorry; it occurred to me how this is a gift, a gift from people who understand loss and pain yet rise above it. I'm not promoting my book or anything, but around you are also selections from a work that Amalie helped put together with a…friend. I hope they understand what it means to me." Emma stopped as the lump in her throat grew, "I hope you enjoy my song."

She prayed for God's grace to keep her hands from shaking over the keyboard keys and the grace to be heard. She adjusted her microphone one more time and found the courage to do it. She wasn't alone. With one last breath, she played her song.

In the darkness, it scared me.
To know you understood my heart and revealed how I killed my dreams.
When I thought it was worth nothing to feel or see
How everything I did was worth nothing
You put visions to my words
Words that expressed in good faith
Gave hope when I lost it.
You reached out your hand
Gave me warmth when I forgot my coat
You gave one that fit
Embraced in my fear
And even though pain and distrust stood between us
My tears didn't scare you away
You stretched your hand in love and in hope to lead me to my joy without you.

As Emma sang, her relationship with Christopher flashed across her mind. When he questioned why she broke off her engagement, she explained how she wasn't in love with Martin. But her heart yearned to tell him the truth, and it only came clear to her mind as she sang.

I love him.

CHAPTER 40

Emma retired to her room at the King Edward Hotel before the party ended. If she saw Christopher, her self-control would lose the war to her heart. Hiding in her room all night gave her the time she needed to remind herself that he was in love with someone else. He helped to give her back her confidence to write; the least she could do was to accept the reality he was in love with Beth. She loved him without conditions where she could let him go to have the joy and happiness God had in store for him, even if it meant it wasn't with her. It was her mantra this morning as she waited for the valet to bring her car.

"Your song was brilliant." Beth nudged her shoulder as she stood behind her.

"Beth! What are you doing here?" Emma tried to sound casual.

"I had a room. I'm waiting for my car. It was a beautiful evening. Shame you had to leave early."

"It was a long day."

With a genuine and pleasant smile, she nodded and hoped her car would arrive soon. Emma needed to get into her car and leave. Seeing Christopher and Beth together was too much for her heart. As much as she had decided not to declare her feelings for his sake, it still hurt.

"Your song was inspiring. Can't wait to read your book."

"Yes, Amalie and um… Sorry. Yes. I wrote a book. Actually, I'm taking a break from my job to see if I can do this professionally. The showcase featured my poetry and quirky sayings, and maybe there is something there that I can use to write something else."

"Christopher mentioned it."

"Right. Amalie's mother is a publisher, and when Amalie showed it to her, they wanted to publish it. I'm going to dedicate it to Amalie, seeing how she found my journals and pieced most of it together."

"Can't wait to read it. If it's like your song, it'll be inspirational. Send me a copy, and I'll get my fans to check it out."

"Thank you. I hope you enjoy living in London," Emma blurted out.

"Excuse me?"

"Christopher told me. You're moving to London."

"He is. I'm not."

"Ma'am, your car."

Emma handed her ticket to the valet and pointed to her luggage and garment bag to be placed in the trunk. Her heart was beating with a speed she didn't realize was possible. Emma squinted her eyes at Beth. "I don't understand."

"I'm moving to Vancouver. I found this great little inn in the mountains that I'm converting to a retreat house. Plus, my fiancé lives in Vancouver."

"How is that possible? Aren't you engaged to Christopher?"

"No, I'm marrying Justin Christopher Lyme."

"But, you were dating Christopher a few months ago."

"It's a long story. My promoter, Edward, thought it was a good idea, something to help my brand. I'm not sure, but it always felt wrong. Dishonest. Christopher was a good sport and was helping me out, and I had just broken up with my fiancé, and well, we went on a date or two. It was nice hanging out with him, and I thought maybe he was the one, but after we watched *Twelfth Night*, I realized I've only looked at one man the way Christopher looks at you. Seeing you two together helped me realize how much I love Justin." She pointed to a man waiting in a car.

"You're all set." The valet dangled Emma's key in front of her.

"Thank you," Emma tipped the valet.

"You should tell him." Beth grabbed Emma's arm. "He won't tell you because you're engaged to Martin. I told him it hurts no one to hear someone say they love you. Leave it to the other person to decide what they want to do with the declaration."

She rested her hand on Beth's and conceded she was right. "Regardless, if the person doesn't say it in return, you can't control a person's response."

"That's wise, but you don't have to worry about how he'll respond."

CHAPTER 41

Emma snuck into Christopher's condo building. As she rode the elevator, panic and anxiety flared through her. But her fear didn't paralyze her into silence. She had to tell him the truth and risk her heart.

She tried calling him, but her calls went straight to his voicemail. Frustration blazed through her blood. When she needed him, he didn't have his phone near him.

"Excuse me, miss."

Checking out his name tag, she interrogated Timothy. "Is this apartment 14-427?"

"The open door. Paul, someone's coming in," Timothy shouted.

Paul leaned his head to the right. As she entered, she found packed boxes and plastic sealed furniture.

"Are you checking the place out?" Paul inquired.

"I'm not buying. Is the previous owner here?"

"He left already."

"Right."

"This must be you. It fell from one of these boxes," he commented as he rolled his load of boxes out of the condo.

"Thank you."

Reviewing the picture, her heart exploded with emotion. She was unsure when he took the picture, but as she reflected on the girl who wrote under a tree, she remembered how everything in the world made sense at that time. She recalled how she loved writing with him by her side and how much she loved sharing stories with him or simply sitting silently with him. She flipped the picture over and was in awe of what was written on the back.

In his writing were her words:

In truth, when you find your best friend to love, everything will hurt more, but even in the disappointments and imperfections, you find a way to love unconditionally, ready to give your life to them, perfectly bound in sacred vows to your other self.

Gasping for air, she remembered writing those words and showing him. Her influence had led him to find God, and it was God who was guiding her back to herself and to have the courage and grace to love Christopher—a man who had always valued her for her mind and spirit and who loved her.

"Where are you forwarding these items?" She grabbed Timothy's arm.

"He donated the furniture. The personal effects are off to storage."

"No fixed address?"

"Sorry."

"Thank you."

"You okay?" His voice sounded concerned as Emma gripped the picture in her hand.

"I will be."

CHAPTER 42

As Emma rode the elevator up to her place, she was already searching for flights to London. She was going to interrogate his staff until they provided her with the information to find him. She had to tell him that she loved him and hoped he felt the same way.

Walking down the corridor, she noticed a slumped-over figure sitting in front of her door. She recognized the tuxedo and the figure inside of it. He glanced up and stared hopefully into her eyes. His gaze paralyzed her as he rose to his feet. Without words, he kissed her beyond sentiment and reason.

"Hmm..."

Emma's neighbour Gwen coughed and shoved her way around them.

"Sorry," Emma apologized.

She took Christopher's hand, and he grabbed her luggage. Entering her condo, she zipped into the kitchen. As tantalizing as his greeting was, they needed to talk. It was too easy to give in to their physical desires. But, she wanted something more than to feed her primal need when there was still so much to say to each other.

"Can I get you a drink?" She plugged in the kettle and pulled cups from the cupboard.

He braced her between the countertop and himself. His touch felt warm against her skin. After spending a whole night in front of her door, Christopher wasn't thirsty for a drink.

"Not what I'm thinking." He tried to kiss her again, but she placed her hand over his mouth.

"I know you're not engaged."

Taking her hand, he gently kissed the inside of it with a warm kiss. "If I was, I wouldn't be kissing you in a hallway, nor wanting to really do it again. I wanted to explain it to you as soon as you finished singing, but you disappeared. Figured we needed privacy to have this conversation. But I chose the wrong door to wait for you. I'm glad you found out."

"You slept here? In front of my place, and my neighbours didn't throw you out?"

"I told them I was preparing for a grand gesture to express my feelings in the hopes I could be your boyfriend."

"Hmm," she pecked him on the lips. "But, I was engaged to Martin."

Releasing a euphoric breath, he raised his head to the ceiling, "I don't want to talk about him."

"Hence the kiss?" She was teasing him and relishing in the truth that she could trust him with every part of her heart.

"Em, I've been waiting a long time to say this to you." He grinned and whispered as he placed his mouth closer to her lips. "I have never stopped loving you." Closing the gap between them, he kissed her, and she forgot her name at that point. "That's better."

"Wait."

"You're killing me, Em."

"I need to tell you what I'm thinking and feeling."

He took a step back and raised his hands in surrender to her wishes.

"What I did to you was heartless. When I heard you made a bet, it devastated me to learn how the time we spent together meant nothing to you. I convinced myself how I was nothing to you and how it changed me to never trust my relationships or my instincts because when I did, with you, I was wrong. I didn't want to feel that way again, so I stopped trusting myself in everything. And I blamed you entirely, and that wasn't fair. I'm sorry."

Taking both her hands into his own, he brought them to his lips and kissed them. "The first time I saw you, I knew you were the one. But being a coward, I took the bet because it was easier than being honest with my feelings. I never thought you could ever consider me as someone to be friends with or love. And now, working with you and when we started to be friends, I realized I never stopped loving you. Every day, I fall more deeply in love with you. I didn't want to admit it because you and Martin were together. Your happiness means everything. Even if we weren't together, I needed you to be loved and for you to love someone. I didn't want to lose you, but I bore the loss of accepting you were happy and in love with Martin."

Emma tried to interrupt. "Can I finish?"

"Sorry, I've been wanting to tell you for the longest time, and the fact that I get this chance," he responded as he encircled her in his arms.

She kissed him on the cheek. "I might have saved you in the past, but you returned when I needed someone to save me from myself. Not like save me by doing everything for me. But, you reminded me of who I am. You helped me discover how I had a voice and needed to trust it again. I broke my engagement with Martin because my voice told me that I wasn't in love with him. But, you were engaged. It was inappropriate to tell you—"

"Tell me what?"

"Stay." She rested her hands on his chest.

"Stay?"

"You're moving to London."

"Not anymore. I was moving because I didn't want to see you with Martin on the news or billboards. Understand, I wanted your happiness, but I didn't have the strength to see you with him every day. I told Mr. X that working in London was better for me. He said I was stupid. Suggested I tell you the truth."

"Shouldn't you call him?"

"Not important."

"This isn't important? You need to call and tell him."

"He is aware. I talked to him as I waited for you. Killed my battery. Em, I need to kiss you again."

"Wait." She placed her hand over his mouth.

"Seriously," he mumbled against her hand.

"Mr. Christopher Riley Gomes," she whispered as she moved her hands behind his neck.

"I," she whispered, kissing him on the lips, "love," kissing him longer this time, "you."

They both expressed tenderness in each kiss. As they held each other, Emma felt loved and safe. There was no hidden agenda nor regret or pain to hold them back from love and reconciliation. But, life always interrupts romantic moments. A blaring knock came through her place.

"Emma, it's your mom and dad," Beatrice yelled through the door.

"And Annabelle."

"Annabelle told us that you broke off the engagement. We're here for you."

"Your parents?" He turned towards the door.

"Package deal."

"I'll take it."

"You need to tell my parents the truth and make peace with Annabelle, Lillian, Charlotte, and Sonja. You need to impress them." She was teasing him.

"Honey, are you home?" Beatrice's voice came booming through the air again.

"Coming," Emma shouted.

"Bring it on. I'm not going anywhere." He kissed her on the lips. They kissed for a few minutes longer.

"They won't blame me for breaking your engagement with Martin?"

"Absolutely."

"Martin fans?"

"They'll blame you, then shake your hand in thanksgiving."

"Finally, people who aren't on team Martin!"

"They'll thank you for helping me find my voice and heart again."

"Emma, open the door, so we can meet Christopher." Beatrice knocked harder on the door. They exchanged glances.

"She's my mom, and you can't hide the truth from her."

"I'll remember that. I'm telling them how your happiness is everything to me. Are you happy, Em?"

"No." She kissed him before he could respond. "I'm filled with undeniable joy."

"See, I keep my promises."

Smiling, she recognized this love was more than a feeling. It was a love which they earned from forgiveness, self-sacrifice, and understanding. A love that illustrated what it means to sacrifice for your beloved's well-being. Yes, they would hurt each other, but over time, experience, reflection, and discernment encased in love for God and for each other would always lead them to forgiveness and reconciliation. In their love for each other and in their suffering, they found what it means to love like God.

Coming Soon, Book 2: Can Ashlyn and Simon find love when their lies have ruined the reputation of the other?

Acknowledgements

I would like to thank God the Father, Son, and Holy Spirit who kept inspiring me to finish this story, especially when I lost faith in my ability and joy to write a story that reflects my studies in Catholic Theology.

A heartfelt thank you to my mom and dad who sat with every night until I learned how to read and never discouraged me to write stories. For a marriage that reflects what a committed relationship looks like, which includes a commitment rooted in faith to God and each other. Thank you for always supporting my academic and artistic aspirations.

To a wonderful sister who has been my toughest critic and cheerleader in my pursuits as an artist. Your honesty and support have helped me develop my craft and toughened my heart to deal with criticisms and rejections. I continue to enjoy our discussions from popular culture to theology.

To every aunt, uncle, and cousin, thank you for your encouragement and willingness to always share your opinion and attend my various events. Although I would love to list all of your names, I would need to publish another book. Your lives have inspired me to write and document how your love and commitment to each other are stories that others need to hear.

Thank you to every friend who has had to read anything I wrote. Thank you for your time and patience and continued support. My apologizes for every ill-written sentence you had to correct.

Of course, thank you to the multiple editors and readers who had to review the early drafts or excerpts of this story. Each of you breathed either new life into these characters and enriched the story with your wisdom. A special thank you to Ellen Hrkach, whose words of encouragement and keen eye helped to return the story to its original purpose and heart. I have learned a lot from you. I am also very grateful to James Hrkach who offered much needed design and technical support.

Lastly, to you, the reader who took the journey of love and forgiveness through Emma and Christopher. May you find love and when you forgive, thank God for doing either in your lifetime.

About the Author

Eliza Mae Albano lives in the Greater Toronto Area, serving the Lord in word and deed as a Chaplaincy Leader and Music Minister. She is a graduate of St. Augustine Seminary and the University of Toronto where she holds a Master's in Theological Studies and Honours Bachelor's Degree in English, Theatrical Studies, and Political Science. She enjoys discovering how God reveals Himself through stories and reflecting on scripture and Church teachings. Using her vast knowledge and experience as a former Youth Minister, Sacramental Coordinator, and actor, she produces work that reflects how God's love is unending and how we can live our lives accordingly, even through heartache, loss, and celebration. Through daily reflections and stories, she helps people understand their relationship with God and others. She is always open to hearing and sharing stories with others. Her debut novel '*I Hope You Find Joy'*, is part of a new series *Stories of Love and Forgiveness*, which explores how our small acts of kindness is how God shows Himself to us and in His time is how He calls us back to Him when we lose our way.

You can view some of her body of work:
website: witnesstogodsgrace.com
Or follow her on
instagram: awitnesstogods_grace,
twitter: @EMAlbano1